WEST SUSSEX COUNTY CO

This book is due for retu ~~~~ ~~~ ~~~ the last
date stamped below. If it is not required by
another borrower it may be renewed by post,
telephone or personal visit to the library.

Fines will be charged on overdue books.

R628 Lib.10

Please return to:

BOGNOR REGIS
01243 864638

05. APR 01	12 MAR 2003		13. NOV 04
095 26 H 01	12 JLY	23. JUN 04	08. JAN 05
26. MAY 01		14 JUL 04	
	14 JUN 2003	11	
21. JUN 01. 09. AUG 01.	28 JUN 2003	20. AUG 04	
08. SEP 01	30. AUG 03 08 OCT 03	13. SEP 04	
09. OCT 01.		25. SEP 04	
11. APR 02	18. OCT 03		
14. AUG 02	11. JUN 04 05. OCT 04		

Recent Titles by Margaret Hinxman

LOSING TOUCH

Margaret Hinxman

This first world edition published in Great Britain 1996 by
SEVERN HOUSE PUBLISHERS LTD of
9–15 High Street, Sutton, Surrey SM1 1DF.
First published in the USA 1996 by
SEVERN HOUSE PUBLISHERS INC. of
595 Madison Avenue, New York, NY 10022.

British Library Cataloguing in Publication Data

Hinxman, Margaret
    Losing touch
    1. English fiction – 20th century
    I. Title
    823.9'14 [F]

ISBN 0-7278-5100-4

All situations in this publication are fictitious and
any resemblance to living persons is purely coincidental.

Typeset by Palimpsest Book Production Limited,
Polmont, Stirlingshire, Scotland.
Printed and bound in Great Britain by
Hartnolls Ltd, Bodmin, Cornwall.

Chapter One

"Watch it!"

The boy – trainers, torn jeans, black sweat shirt with the message 'Up Yours' stamped on the front in electric pink letters – elbowed her sharply in the ribs and gripped her wrist.

It didn't hurt much. But she winced out loud, more from surprise than from any actual pain.

A girl's voice cut in. "Leave off, Tone. She ain't all there. See!"

The girl was barely distinguishable from the boy. Matching clothes, matching jet black hair, centre-parted and scraped back in pigtails; only the black sweat shirt asserted its independence, proclaiming 'Down With Everything' in stark white.

Connie Remick looked up at the pair of them, bewilderment tempered with indignation. ("Ain't all there", indeed!) What had she done? She couldn't think. But she didn't doubt that she had done something. It happened a lot lately. Just drifting and forgetting.

The boy, Tone, hadn't relaxed his grip on her wrist. A few people in the shopping precinct were beginning to pay attention and Connie sensed he was getting nervous. He couldn't have been older than Colin, but tougher, more aggressive, although just a little scared now and perhaps not as brutish as he appeared.

"Just give it back. We don't want no trouble!" He lowered his voice, presumably so that he shouldn't draw any more attention to himself. But it was too late for caution. A small crowd was gathering, not interfering, just curious.

1

"Give back what?" She smiled what she hoped was a beguiling smile. She really, honestly, couldn't think.

"The *tape*! Stupid cow! In your bag." He was no longer scared, but angry. "Look!"

He pointed to the pretty raffia shopping bag she was carrying and forced her to look inside. He had sense enough not to handle her property. If it came to a confrontation, the law would certainly take her word against his.

"That!" He touched the music cassette lying face upward at the bottom of her bag, beside her purse.

She stared at it for what seemed like a long time as if it were some strange, unidentifiable object, which in a sense, to her, it was.

"U2." She turned to the boy with a puzzled expression on her face. "U2?" she repeated. "I'm not sure . . ."

He stopped being angry, his attitude less threatening. "You nicked it," he hissed. He was beginning to feel sorry for her, not an emotion with which he felt comfortable. "From my back pocket. I felt you take it." He grinned or maybe it was just a grimace. "You're not good at it, duckie!"

Connie passed her hand over her forehead and down the side of her face. Her fingers, she saw, were trembling.

"I don't remember. Silly! I'm so sorry," she murmured, almost to herself.

"Don't worry," said the girl, her small, thrusting breasts mapping a hilly landscape under the 'Down With Everything' sweat shirt. "His gran does it all the time. Trick is not to get caught. Ouch! That hurt!"

She looked at Tone, aggrieved, as he grabbed her roughly by the arm.

"Forget it!" he said brusquely to Connie, recovering his swaggering poise.

"Are you in trouble?" An elderly, upright man in a tired tweed suit of ancient pedigree had plucked up the courage to come forward. There were murmurs of support behind him.

"No, *no*!" The note of hysteria in her voice alarmingly

2

echoed in her ears. "Cool it, Connie!" That's what her son Colin would have said before he stopped saying much of anything to her.

"I could call the police," the man suggested anxiously.

"Good God, no. It's my fault. A mistake. My fault."

"Oh!" he said, relieved. The group of bystanders started to drift away.

"Sure?" he persisted. His voice had a tinny sound like an out of tune piano. Maybe she was the only person he'd spoken to that morning, Connie speculated. He had that lonely, bed-sitter look about him.

"Sure!" She nodded vigorously.

She looked around, but Tone and his girlfriend had disappeared with the U2 tape.

It was all over, no more than a couple of minutes.

The elderly man in his faded glad rags hovered for a moment or two, but, receiving no encouragement from her, marched off in the direction of Woolworths. She noticed, idly, that he had a limp which his military bearing couldn't quite conceal.

Then the passers-by and shoppers merged into a background that seemed to grow hazier and hazier. She felt disembodied. At least when Tone was accusing her of theft she had experienced a sense of being, here and now. Strangers were so much safer than friends or family who could draw on a shared past for their terms of reference. They were always so pat about the past: put it behind you, confront it head on, never does to dwell on it!

But strangers – the Tones and their girlfriends – didn't know and didn't care. They only related to the present. The present in which she had pinched a tape for no imaginable reason than that it happened to be sticking invitingly out of someone's pocket.

Well, at least that was a first. She couldn't recall committing a felony before – or was it a misdemeanour? She thought it probably was. Her daughter Amy would be able to put a legal name to the crime, as well as one or two others less formal – like disgraceful and humiliating.

Of course she had lied a little. Not that she could

3

recall actually taking the thing. But she remembered the moment. The walking through the precinct, idling as she often did these days. And her mind floating, bumping into odd bits of flotsam, the debris of her life: things done, things undone and always coming back to the last sight of Colin with that hurt accusing expression in his eyes. It was at times like this that she couldn't be relied upon. Not herself, her elder daughter Amy would explain when explanations were called for; her youngest, Holly, would simply distance herself from the whole sorry business.

It wasn't fair, she thought. To Amy, to anyone who cared about her. Two years was surely long enough to get a grip on herself, revert back to being the old Connie Remick, whoever 'old Connie Remick' might have been.

She sat on a bench and gradually the precinct and the people became alive and in focus again. She stared at a reflection of herself in the shop window opposite: a neat, well-dressed middle-aged woman with a raffia bag, taking her ease between spurts of shopping on a warm, summer morning. Nothing odd or unusual about that. Why had the girl said she wasn't 'all there'? She stood up and inspected herself more closely in the shop window. Did she look older than her forty-eight years? Maybe! Too thin, certainly, almost gaunt. But so were lots of other women.

Maybe it had just been the girl's way of avoiding a scene that might have had awkward repercussions. Or maybe she had seen in Connie a replica of Tone's gran, who nicked things all the time, and had taken pity on her.

She suddenly realised that the window into which she had been staring so intently belonged to a video and record superstore. Her reflection was superimposed on a bargain promotion display for U2 CDs and cassettes. She hadn't even heard of the group before today and had never consciously heard the sound they produced. Perhaps she should make an effort to listen to it. It could be the turning point of her life. Joke!

4

The idea of Constance Remick, who tended to find Wagner wearing and had never embraced anything more radical than the Beatles in pop music, voluntarily submitting to an onslaught of ear-splitting rock tickled her no end. That would give Amy something to think about.

She became aware that a burly man inside the store, who had been riffling through the jazz classics, was staring right back at her, an amused expression on his face. Amused – and faintly amazed. Or was it her imagination? She persuaded herself that he was probably one of the people who had witnessed the episode with Tone and the tape and, blushing at the memory, she walked briskly away from the store and his curious gaze.

It was then that she noticed she was wearing one mink brown suede pump on her left foot and a navy blue calf pump on the right. The sight of her mismatched feet struck her as wonderfully comic and she laughed out loud. When the laughter was spent she felt a light-hearted sense of release and didn't even mind the nervous attention of a cluster of pensioners who were whispering among themselves. "The same one," she heard – the rest was a mumble. They looked like mid-week day-trippers to sunny Southdean, down by coach, with plenty of time to fill in before the return journey. And she supposed they had her down as a menopausal neurotic.

She marvelled at how much, how many small details, she was registering today. The past months, even years, had been so blank. She could barely recall a single incident after Colin's death. But there was a clarity about today for which she couldn't account. And at least she had solved the 'ain't all there' mystery, she thought, regarding her feet. They must have looked peculiar to the girl in the unisex uniform.

She wouldn't go back yet, she decided. It was all still too fresh in her mind – the tape, Tone, the girl, the 'Up Yours' and 'Down With Everything' sweat shirts. And now the odd shoes. Without wanting to she would find herself telling Amy all about it. As a joke. Although Amy wouldn't laugh.

5

In the old days it was the sort of story she could dine out on because her absent-mindedness about everything she didn't consider immediately important had been legendary. An endearing trait. Like directors of companies who turned up at board meetings wearing odd socks and academics who were chronically unpunctual and spread strawberry jam on their kippers.

But not any more. Now that she was no longer a positive force, a doer in society, those little idiosyncrasies were major causes for concern.

She spotted a McDonald's, bright and pleasantly full. She'd never been in a McDonald's and felt an overwhelming urge to try it. Another first. U2 and McDonald's.

She queued for her coffee in a polystyrene container and, suddenly hungry, ordered a bacon and egg McMuffin. She found an empty table by the window overlooking the precinct and tucked in, relishing every mouthful. It was the most delicious food she had ever tasted, better than the Savoy Grill. The coffee was more flavoursome than the finest Kenyan blend she used to buy from Fortnums. The surroundings were light and airy and spotless because people remembered to dump their wrappings in the bins. Best of all no one was looking at her, observing her, judging her, worrying about her. They were all engaged in munching, chewing and gurgling down to their last drip of triple thick milkshake. Either that or chatting and minding their own business.

She smiled with pleasure at the stroke of strange fate that had brought her here. Another world.

I will sit here and compose myself and then I'll go back as if nothing had happened. Only something has. Happened. Today I shall make a real effort to begin to reinvent myself, she resolved.

At this purposeful moment she saw the child staring at her balefully over the remains of a Big Mac, the dismembered burger temporarily forgotten as her eyes beamed first on Connie's oddly clad feet and then straight into her eyes. The disconcerting stare, Connie recognised, was all part of a kid's game. Whoever blinked first was

6

the loser. Adults could play, too, but they seldom won. Children had it down to a fine art.

Well, why not? she thought. I'm enjoying myself. For the first time in so long I'm enjoying myself. Two pairs of eyes – hers and the child's – locked in a battle of wills.

She was a glum-looking little girl of six or seven, maybe more, just undersized. But there was a monkey cleverness in her expression that was unnerving. It was as if she instinctively understood everything about the woman with the shoes that didn't match.

"Why's she got one brown shoe and one blue shoe?" she demanded of her companion, presumably her mother. These days it was hard to tell, thought Connie. Girls had babies so young.

Getting no answer the child changed the subject without taking her eyes off Connie.

"What's reduced circumstances?"

Reduced circumstances! Where on earth had she picked up an expression as genteel as that? Connie smiled again, still feeling good about herself, but trying not to blink, not to finish the game and admit defeat.

The mother wiped the child's lips roughly with a paper napkin, but traces of tomato ketchup and mustard clung to the thin, stubborn line of her mouth. During the mopping up operation her gaze never wavered.

"It's rude to stare." It was hardly a reprimand, more a dimly remembered rule of manners that required to be stated but no longer applied. "Who said that? About the reduced circumstances?"

The child considered. "Dunno." Then: "Telly. What's it mean?"

"Skint," said the mother. It didn't sound like a word that came easily to her and she seemed vaguely embarrassed at having uttered it.

"Like us?"

No comment.

The child shrugged. "*She's* not. Skint." She pointed across the crowded McDonald's at the object of her unflinching inspection perched on a stool by the window

7

and wearing two odd shoes. Then, with no particular malice, the child poked out her tongue and skewed her eyes.

"You'll be struck like it," said her mother absently. "Eat your burger. You keep nagging and nagging and then you don't eat it. I hate these places." She looked around her with a suggestion of panic. "You can never miss the rush." She sounded worried and much older than she looked, as if the 'rush' had targeted her personally for constant harassment.

The little girl affected not to hear, maintaining her gesture of defiance toward the woman who plainly wasn't skint.

"Vicky!"

So that was her name, thought Connie. Victoria! By what stretch of the imagination or wishful thinking had her parents elected to name her after the Queen whose sculpted likeness peered down majestically at the pigeons from her plinth in the town square – and from how many other plinths in how many other squares all over what used to be the British Empire?

Why she should find this pugnacious child so fascinating she couldn't imagine. It seemed that all the interest in anyone other than herself that had been so conspicuously lacking in her life lately had now found an unlikely focus.

What a curious day it was proving to be! Curiouser and curiouser! Quite suddenly, in response to the child, she, too, poked out her tongue and crossed her eyes. I really must be going out of my mind, she thought. But it was amazing how gratifying it felt to make a fool of herself so publicly and with such abandon.

Queen Victoria smirked with stately satisfaction at having won another round in the endless battle with the grown-up world. She returned to the serious business of demolishing the remains of her burger, paying no further attention to her victim – or seeming not to.

But Connie knew she wouldn't escape the child's surveillance, covert but persistent, all the time she sat there.

She looked down at her hands nursing the container of lukewarm coffee and realised they were trembling, just as they had when she'd been accused of stealing the tape. The atmosphere in the restaurant seemed to darken, no longer so bright and cheerful, the customers no longer so benignly incurious about her, just brutally indifferent.

Why am I here? she wondered. What compulsion had brought her here? What had she expected to find, hoped to find? Nothing much had changed. The McDonald's was new and the video superstore and the cut price Quality Seconds. The boarded up shopfronts of businesses that had gone into receivership were new, too.

But basically it was the same shopping precinct that she'd declared open, ten years before, acknowledging polite municipal applause as she unveiled the plaque beneath the contentious example of modern sculpture that stood guard over the entrance. She doubted whether more than a handful of people even noticed it now. (But what a furore it had caused then: '*Who is this Elisabeth Frink*!' thundered the local paper, affecting not to know in the hope – justified as it happened – of provoking an ongoing controversy.)

And who among those shoppers, now so busily going about their business, would be remotely interested in knowing that Constance Remick MBE, had presided over the opening ceremony? A woman of means, a woman of consequence, "a woman" – in the words of the mayor's plummy introduction – "who is a credit to Southdean". Except, of course, she hadn't been born here, but that was of no significance. The important thing was she had spent money here, created jobs here, bossed the old boys on the council around like Margaret Thatcher in the days when that comparison was considered a compliment, before the rot and the recession set in.

But that was then.

It didn't answer the question: what was she doing here now? Had she crazily hoped, perhaps, to find Colin or at least a little peace from the memory of him? She knew she shouldn't have kept this bottled up inside, not discussing it with Amy, or anyone else. That was half the trouble.

I have to get a grip on myself, she thought. But she couldn't will her hands to stop trembling or her legs to support her when she tried to stand up. And all the time she kept being aware of the child who stared at her with such knowing cunning.

The mother had disposed of the debris of their meal and was hustling her offspring to the door. "Don't dawdle, Vicky!" Irritably.

As the rest of the faces around Connie seemed to recede, the little girl's grew larger and larger until finally it appeared to be isolated in a black vacuum, like the Cheshire Cat's, grinning. She wanted to embrace that grin, absorb it, possess it, make it part of herself. It became terribly urgent that she should make contact with the child before it was too late.

She put out her hand to touch the face. That's all. Just to touch the face.

"What are you doing?" screamed the mother. "Leave her alone! You're mad! She's mad!" She turned round, urging the crowd in the restaurant to bear witness. "She's mad!"

She wrenched the wriggling girl, squealing half with pleasure and half with fright, from the arms of the strange woman wearing odd shoes who was attempting to push through the door with her child.

Someone from behind forced Connie back on to her stool and pinned her hands behind her. A large but surprisingly nimble lady.

"You can't be too careful, these days," she said to Vicky's mother and tightened her grip on Connie. "Best call the police. Let the buggers do something useful for a change. She tried to snatch the kid," she announced to the restaurant at large.

"It was a game," said the child. But no one listened to her.

It's a nightmare, thought Connie. I'm living in a nightmare. If only I could remember. A second, half

10

a second, ago. That's all. If only I could remember. I just wanted to touch her face. How could they think I wanted to abduct her?

Faces crowded in around her. Another crowd, with her as the centre of attention again. She imagined she saw the boy and the girl with the tape peering down at her, recognising her.

She could hardly breathe and her heart was pounding as if it were about to erupt out of her body like some malign thing in a horror movie. Pins and needles pricked her skin.

"She's going to faint," volunteered a man's voice, authoritative, and she felt her head pushed down hard between her knees.

As she lost consciousness, the last thing Connie heard was the child repeating softly: "It was only a game."

Chapter Two

She must have banged her head when she fainted, because she was unconscious for quite a while.

When she came to she was stretched out on a couch in the staff rest room at the back of McDonald's. A good deal seemed to be going on around her. Her head throbbed merrily and the pain intensified as she opened her eyes. What she saw and heard made her wish she could pass out again.

The large lady – fat, really – who had tackled her in the restaurant was giving a uniformed policeman the benefit of some highly charged attitude.

"Well, how were we to know she was somebody?" she demanded. Then, even more truculently, as the qualifying thought came to her: "And even if she is, that's no excuse for going around interfering with children. Anyway, *I've* never heard of her." The implication being that, as she'd never heard of her, Constance Remick was of no more account than the rest of them. Quite right, thought Connie, mentally applauding her own grasp of the woman's logic, even in her present muzzy state of mind.

Her 'crime', she realised, as she lay on the couch listening, had seemingly taken on new, alarming proportions during the time since she'd passed out. How long ago? Long enough anyway for her to be transported to the staff room and for a policeman to be summoned from somewhere. It was he presumably who had decided she was 'somebody', probably after inspecting the contents of her bag.

He was very young and black in the all purpose current definition of the term, although his skin, glowing like

12

polished mahogany, was no more black than the large lady's bright puce face was white.

He knew he was enough of a rarity in Southdean to warrant a second glance if not actually to cause comment. While he privately suspected that this was a fuss over nothing very much, having been brought up in a demonstrative Jamaican family that didn't think there was anything innately wrong in reaching out to other people's children, he was prepared to treat the incident with proper seriousness. There had, after all, been some rum cases even in his limited experience. And he was determined to maintain a correct impartiality, however much he might be provoked.

"Was that what she was doing?" Just the facts, ma'am! Nothing fancy! To Connie's ear he sounded comfortingly pragmatic.

"It was hardly what you'd call interfering. Just – well, odd. Really, no harm done. I mean – sort of sad, don't you think?" Connie recognised the tentative tone, with its underlying hint of misplaced breeding. It was Vicky's mum who, she noted thankfully, appeared to be having second thoughts.

"Mad, you said. Mad!" The large lady sounded aggrieved as she heard her evidence of criminal intent wasting away for lack of support from the principal witness.

"I can't remember what I said. It was so sudden. Odd, I said, odd."

The young officer sighed and Connie groaned. She was fully conscious now and her head was still throbbing as if a mechanical drill were pounding away inside her skull. She couldn't delay whatever accounting she might have to face any longer. Please God, don't let them have called Amy! Holly would have been unreachable.

"An ambulance is on its way." Another voice chimed in. Young, too, but in command. The manager maybe. Like policemen they always seemed to be so young these days.

"I don't need an ambulance." Connie tried to sit up

on the couch, winced with pain and sank back again. "I'm perfectly all right. And I didn't try to abduct that child," she said feebly, as if she half wondered whether perhaps she had.

"I think it's better they take a look at you in the hospital. Just you lie there." The officer looked down at her. Poor, sad, silly soul and she had been somebody once, although he personally had no recollection of her.

He took the young mother aside. "Do you want to press charges?" It was the right thing to ask, but his tone plainly said: "You don't want to press charges, do you?"

She shook her head. "No. There's enough misery," she added, for no apparent reason. But the policeman understood. Even in relatively prosperous Southdean there was enough misery. The child, the object of the fuss, had been quietly taking it all in, almost forgotten.

She stood at the foot of the couch, gnawing her nails furiously and staring at Connie. When Connie opened her eyes and looked back at her, she giggled.

"Don't, Vicky! She can't help it," said her mother.

Help what? thought the child. It's only a game.

"She *was* acting strange." It was Tone of the U2 tape. She hadn't been wrong. Connie recollected having seen him before she fainted. If that came out . . .

"How strange?" It was an obligatory question but the officer didn't seem much interested in the answer.

The boy thought about that for a bit. "Nothing," he said finally, motivated perhaps by pity. He nodded at Connie's feet. "Odd shoes."

She heard the wail of the ambulance as it mounted the incline to the shopping precinct, scattering pedestrians on either side. She was aware of experienced hands loading her onto a stretcher and soothing voices assuring her that she'd be all right. Of course I'll be all right, she thought irritably. I banged my head. That's all. Mild concussion at most.

But if only that were all. What ailed her wouldn't show up in any X-ray.

She felt a small, bunched fist kneading into the

14

palm of her hand. "I expect you'll get well," said the child, carelessly. Her greedy little eyes locked into Connie's again.

"I expect so," said Connie. "What's your name?"

"Victoria Marilyn Dowling. Six years, eight months, two days. 28 Plum Close, Brighton, Sussex. England. Europe. The World." She enunciated the litany of identification in a high, clear voice as if giving a recitation.

"That's *enough*, Vicky! I've told you before about being free with strangers."

"Don't go," said Connie as they shut the ambulance door.

But she wasn't sure whether Vicky and her mother had heard her.

She sipped her herbal tea, snuggled down into the cushions of the settee and gazed up into her own eyes staring serenely out of the painting over the fireplace. Had she ever been that young? she thought, looking at that confident, unblemished face. No lines, no doubts, no fears, not even the merest trace of a sag around the chin or an untidy hair in the eyebrow. All rosy glow and rosy future. Unnatural golden hair – except it hadn't been unnatural then – centre-parted and falling decoratively to her shoulders. Those square tanned shoulders holding up the halter top of some sort of flowery frock.

"I want to reveal the feminist beneath the femininity." The painter, fresh out of art school, had been determined to impress with the depth of his understanding of his subject. It was his first paid commission and not really his 'thing' he had later confided to Connie when cheque and painting had been exchanged and they'd both privately conceded the result had not been an unqualified success. But Sam had liked it. Sam would. And that, she supposed, was what mattered. If he could bear to have this idealised portrait of his wife forever looking down at him from above the mantelpiece, then who was she to argue? Not even his wife any more, not for how many years? Three? Four?

"I can't think Karen is overjoyed at seeing *that* every day," she said to her ex-husband.

"I don't think it bothers her. More tea?" He was wearing the same sloppy Fair Isle cardigan he always wore, summer or winter. Well, probably not exactly the same cardigan. Having found a garment in which he felt comfortable he tended to buy identical twins in bulk until the manufacturer ran out of stock, changed the design or went bust, she recollected. Indeed if she had to describe her ex-husband in one simple term it would be as a sloppy Fair Isle cardigan: honest, unpretentious, old-fashioned and reliable to a fault. How his unrelenting reliability had aggravated her in the old days!

She declined the tea. "You mean she doesn't even notice it? Karen? The portrait?"

He wrinkled his brow. Even his face arranged itself in a Fair Isle pattern it seemed. "No. I don't suppose she does."

"Part of the furniture?"

He didn't attempt to answer that. She remembered that, too. His amiable retreat from any kind of confrontation, which had always left her feeling he had won the argument by default.

She didn't know why she was goading him now. Probably out of habit. It was her only way of indicating her displeasure that the receptionist at the emergency department of the local hospital should have called Sam after they'd trundled her along to have her head examined and an X-ray taken. After consultation, no doubt, with the policeman who had insisted on seeing her admitted.

It was none of their damned business. She'd said she was perfectly all right. Just a bump. Ninety-nine people out of a hundred had to wait patiently and endlessly for attention from the NHS and the police and she had to be the one who got the full treatment instantly.

Didn't they think she was capable of calling a cab and getting herself off home on her own? Presumably not.

"You're angry they got in touch with me," he said in that mild voice that managed at the same time to

16

sound so penetrating to her. Penetrating in intuition, too. Of course he'd got it right. It had nothing to do with Karen or the silly portrait. It was the fact that he should be made privy to her stupidity. Her vulnerability. She'd always hated that word. Vulnerability! It was like Bisto or custard: all purpose slush. Anyone from Marilyn Monroe and the Princess of Wales to a stray dog or a Muslim refugee was vulnerable. Call it vulnerable and you didn't have to address the real problem.

"Yes, I'm angry," she admitted. She held out her cup. "I don't suppose you've got anything stronger than tea with bits of grass in it." Cow, she cursed herself.

He looked at her doubtfully, seriously considering the advisability of something stronger and ignoring the aspersion cast on his herbal tea. "They said at the hospital you should take it easy for a while, rest, liquids, lay off alcohol."

"They always say that."

"They've also given you a note for your own doctor. About the mild concussion—"

"I knew it was just mild concussion—"

"And the blood pressure."

"Oh!"

"It's up. You'll probably have to have some medication for it. Candidate for a stroke, they said."

She sighed deeply. "Why didn't they say all this to me? Did they think I wasn't competent to take it in?"

He shrugged. "Of course not." But the shrug was more eloquent. They probably didn't think she was competent. After all – if the policeman had passed on the message – she had been practically accused of stealing a child and God knew what else. And anyone could see she was wearing odd shoes, even Sam, although he considerately averted his eyes from her feet.

She kicked off the mismatched pumps viciously so that he had to take notice of them. "You see what a wreck I've become. Can't even dress myself properly. And what's more I even tried to pinch some boy's music tape in the precinct. I'll bet you didn't know *that*." Her

17

voice was heavy with sarcasm, telling the joke against herself and inducing embarrassment in him. Except, of course, Sam never got embarrassed, either for himself or anyone else. Life in all its forms was a gift from God and only God required an explanation as to how you conducted that life. God – and maybe the Director of Public Prosecutions.

He picked up the shoes, bending carefully to favour one side. She felt a momentary pang when she recalled how she'd heard he had had a hip replacement, but she'd forgotten or hadn't bothered to enquire how he was adjusting to it.

"It's a natural mistake. I have the greatest difficulty deciding which cardigan to put on in the morning." He screwed up his mouth, the smile lighting up those reflective eyes.

It never failed. She smiled back. He hadn't lost that endearing knack of making mock of his own foibles. Cardigans had been a bone of contention between them, until it had lost its novelty value and become – like everything else in their marriage including that ridiculous portrait – part of the furniture.

"You're a lovely man, Sam," she said. "And I treated you shamefully. It's just – just you were never *my* man. If there is such an animal."

"I know Con." He sat down gingerly on the side of the settee and took her hand in his. "You mustn't mind that they called me. Same surname, after all. And there are a lot of people in Southdean who remember you, remember we were married, perhaps still think we are. You'd had a rough do and I imagine they thought someone should be around to see you home."

"Except it's not my home any more, Sam. It's yours and Karen's. I couldn't wait to get out of it when we split up. It summed up everything: the divorce, the business being taken over, Colin. Every nook and cranny seemed to hide some memory I wanted to forget." She snorted. "Memory! Who am I kidding? Guilt."

A flicker of amusement came into his eyes, was quickly

suppressed but not quick enough to escape Connie's notice. "You think I don't feel guilt?" she said, the old edge sharpening her tone.

"I'm sure you do," he agreed. "We all do at some time or another. And there's nothing like a good old wallow in guilt to let you off the hook."

"What hook?" Even more abrasive now.

"There's not much point in feeling guilty if you don't do anything about it. Otherwise it's just an exercise in self-indulgence."

"I didn't ask for a lecture," she snapped. "God preserve us from the reasonable man. It must be all that talking to plants. Words, words, words! Blah, blah, blah!" He'd sounded so complacent yet non-judgemental that she'd wanted to throw something at him, as she had on occasions of extreme provocation in the past. But he would only have ducked and laughed at her childish bad temper.

"Well, God preserved you from this one, so that's all right, isn't it?" he remarked – reasonably.

She sighed, wondering whether his new wife, Karen, found living with such an equable temperament as Sam's as trying as she had. Or perhaps Karen was as saintly as Sam, saving her venom for all the aphids, mites and other ravenous pests that might endanger their prize fuchsias.

"I really could do with that drink."

"A small one," he agreed, adding pointedly, "Where did you park your car?"

"Not just a reasonable man, a cautious one, too." She accepted with ill humour the minute brandy which looked even tinier than it was, drizzling around at the bottom of the bulbous glass. "I didn't park it. I didn't drive. I came down by train. It was revolting. Dirty windows, no buffet car and it filled up at Gatwick with an army of huge, young German back-packers who got out at Hove. I can't imagine what they'd find to do in Hove – actually." Why was she rattling on like this, as if she gave a damn about a bunch of husky Germans in Hove? There was so much more she wanted, needed, to say to Sam. He knew

19

it. She knew it. Maybe that silly business in McDonald's had created the opportunity she hadn't dared face: the involuntary cry for help about which psychiatrists and social workers talk so glibly.

He shook his head, a puzzled expression on his face which she remembered well from the many times he'd been baffled by some unconsidered action of hers. "Con, what on earth made you come by train? You always said you loathed travelling by train. Only did it when you had to. More to the point," – for the first time he seemed hesitant – "frankly, why did you come down anyway?" he blurted out, regretting it instantly. "Sorry, that sounds . . ."

"Perfectly natural." She shrugged. "Whim! Or something. I wonder who first thought up that 'Hove – actually' thing? Someone who wouldn't be seen dead next door in Brighton, I suppose." There she was, at it again, rattling on irrelevantly. She mustn't waste this precious time.

She set down the glass carefully on the creamy-minky rug, reflecting how well it had stood up to the years of wear and tear, considering it had been one of the first things they'd bought for that comic rented flat when they'd married twenty-eight years ago.

She took a deep breath. "Sam . . ."

"Connie, don't torment yourself. We're both to blame for Colin – in our way."

"You always could tell when I was bracing myself to say something awkward." She was half relieved that he'd taken the initiative and half angry with herself for not having the guts to come out with it first. "It's just . . . I haven't . . . to anyone . . . even Amy . . . about Colin. . . ." The words, coming out in fits and starts, kept choking in her throat and she realised she had no control over the tears that were welling up in her eyes and starting to trickle down her cheeks. "Sam, where did it all go wrong?" she managed to say before the floodgates opened and the great, racking sobs that had been held at bay shuddered through her body. She felt his arm around her and a hankie stuffed into her hand.

All her life she'd ridiculed those women who had had to be coddled and cared for. "The one lesson you need to learn is never to rely on anyone but yourself," her ferociously ambitious mother had drummed into her. And how well she had learned that lesson!

The trouble was it didn't teach you how to survive unaided when everything started to fall apart. For two years she'd tried to go it alone – Lord, how she'd tried! – and what a humiliating failure that had been!

And now here she was behaving like some helpless Victorian maiden grateful for a manly shoulder to cry on and a manly handkerchief to mop up the tears. How appalled that indomitable old lady, her mother Beattie, would have been to see it; except at the last in that distressing twilight of her life she hadn't even recognised Connie, let alone been capable of approving or disapproving of anything she did.

Thinking of Beattie made it worse. Beattie, Colin, the business – three knock-out blows. Why me? She felt him withdraw his arm and realised she'd been whimpering out loud. "Why me?"

"Why *not* you, Con?" he said. "It's a rough world out there."

He'd judged the right, reproachful response. If he'd been sympathetic she'd probably have gone on weeping indefinitely. She straightened up and scrubbed her eyes viciously with the damp handkerchief.

"How would you know? You're sitting pretty."

"Touch of the old acid!" He cocked his head on one side. "You look terrible."

She ignored that. She knew very well that she looked terrible, but at least she didn't feel dozy and half not here as she had earlier. Whatever Beattie might have said, when she laid down the law about any and everything, a good cry really could be therapeutic.

"I can't stand self-pity," she said primly.

21

"No, you just enjoy it. In other people it's self-pity; with you it's self-justification."

"That's right, rub it in. . . ."

". . . Kick a dog when it's down."

As if on cue a very elderly red setter plodded into the sitting-room, sniffed at Sam and then, turning his rheumy old eyes on Connie, lumbered across to her with as much energy as he could muster.

He nuzzled his moist nose into her lap and looked up at her mournfully.

She ran her fingers over his floppy ears. "Jagger, you old reprobate! You remember me. He remembers me." (Had it been Colin or Holly who had christened him 'Jagger'? Certainly not strait-laced Amy.)

"Dogs don't forget. Do you Jagger?" The voice, with its faint Sussex country burr, implied that on the whole dogs were preferable to people in the memory department.

Karen Remick was in her late twenties. She was a rawboned young woman with a ruddy complexion, capable hands like a navvy's and a nature so sweet that it should – in Connie's biased opinion – carry a Government health warning. She had worked for and then with Sam Remick at his nursery ever since she'd left horticultural college. They'd married a decent year after Connie and Sam had divorced. She was, Connie could hardly fail to notice, heavily pregnant and wonderfully happy and healthy with it. Connie's pregnancies had been fraught and miserable and thoroughly upsetting.

"Lovely to see you, Connie," she enthused as if she really meant it, which she almost certainly did. It would not have occurred to her to think otherwise about her husband's ex-wife who, at some stage in her life, must have been nice, otherwise why would Sam have fallen in love with her?

"Con had an accident in town," Sam explained.

"Con made a fool of herself in town," Connie corrected him. Let's get the record straight. Neither version dented Karen's even, welcoming smile.

"She's all right. A bit concussed. I think it's better she stay the night."

"Of course you must." Karen managed to sound both sorry about Connie's misfortune and delighted to offer her bed and board for the night.

"I'd rather not." I *am* being ungracious, thought Connie. Why should she be so hostile to a young woman who so obviously cherished her discarded husband and whose only crime was in being unfailingly agreeable?

"Nonsense. I can call Amy and she can come and collect you tomorrow. Or whenever. You really ought to let her know."

"I don't *need* to be collected," she exploded. "I don't *need* to be looked after. I just want to be alone. I just want to be *left* alone."

"That's the trouble, Con. Alone is no good. Alone alienated practically everyone who gives a damn about you – *and* drove Colin away."

She was surprised. Twisting knives in wounds wasn't Sam's style at all. His ugly reference to her relationship – or lack of it – with Colin pulled her up sharply. She felt suddenly awfully weary, tired of being prickly, on her guard. It would actually be quite pleasant to spend a night in the old house; they'd been so proud of it when they had picked it up at well below market value, because so much needed doing to it, all those years ago.

He wasn't finished, not understanding that she had already decided to give in. "Alone is dangerous."

That way lies madness, she felt he wanted to add but hadn't dared to.

"Whom God destroys He first makes hopping mad!" She loved the 'hopping' bit that ridiculed the doom of the gloomy prognostication. She couldn't think why the pun she'd read in a magazine should pop into her mind at that moment. But it seemed somehow appropriate.

Sam and Karen exchanged anxious glances over her

head. Poor Con, maybe she is going off her rocker! But Jagger barked enthusiastically. At least *he* knew a good pun when he heard one.

Chapter Three

She awoke abruptly. Someone was shouting. Not loudly, but close by. It took a moment or two, as she recalled why she should be back in these once familiar surroundings, before she realised it had been she who was shouting. An extension into reality of a bad dream in which she had been trying and failing to scream, the sound stifled in her throat until it had forced through her unconscious and pierced the night silence.

There was a patter of feet and a timid knock on the door.

"Connie? Are you awake? I thought I heard a noise."

It was Karen's voice, not Sam's. Karen, who had cooked the delicious supper bursting with nourishing, organically grown home produce. Karen, who had thoughtfully made up the bed in Amy's old room, the one least likely to hold uncomfortable memories for Connie. Karen, who had brought her a hot milky drink and a hot water bottle, as it was so unseasonably chilly, apologising for the lack of an electric blanket because it was one of those energy consuming comforts the Western world should learn to do without. Karen, who had won over her stepchildren by her sheer niceness without appearing to alienate them from their mother (it was Connie, she was forced to admit, who had done the alienating). Karen, who had assured her she could stay as long as she cared to, until she felt quite better and wouldn't she like to see their GP, a marvellous doctor who practised medicine nature's way? Karen, in whom at this very moment Sam's child was growing some tiny organism to fit into the miraculous process of creating a new life. Karen, who would rather not know whether it was a he or a she because it would be like second guessing God. Karen, who would wake at the slightest sound in the night and feel concerned for the safety – or sanity? – of her guest.

There seemed no end to Karen's allotment of virtues, not least of them the quality of being and doing good with such self-effacing modesty. And she would probably have been appalled if she'd realised how intimidated Connie always felt in her company, intimidated by so much unforced decency in one person.

But now, in this pre-dawn limbo, before the old resentments and defences had time to invade her consciousness, Connie had to concede that Sam had struck lucky in his second wife: far more the woman he deserved than Connie.

She faked a yawn and a story. "Sorry, Karen. Went to sleep with a book open and woke up with a start."

"You're sure?"

Caring Karen! Stop sounding so doubtful! "Absolutely sure. Sorry I got you out of bed." She yawned again, very loudly. "Sleepy now!"

That did it. The patter of feet receded.

But the dream wouldn't go away now. She would have to examine it before she could hope to nod off again. And the last thing she wanted was to have to relate it to an understanding successor who was almost half her age and a source of more happiness to her ex-husband than she had ever been.

Where had she been? A courtroom. Trial by jury. Had she been arrested for stealing the silly tape and kidnapping the child with the knowing eyes? That would have made a kind of sense; after all, you can usually relate the remembered bits of dreams to some incident or thought you'd experienced during the preceding day.

But it hadn't been that sort of trial at all. Nothing incriminating in the legal sense had taken place. She'd been standing in a cramped, glass-sided cage. For some reason she hadn't been allowed to sit. The cage was suspended several feet above the floor and she was the focus of attention, like a war criminal. Hundreds of spectators crowded the courtroom which was the size of a cricket pitch. And, fenced off in a jury box, were the faces, judging her. Faces she knew well: Colin, Amy, Holly, Beattie, Sam. Faces she barely recognised: the child in McDonald's and her mother. And the face of a stranger who, for a fleeting familiar moment, wasn't a stranger at all but a disturbing presence from the past; try as she may, though, she couldn't give form or identity to the familiarity.

The faces were mouthing words at her which she couldn't hear through the thick glass walls of her cage. She had clenched her fists and battered them against the walls. There was blood on her hands and trickling down her arms. She tried to scream – and then the scream had become real, here in this peaceful old house, flanked by woodland.

She marvelled that she could remember it all so vividly, something that hadn't happened except in her head; although her everyday life was littered with the debris of her forgetfulness.

She doubted whether a psychiatrist would have much trouble explaining the dream; indeed she was sure she could explain it perfectly well herself. Dreams weren't hard. She recalled that when she used to travel a lot in the early years of the business she kept having a recurring one about losing her handbag without which she would have had no money or credit or means of identification. When she stopped travelling so much, settled and safe, she stopped having the dream. Simple!

But if it were that simple, why did she always break out in a cold sweat at the thought of it? And why did the sight of those accusatory faces in the enormous courtroom fill her with such dread?

She turned her face toward the window. Through the half-drawn curtains she could see the dawn lightening the night sky. Some early birds, probably tits, had started chattering to each other. She heard Jagger wheeze and bark, still half asleep. Someone was moving around

27

downstairs quietly, not in a sinister way like a burglar, but considerately, so as not to wake anyone else.

It was all pleasantly reassuring. She closed her eyes and was agreeably surprised when she opened them again to realise that it was eight o'clock and a tray of tea and biscuits had been thoughtfully placed by her bedside.

She sat up and surveyed the room. Amy's room.

Little had been changed in it since her daughter had left to set up on her own and no doubt she enjoyed coming back to it on her visits, finding everything more or less undisturbed. Karen would be very scrupulous about that. The books were neatly lined up on the bookshelves that took up practically an entire wall: serious books, reference books, the only fiction the kind that other people found difficult, graded by size not alphabetically by author. On the small desk under the large bay window was the Olympia portable typewriter they had given her on her eleventh birthday. The vivid red and grey striped wallpaper she had chosen when the room was redecorated, giving it the family nickname of 'hangover alley'. And Connie had had to concede that, once you got used to it, it was really quite fetching in an aggressive kind of way. She had drawn the line at matching curtains and, disgruntled, Amy had settled for a pinkish dove grey which was surprisingly complementary.

Amy had never been a girlish girl and the room reflected it. A strictly business room for homework and study. No knick-knacks or cuddly relics of child-hood. Not a room for mooning around in on scatter cushions, listening to pop records and dreaming of rock singers who sweated obscenely, took drugs and stripped down to their Y-fronts on stage. Amy had always known exactly where she was going. In a way she was more like Beattie than Connie had ever been. Connie had conformed to her mother's ideal of a liberated, independent woman; choices had never been an option, even considered. But Amy had embraced that ideal whole-heartedly and single-mindedly. She had plotted her course with calculated determination: more than ample A levels, business studies, accountancy, economics, a swift rise in the ranks of one of those august city financial institutions that could ride out any crisis in the money market short of bloody revolution.

She was now a respected small firms' consultant within the company, a job she found absorbing but confining. On the back burner of her life was an ambition, when the time was right, to go into politics. But if she saw herself as a future Chancellor of the Exchequer she kept quiet about it. She was wise enough in the ways of getting ahead in a man's world to know when to keep her mouth shut. The use of subterfuge, even feminine wiles but only in extreme cases, when she deemed it necessary, didn't bother her at all. Unlike her young sister Holly she was no militant feminist. When challenged, Amy would explain, quite reasonably she thought: "I'm a feminist for me. You fight your own battles. I did." Of course Holly would argue back: "What about those who can't fight their own battles? It's up to the strong to support the weak." But she made no dent in what she considered Amy's pragmatic callousness.

Her achievement had not gone unnoticed. When a journalist had written an approving paragraph about her in the *Sunday Times* Business Section, she had cited her mother as her example (although Connie had always scrupulously ignored her pushy daughter's shrewd professional advice – a neglect she later regretted). At the time Connie had doubted whether Amy had actually meant it or whether it had simply been one of those bogus little touches that persuade the reader there is a human side to such impressive efficiency. Now, she realised, it was probably quite true.

Connie – or, rather, CC Connections – had been undeniably one of the Eighties' small success stories. Not in the Anita Roddick league, but still a notable testimony to the Thatcher theory of free, unbridled enterprise.

Ingenuity and initiative. Spot the demand and supply

29

the need. That's what they had said about Connie Connor. She had used her maiden name because it produced a pleasingly alliterative logo. CCC – separates with style, beachwear with bezazz!

In time the 'Connections' had been dropped from the marketing as too formal. 'CCC' was sufficient to identify the product: quality design combined with street cred and low price. The look that's ahead of the look! Whatever that might mean. Who, she wondered, had thought up that nonsense slogan that had somehow caught on?

It had all been so easy, as if it were meant, from the beginning. A logical progression, with no ruts on the way, no unforeseen detours. Every corner had seemed to open up new, exciting vistas, except the final one that had ended in a dead end. But that was in the future, a grim future she had been too blind, too stubborn, to countenance even during those three o'clock in the morning sweats. Before that it had been an exhilarating run. Even now that it was all over, long over, she could still sometimes feel the thrill of it, of being that 'somebody' about whom the woman in McDonald's had been so dismissive.

Hadn't she inherited from Beattie her instinctive flair for fashion? And it was Beattie who had encouraged her to take the City and Guild's course in design and clothing craft. As there hadn't been much money in the kitty after the death of Connie's father, they had made their own clothes, at first from necessity and then for pleasure. When friends admired them, they had started buying up job lots of cheap fabric from the mill shops and adapting *Vogue* couture patterns, selling the finished articles to friends of those friends and, finally, to total strangers.

"You're away, girl," Beattie had said. Not 'we'. She'd abdicated her own right to success in nurturing the hunger for it in her daughter. It was enough to see herself in Connie or the self she projected into Connie. It had never occurred to her that maybe Connie hadn't the stamina or foresight to survive as she would have survived, that her child wasn't a replica of herself.

When the Inland Revenue and VAT inspectors had started taking an interest in the enterprise, they had set up as a fully-blown business, with a loan from the bank and a small factory on the outskirts of the nearby seaside town, Southdean.

Gradually, Beattie had receded into the background and it was Connie up front all the way. They were heady times when it seemed she could do no wrong; plus the lucky coincidence of an unsolicited endorsement for CCC from a well-known TV actress who had just landed the lead in a popular soap. (That the TV actress was an old pal from childhood who owed Connie a favour didn't detract from the boost she gave to the product.) Caution, as advocated by Sam, even Beattie, was for wimps and Connie was enjoying proving to herself as much as to anyone else that she was no faint-heart. She expanded the business, took on new employees and new premises, engaged a PR firm and a management team that was only too happy to earn its keep by advising her to open CCC retail outlets in department stores to cash in on all that expensive advertising which seemed obligatory at the time.

Oh yes, she'd been an example all right to a bright girl like Amy. But an example of what? Success turned sour, a life so focused that, when the focus was removed, there was nothing left to take its place?

She sipped the lukewarm tea and looked at the garishly striped wall opposite her. Square in the centre was the original poster of the first CCC advertisement, the three letters swirling into the shapes of three female forms, not wearing any distinguishable garments, but daubed in the distinctive blending colours that had been Connie's trademark. She supposed it had been decorating the wall for years; the first thing Amy would have seen when she had woken up, an ambitious teenager with all those big plans which she was now busily putting into operation. And maybe wide-awake Amy wouldn't

31

make the mistakes she'd made. At least she didn't appear to be interested in acquiring a husband or a long-term partner, let alone a family. But then career women didn't, these days, it seemed to Connie: they put their maternal instincts on to hold until they were forty and then made up the time in their race against the biological clock by producing a couple of infants in quick succession. Maybe it was better that way.

She was conscious of scratchy sounds of activity in and around the house. She supposed she should put in an appearance, although she dreaded it. The memory of the day before came flooding back. Yesterday she had simply felt tremendously foolish; now, she realised, she must appear to have been unhinged, even dangerously so. "Mad," the woman had said.

It was Thursday; that much she remembered. She was supposed to have had lunch with Amy on Wednesday but her daughter had had to call it off and another endless day of nothing much had seemed to stretch to infinity. So, on an impulse, she had left her small flat in the purpose-built block in Richmond and taken the train to Southdean.

There could have been only one reason for the sudden decision, although she wasn't fully conscious of it then. She could have gone to the Royal costume exhibition at the V & A or taken in a matinée or even visited one of the few equally aimless friends she had made in this new idle existence. She didn't particularly like Southdean very much. But everything of consequence in her life was locked up in this small town and maybe she had actually hoped to recover some sense of herself if she could spend some time there again. That had to be the answer and look where it had landed her! Narrowly escaping being charged with attempted theft and abduction, forced to accept the hospitality of an ex-husband and his new wife, with nothing to wear but yesterday's clothes and two odd shoes.

Gingerly she tested the tender spot on her head and pattered into the adjoining bathroom. A selection of Amy's bath essences and cosmetics were scattered around, so at least she could put on a fairly decent face and present a clean body. It was the shoes that bothered her. Amy had smaller feet even supposing she'd left any shoes behind in the wardrobe. In the old days mismatched feet would have been a cute marketing ploy. But that was then. This was reality, normality, not an ad in a glossy magazine.

She made her way downstairs to the kitchen. It was much less neat than it had been when she had been mistress of the house. A working kitchen, warm, comfortable, the smell of fresh baking still clinging to the atmosphere. Obviously, Karen had been busy before going off early to help in the nursery which had grown substantially in size and reputation in the twenty years of Sam's proprietorship.

Sam had resolutely refused to term it a garden centre, with all its expectations of children's play area, plaster gnomerie, mock Victorian preserves, cafeterias and lavatories. Real gardeners bought plants, shrubs and trees with reliable pedigrees, not conceptual experiences.

These days he occasionally put in an appearance at the nursery but not too often. His face was too well known. The request to pose for a photograph beside a grinning customer and his chosen pot plant amused him at first, then irritated him. He was a gardener – all right a gardening expert, he conceded – not a celebrity. His attitude used to baffle Connie who allowed herself to be used in every possible way to promote her business. Now she understood it. Sam had refused to go against the grain, his grain.

As she brewed up a pot of coffee and made herself some toast, she wondered where he was. Probably in his study composing one of the several gardening columns he wrote each week for various publications or plotting out a feature item for *Gardeners' World* on growing the fuchsias he was so passionate about. Channel 4 had approached him to host a gardening programme of his own, for he had an earthy, slightly curmudgeonly image on screen which, though at odds with his private personality, seemed to please the viewers. He had turned down the offer as he turned down all offers that smacked of personal publicity. He was, Connie had to admit, a contented man.

"How are you in yourself?" a naïve interviewer had once rashly asked him.

"A contented man," had been his crusty reply. And that's what had been the headline the subs had used on her rather thin feature.

"You knew damn well it would be," Connie had challenged him, "that's why you said it."

"No I didn't," he said, genuinely surprised. "It's the truth."

And he had said it with such confidence. The one lucky man or woman in a million who knew the truth about himself.

She wandered out into the garden nursing her coffee cup. Despite the brilliant sunshine the air was fresh and a brisk breeze was blowing.

She heard the monotonous whine of an electric saw nearby. Obviously a tree was being lopped, probably the untidy old oak that might have a local preservation order on it but was well past its dead-by date and in constant need of care and attention. She remembered it well. Even Sam, who always had excuses for nature's waywardness, had been known to curse its persistent refusal to give up the ghost and die gracefully. It was much too close to the house and the lawnmower regularly sliced roots that, during recent scorchingly dry years, had poked through the earth sucking up whatever moisture was around. It was an odd time of year to be lopping though, she thought idly. She was no gardener, but she could hardly have helped picking up a few basic rules from Sam.

She supposed she ought to ring Amy while immediately deciding to put off the call for a bit until she felt stronger. Amy, at full throttle, was too daunting a prospect for her to contemplate just now. ("It's a pity you didn't salt more away when the going was good.

For someone with a decent business head it was very stupid." "How dare you speak to me like that," she'd replied, on her remaining dignity. But of course Amy had dared because Amy was right. And there was no point in regretting her euphoric miscalculation that the going would never not be good now.)

There was always the faint possibility that Amy might not be aware that Connie hadn't spent the night in her flat, but it didn't seem likely, given her habit of looking in on her mother before going to the office. She lived only a few minutes away in a rather grander flat, the better to keep an eye on her erratic parent while not actually having to share living space with her.

The sound of the electric saw grew louder and she realised she'd been drawn toward the oak which dominated the rear garden with such stately disdain.

Then she heard Sam's agitated voice from the terrace. "For Christ's sake, Connie, *move!*"

She looked at him, alarmed, and up at the tree. A large chunk of blighted oak missed her by inches, showering her with brown, crackling leaves and shreds of bark. The coffee cup fell from her shaking hand to the ground, shattering on impact. She stared at it, horrified.

"Are you OK?" Sam was beside her, brushing the bits of leaf and bark from her blouse and skirt. He sounded worried. She could have been hurt.

"I'm so sorry, Sam."

"Sorry? For what?"

"The cup." She kept staring at the pieces of china.

"Don't be ridiculous. It's just a cup."

"No, really, Sam. It's . . ."

"It's just a cup," he repeated firmly. Then, raising his voice, he bellowed up into the tree, "Bill, what the hell's got into you? I told you to leave it till autumn. How could you be so careless?"

A wiry little gnome of a man shinnied down the oak. He was in his fifties and there was no remorse in the beady eyes he turned on Connie. "I must have misunderstood," he said by way of apology.

35

Something, a familiar tone, deflected her concentration from the shattered cup.

He looked her boldly in the eyes, equal to equal, ignoring Sam for the moment.

"You don't recall me, do you?" he said. "I was the sample cutter in your factory. First you hired."

There was a bravado in the remarks that made her feel threatened. She took a step back wanting to sense Sam's comforting presence behind her.

"I remember you," she said carefully. "Bill Daley. How are you Bill? Who are you working for now?" That was a mistake.

Nervously, she extended her hand, but he didn't reciprocate.

"Mr Remick. I work for Mr Remick. He hired several of us when we were made redundant. No other jobs around here."

"I didn't know."

He paused, pursing his mouth and wrinkling his nose, pondering a suitable response.

"No, I suppose you wouldn't," he said finally. "I'll finish up later," he said to Sam. "It'll be all right," he assured him. "That old thing," – he jerked his thumb up at the denuded oak – "you can't do that old thing any harm."

He trotted off across the lawn to the greenhouse, stopping half-way to look across his shoulder at Connie.

She stared at his bouncy little body. He had the build of a flyweight boxer past his prime but still raring for a fight.

"He hates me," she said. "They all hate me. Colin hated me."

Sam shook his head. "Poor Con, it's not that simple. You still don't understand, do you, even now?"

Chapter Four

Trust Sam to state the obvious with the blunt compassion of an honest man. She had never been strong on understanding. Everyone knew that. Even she had gleaned that much after a year in analysis when her whole world had seemed suddenly to be collapsing around her.

"What don't you understand?"

He hadn't been at all what she'd expected of a psychotherapist. Mild-mannered, almost sleepy, peering at her through lidded eyes, prompting her with what seemed trite questions, as unimpressive as his flat Midlands accent. But then her experience of psychiatry had been limited to the movies and Montgomery Clift as a bearded and mesmeric Freud.

"Me. Why Colin died. Why the business went bust. Why my marriage broke up. Everything."

So, give me some answers!

Oh no, that's not the way the game's played. You have to supply the answers for yourself. You have to discover the understanding. The chap behind the leather-topped Victorian desk in the nice Harley Street office just did a lot of listening and a little prodding. He had a habit of fingering the bridge of his nose as if to ease a persistent ache; she found it a worrisome trait, not conducive to trust.

If he'd been Montgomery Clift with the beard she might have stuck it out. But one day she had arbitrarily decided that she would rather suffer a nervous breakdown in stressful ignorance than endure any more seemingly useless hours of therapy at enormous cost to someone –

probably Sam, who would feel responsible for her even though he legally wasn't.

She felt Sam's hand gently patting her shoulder. Already he was regretting reproaching her for expecting life to be simple, for not understanding.

She would like to have melted into the comforting warmth of his sympathy, but she no longer had the right and she shrugged him away brusquely. If he was hurt by her rejection he didn't show it, but then, being Sam, he wouldn't.

"You didn't tell me you took on some of the people they let go at the factory." She made it sound like an accusation of deceit.

"It wasn't important and you have enough on your plate."

"You mean I wasn't expected to care about my former employees!" That's right, Connie, stir it up.

"No. I mean what with one thing and another you weren't well."

"That's a delicate way of putting it. One thing and another." She looked around the garden, taking in the untidy beds, the straggly shrubs and, finally, fixing her eyes on the offending oak. Oddly, it didn't appear uncared for or abandoned, just pleasantly disordered as if that were the way Sam had planned it. It had been neater in her time, like the kitchen. ("That's what we'll put on your gravestone," Sam had joked. "Here Lies Connie Remick. She Was Neat." That was in the days when they could share jokes.)

"What a fright all those fans of yours would have if they could see your own garden, after all that expert advice you give on how to manage their own! It's a mess, Sam," she said irritably.

"You're right," he agreed amiably. "But it's my mess. My own private mess. My own private woodland mess. It's where I make my mistakes away from curious eyes. Didn't you ever wear jeans and a baggy sweater when you were off duty?"

She frowned, not quite getting the connection. When

she did, she thought for a moment and shook her head. "No." Eccentric maybe, but messy, no. She was suddenly acutely aware again of the odd shoes.

"No, I don't suppose you did. Come to think of it I can't ever remember you being off duty – even when you were!"

It was another of his convoluted connections, but this time she knew exactly what he meant. During most of their marriage when she was occupied with the business she could never wind down, relax, be something other than a highly successful career woman. She was always putting herself about, taking up local issues, graciously allowing herself to be persuaded to stand as councillor in the borough elections. She was a prized speaker at schools, painting a picture of a glowing future for pupils with her energy and drive.

Even on their rare holidays she could never allow herself to forget what she had left behind and simply enjoy being with Sam and the children. If she ever felt a moment's unease about neglecting them she would immediately reassure herself that, after all, wasn't she doing it all for the family, weren't they benefiting materially from her efforts? (Sacrifice, she decided, trying it on for size, was too strong a word.) "That's the classic workaholic's excuse," the mild man behind the Victorian desk had told her in one of his exceptional expressions of confidence in her ability to take in an unpalatable fact.

"What on earth did you find for Bill and those others to do in the nursery?" It still rankled that it should have been Sam who had shown more concern for her redundant workforce than she had.

"Bill's a good mechanic, electrician."

"Except when I'm around."

"That was an accident. With the oak. So, don't start getting paranoid about Bill."

She detected the hint of the martinet she'd forgotten. Not all sweetness and light, our Sam!

"And the others?"

"Maisie, Phyllis, help out with customers. I was surprised how knowledgeable they are about plants, what grows well in local soil and what to avoid. I suppose it was always there. They seem happy and the nursery was expanding. I'd have had to take on more staff anyway."

She remembered Maisie and Phyllis, two plump, cheery girls she had taken on as trainee machinists on a youth training scheme when they left school, larking about with the drivers in the yard during the tea break and sneaking a fag in the loo. They'd been quick and bright and anxious to learn and she felt ashamed that she hadn't thought about them in years since CCC had been taken over.

"Do they ever talk about me?" Silly question. She didn't know why she had asked it. Yet it would be consoling – although hardly likely – if they did remember her not unkindly.

"Why should they?" He avoided her eyes and she knew that whatever had been said in Sam's hearing probably wasn't complimentary. More along the lines of: "Bloody bitch dumped us – and I don't see her having to queue up at the Job Centre."

But they had shared some good times – she and the crew at the factory – before she had distanced herself from the nuts and bolts of running her own show, that part of the job that had been her prime reason for starting the business in the first place. The designing. The haggling with suppliers. The sweet-talking of buyers. The sense of triumph when a new line clicked. The rapport and chit-chat with the machinists and cutters and finishers and packers on the shop floor.

But all that was before she had been beguiled by the magic word, expansion, when the bank was begging her to take its money, go public, invest in growth and diversification. "Think big," they said. "Big is beautiful." And she believed them, the clever young men in their suits and ties whom she paid handsomely to advise her.

When the crash came it was sudden but not unexpected. Heaven knows, there had been plenty of ominous signs with the economy sliding into stagnation. "You're over-extending yourself, Con," Sam had cautioned, but he had another life now which didn't include her. Amy was blunter, if less comprehensible, warning her about "overheating" and the bubble having to burst sooner or later because there was no such thing as "hurry money" – whatever that might mean – on a long-term basis.

Why hadn't she paid attention? Perhaps because she wasn't as shrewd as she thought she was; perhaps because at the time she seemed to be on a perpetual high as potent as any drug addiction.

If the CCC retail outlets were starting to lose money they would surely pick up soon. If other cost-cutting manufacturers were starting to corner the cheap leisure-wear market she could win back her share of it somehow. If the business could no longer sustain its overheads all that was needed was a practical economy drive.

Only there was no picking up and winning back and economy drives.

At least she had been spared the humiliation of receivership or bankruptcy. When the truth had finally sunk in, it seemed only sensible to accept the offer of one of those opposition manufacturers, who had read the future more astutely than she had, to buy her out, retaining the CCC name. She had even come out of the deal with a tidy income from shares in the parent company. But that had somehow made it worse. She should have suffered more.

Suddenly she was no longer the admirable Constance Remick *née* Connor. She was the woman who had mismanaged a flourishing business. She was the woman who had sold out and in doing so added to the growing unemployment figures. Connie Remick and the recession, it had seemed, were one and the same thing.

And where were those clever young men in their suits and ties? Shaking their heads and swearing blind they had told her so in the boardrooms of rival companies? No, that

41

wasn't fair. They may not have been right, but they hadn't been venal. She was the one who was supposed to be in charge and she'd let them down, just as in different ways she had let down Sam and Amy and Holly and Colin – above all, Colin.

"Wallowing in self-pity again, are we, Con?"

He sounded amused and removed at the same time. He was checking his watch ostentatiously, not saying that his time was precious but implying it. Some printer's proofs perhaps that had to meet a deadline.

"Don't mind me. I'll just potter for a bit. You're busy."

"No. Well – yes." He smiled, grateful that she'd noticed.

"It's funny the way things turn out, Sam. You were the grubby gardener who was perfectly happy to spend the rest of his life in the council Parks' Department and I was supposed to be the high flyer. Now you're the high priest of horticultural know-how with the growth business, the best-selling coffee table books and the medals from Chelsea and I'm the idiot who blew it all and behaves half the time like a crazy woman. You have to admit there's a certain irony about it all."

"Oh, Con," he sighed. "Why do you dwell on everything so much? It's all past history."

"That's where the bodies are buried, according to that miserable Brummie therapist you sent me to. At least, I assume it was you." What was she saying! Where the bodies are buried. She tried not to wince at her own insensitivity. Some day they'd all have to talk, really talk, about Colin. But she wasn't sure she could face it yet.

Either Sam didn't pay any mind to her reference to buried bodies or he preferred to ignore it. "It seemed the right thing. You needed help."

"It didn't. Help."

He sighed again. "I gather not."

"Actually I was a lot better when I decided to sort out my own head. At least I thought I was, until I found

42

myself in Southdean shopping precinct being peculiar. And oddly enough I really feel it did me a power of good." She looked up at him, her eyes pensive, trying to recapture that fleeting feeling of being alive again, part of the human race. "Did I tell you about this child? Funny, crooked-looking little thing. You know, Sam, I swear she had me pegged better than that psychiatrist ever could. I remember . . ."

"Con, I've work to do."

". . . where she lived. Plum Lane. Something. It'll come to me."

"*Con*!"

"I know." She waved him away. "You said. I'll just get myself together and be off. Thank Karen for me. She's been so kind. No – bloody wonderfully kind."

"She's always admired you."

"That's very charitable of her." She said it off the top of her head, not thinking how it might sound. Cool, patronising. It was the sort of remark the old Connie used to toss off, uncaring of its effect, while her mind was occupied with a dozen more urgent matters.

It wasn't the slap that winded her, but the shock that it should have been administered by Sam who had never so much as lifted a hand to his children at their most mischievous or contrary.

She touched her cheek in amazement and felt the delayed sting. She wasn't sure whether to be angry or amused. And did it really matter anyway? Even now Sam would certainly be mentally phrasing an apology, as surprised as she was by his action.

She waited, her hand caressing her reddening cheek.

But he stared back at her with no relaxation in the severity of his expression. "You can say what you like about me, Con. But not Karen. She doesn't deserve it."

"What did I say?" she blustered, feeling cornered. "Charitable! That's what I said. Charitable!"

"It's not what you said. It's how you said it. Me, Amy, even Holly. We know you. But not Karen. She's a simple, good-hearted woman. She couldn't be devious

43

if she tried. She wouldn't even understand if you were taking the mickey and I won't have her being upset, particularly now."

This was an implacable Sam she'd never known and she decided to take the line of least resistance. "Don't be so touchy, Sam. I wouldn't dream of being anything but lovely to Karen."

"There, damn you, you're doing it again. Lovely! Lovely isn't in your nature, Con. It never has been. In many ways you're a monster. In others you're a magnificent woman. People look up to you."

"Used to," she corrected him. She was beginning to feel contrite and not enjoying the experience.

"They still do, if you let them."

"I was nice once, wasn't I Sam?" she wanted to say, but didn't dare for fear that his passion for honesty wouldn't allow him to lie a little, just for old times' sake.

Instead she glared at him pugnaciously. "Well, you won't have to put up with me much longer . . ." she started to say, then suddenly she felt the fight drain out of her. "Sam, I'm so tired."

He peered closely at her as if examining her for some contagious disease, the way he inspected his roses for signs of blackspot. "I know, Con," he said, a relenting tone in his voice. "I shouldn't have done that."

"There are worse things than a slap on the cheek. It hardly qualifies me for battered ex-wife status. And you're right, I can be piggy about people, particularly people who don't know how to get back at me. I'm used to toughies. I had to be, having Beattie for a mother. But you know all that." She paused, hearing herself, the blubbering self-analysis. It's got to stop, she told herself. "What happens next, Sam?"

"You don't have to leave yet, you know. This was once your home. A few days. Amy's bringing a suitcase of clothes for you. I spoke to her this morning and she has to see a client in the area. She won't need her room because she'll be staying at an hotel. We could go over to Chichester to see Holly. She's in the new show at the Minerva. You could see some old friends."

She smiled, no longer tensed up. It wasn't like her to relish being dictated to, but she had to admit she did. "You've got it all organised. Give the old girl a nod, keep her out of harm's way for a bit." She raised her hand, actually laughing. "No, really Sam, I don't mean that facetiously. I just mean it's good of you to care." She pulled a face. "I can just imagine Amy's response when you told her about my – my escapade yesterday."

"Exact words?" he said. She nodded. "'Oh Gawd! Not in McDonald's!'"

She laughed again. Out loud. Two laughs in five minutes! That had to be a recent record.

"'She can't even be trusted to pick a classier venue to play the fool.'" She was mimicking her daughter's brittle accent. "'Now the Ivy or Bertorelli's! *That* wouldn't be so bad.'" She stopped laughing abruptly. "Sam, I'd like to see Colin's room." What had put that into her head? Maybe the laughing. When he was very little and she was young they'd laughed a lot together. About silly, kiddish things. Gertie the giggler, Sam had called her, because Gertrude – named after some dead forgotten relative – was her middle name.

He stroked his uplifted chin in that thoughtful way he had. If he says I shouldn't, I won't, she thought. But then I'll never know, never come to terms with his death and with my culpability.

"It's still exactly as he left it. The cleaning lady keeps it dusted and tidy, but otherwise nothing's been changed. All Karen's idea. I thought we should redecorate it, get rid of his things. It's time. But Karen said we should leave it, at least until you'd seen it again. Frankly I didn't think you'd want to."

"Frankly, neither did I, Sam. But I'm suddenly learning a lot about myself."

She spent the rest of the morning enjoying the unruly garden, breathing the fresh air that somehow never managed to filter through to the city. I've been away too long, she thought. Maybe I never should have uprooted myself so completely and gone to live near London. Lonely London. Well, that's what she wanted at the time. To cuddle up in a shell of depression with nothing but her own failures – Colin, the business, her marriage – to keep her company.

But now she knew why she had come down to Southdean, where it all began, on impulse. It was the sense that finally she had to break out of that stifling shell she'd erected around herself, that finally she would have to pay her dues to the past. She felt exhilarated and dangerously exposed at the same time. Either she'd survive or go totally under.

"Picture! in't it?"

She hadn't heard Bill behind her, but then she hadn't been aware of anything but the private thoughts that had been nagging inside her head.

She realised she had wandered into a terraced-off arbour far removed from the house where Sam had constructed a pond and a rockery surrounded by paving stones and raggedy bits of lawn. There were wooden benches and a table stained with birds' droppings. He'd called it their bit of peace and they'd eaten out there *alfresco* when the youngsters still enjoyed sharing their sausage rolls and jam tarts with wasps and ants.

Bill nodded toward the rockery, prompting her to seriously look at it instead of just idly taking it in. It was, she had to admit, a picture. Well-weathered now, with multi-coloured saxifrages glittering in the sunlight as they tumbled out of the crevices in the rock like streams of rainbow watercolour.

"You're right, Bill. A picture. I'd forgotten what a pretty garden this can be."

He lit a cigarette, wheezed and took a deep drag as if drawing some mental sustenance from it. "Sorry about the tree. He was right. It's much too early to be lopping."

"It didn't matter, Bill. I don't suppose I'd have blamed you if you had wanted to conk me on the head."

He sniffed, enjoying the joke but not disputing it. "I

don't work here all the time," he volunteered. "Just a day now and then when Mr Remick wants something done. Usually I'm at the nursery, out back, in the greenhouses."

"You like it?"

"It's a job. That's something these days. But you don't get the same old feel we had when you started the company. The girls say the same." The 'girls', she assumed, must be Phyllis and Maisie who had to be at least in their late thirties.

"No hard feelings?"

"Plenty. But that's life."

"'Who said life was fair!'"

"Pardon?"

"Joan Crawford. She said that. 'Who said life was fair!'"

"Oh!" He took another puff on the cigarette, flicking the ash on a spongy 'Cloth of Gold' alpine. "Life turns out pretty fair for some," he said quietly, almost whispering to himself. But she heard quite clearly.

"Me?" she said.

He ducked his head and appeared to be busy fingering out a weed on the rockery. Then he straightened up, waving the weed triumphantly. "Damn things get in everywhere." He chucked it onto the grass where it would no doubt happily take root again.

"Not you," he replied finally. "Her."

"Her?" Was she being dense or something? "Her – who?"

"Mrs Remick. The new one," he muttered, plainly irritated that she hadn't been sharp enough to relieve him of the necessity of spelling it out.

"What about Karen?"

"Nothing." His face closed in on itself, his eyes blank. She knew that look from the factory days. There was never any doubt when Bill decided to clam up. "I just said life has turned out pretty fair for her. Well, it has, hasn't it?" he argued, justifying his indiscretion.

She was about to prod him further, although she knew

47

it would be useless, when she heard her name called from the terrace.

It was Sam. He didn't sound too pleased. Another interruption in his morning routine.

"Telephone, Con!"

As she turned her back on him, she saw Bill Daley out of the corner of her eye screwing up his mouth and silently mimicking the call: "Telephone Con!" She wasn't sure whether the mockery was meant for her or for Sam.

"Who is it?" she asked breathlessly, having run the length of the garden to the house. She could never get out of the habit of thinking every phone call would be the bearer of good or ill tidings, particularly the ones you didn't get to answer in time.

"Some chap says you know him. David Levitch. He said that might ring a bell."

She became aware that he was waiting for a reaction and she had difficulty suppressing the prickle of shock the name engendered in her.

Maybe she had communicated it to Sam, after all, for he turned away irritably and feigned annoyance that his valuable time should be squandered by stray phone calls from strangers for a woman who was no longer his wife or his concern.

"Anyway Con," he grumbled, "do me a favour and use the extension in the hall. I've got to get this off before lunchtime."

She passed through the patio door and Sam's study into the hall in a daze. She must have looked strange for she heard Sam call after her: "Con!" In that placating way of his which invariably followed a rare display of what passed for temper with Sam. But she didn't reply.

David Levitch! She conjured up a look, a smile, condescending, amused, but affectionate too. "Constance! That's not a name. That's a middle-class virtue. Constancy!" He'd made it sound like a moral judgement. So that was the face she'd seen in the music store in the shopping precinct.

Chapter Five

Amy Remick checked her make-up in the rear view mirror as she fumed silently in a traffic jam on the approach to the A27 at Arundel. She caught the eye of a red-headed cowboy who was revving up impatiently behind her in an open-topped sports car which he clearly fancied almost as much as he fancied himself. He looked at her disdainfully; not only a woman driver, but a woman driver of a 'safe' car. Dark blue, saloon, four door, 1.8 GLX Mazda. It reeked 'safe'.

He revved up more loudly, clotting the already heavy air with nauseous exhaust fumes. Then he flung a careless arm round a sumptuously pretty companion with long frizzy blonde hair that no doubt caught the motion of the wind fetchingly when they clocked up an illegal 100 mph on the motorway.

"Yob!" muttered Amy and deliberately jerked two fingers up above her head. The red-headed cowboy jerked one back at her and got on with revving up and nuzzling the ear of the blonde beside him.

She turned on the radio. Jenni Murray was rabbiting on about some deeply uninteresting marginal feminist issue on 'Woman's Hour'. She listened for a while. Then, when some shrill smart-ass from UCLA started debating the need to exorcise all traces of political, sexual and racial incorrectness from children's literature with a more sanguine smart-ass from Girton, she switched off.

The traffic inched forward, then came, again, to a seething stop. Behind it, Arundel Castle, looking like a genuinely medieval Disneyland, gazed down serenely on the choking snarl of trucks and coaches and cars. But they paid it no mind. Go, go, go! No time to stand and stare. Except no one was going anywhere for a bit, at least until the police had sorted out a minor collision that was causing maximum disruption up ahead.

Amy fingered her chin and examined it in the mirror. The cover-all make-up had done a good job, but she could still see the yellowish-blue swelling, underneath it, even if other people might be fooled – although they would have to be pretty unobservant.

"Yob!" she repeated. But this time she was referring to the perpetrator of the bruise: a shaven-headed bully boy with swastikas tattooed on both beefy forearms and a Union Jack emblazoned on the chest of his T-shirt.

Lewis and she had spotted him with two similarly intimidating mates throwing punches at a feisty young Asian who was putting up a fight but a losing one.

It was well after midnight on a side street off the Hammersmith Broadway. Lewis had wanted to see an *avant garde* production of something obscure by a Central European playwright with an unpronounceable name in a basement theatre club in the neighbourhood. 'Wanted' was, perhaps, too generous a word. It was more of a duty. Nailed to their seats by Lewis's acquaintanceship with the fiery-eyed director, they had sat through it stoically till the bitter and late end and then been brow-beaten into discussing the show with the cast over spaghetti and rough red wine in an Italian trattoria.

When they finally escaped and started the trek over the bridge to Castlenau where the car was parked, Amy was already feeling nervous. Unfamiliar areas always made her nervous, even in daylight; on her home turf she was fearless.

It was then, in the shadows of a looming block of flats, that they came on the flower of Hitler youth roughing up the Asian.

"Don't get involved," she had hissed at Lewis. But even as she said it she knew it was useless. He would have to get involved.

50

That's when they had turned on him and, by association, her, chanting "Kill the kike!" as a variation on "Paki bastard!"

It was only the lucky appearance of a police car that sent them scattering, and the Asian, Lewis and she nursing their battle scars in the emergency ward of Hammersmith hospital.

"Sorry you got caught in the cross-fire," Lewis had said, not very apologetically, as she tried to staunch the blood from a deep cut over his left eye while tenderly exercising her chin where the wild punch from the tattooed thug had landed.

The Asian boy was admitted for the night with black eyes, a gash on his head and a broken jawbone. He said his name was Ashok and that he wasn't Pakistani anyway, but Hindi, and he'd prefer them not to notify his family. "They worry enough," he volunteered mournfully. "You shouldn't have got involved," he told Lewis as best he could with his injured jaw, echoing Amy's sentiments exactly. "But it was a noble gesture."

He bowed his wounded head slightly. His English was very correct and dignified and it was hard to imagine him provoking any confrontation after midnight in the back streets of London. "All the same," Lewis warned him, "it wasn't very wise walking about alone in the early hours." The expression on the young, pale brown face became suddenly distant and they had the feeling that if he weren't so mannerly he would have told them to mind their own business.

The last they saw of him he was being carted off by a buxom nurse who said, "Well, aren't we a fine mess!" just like Oliver Hardy.

They waited around long enough for them to stitch up Lewis's cut and then managed to get one of the overworked staff to point them in the direction of a pay phone to call a cab to pick up the car.

"I wonder how they knew I was Jewish," said Lewis, feigning surprise as he stroked his imposingly long Semitic nose.

51

"Fool!" she laughed, although it hurt. "How does Dawn French know Lenny Henry is black?"

It was an association of ideas that pleased her. Dawn French and Lenny Henry were famously married. And she was coming around to the idea that it might be nice to be married, or at least securely bonded, to Lewis Diamond. He didn't take up the thought then and there, but she hoped he might give it some consideration. For a long time Lewis had been her secret, a part of herself she kept even from Sam and, particularly, Connie. That's the way she and Lewis had wanted it. But lately she had been aware of a broody desire to put down roots, have a family of her own. It wouldn't have to be the end of her career and, even if it were, would she really mind that much? It was a new and frightening prospect, for the great god Career had governed her life since childhood.

Old Beattie – Gran – would have been appalled. "Any fool can have children," she would grumble, rueing the years she'd spent as a wife and mother which had ill-equipped her for relative penury when her husband died. She would recall the exhilarating freedom she'd enjoyed during the war years, working in an aircraft factory and bringing home a pay packet. As time went by the experience – which couldn't have been that glamorous – became more and more romanticised in Beattie's eyes. The fun, the companionship, the knowledge that you were being valued for your skill and not just regarded as a sex object (although she wouldn't have used that expression then) with housekeeping and breeding potential.

"Then the men came home and it was back to the kitchen for us, wasn't it? They didn't want us in the work place any more. We'd done our bit. Ta-ta, girls! Now brush up on your cooking and make yourself pretty for your man. And all those women's magazines that had been telling us to put our shoulder to the wheel to win the war started lecturing us on how to bring up baby and scrub a floor efficiently and make the most of scrag end of lamb. And what happened the moment your grandpa came home? I got pregnant, didn't I! More fool me."

52

But she didn't mean it. From the moment Connie was born she had been the centre of her mother's life, the focus of all her frustrated ambitions.

Beattie would cuddle little Amy, who tended to be frail, to her enormous bosom and ruffle her hair and feed her butter balls sprinkled with caster sugar when her diet-conscious daughter wasn't looking. "I told your mother and I'm telling you, any fool can have children," she repeated firmly. "But it takes guts and intelligence to have a career. You have to be special for that." Amy, who was only three at the time, would take it all in not knowing what she meant, but enjoying the cuddle (Connie wasn't great on cuddling) and the butter balls. But maybe the idea had lodged in her subconscious, waiting to surface when she was old enough to put it into practise.

If Gran could see her now, even contemplating ditching a fantastic job for a guy or at least putting it on hold, she would probably disown her. But old Beattie was dead. Although Amy had never really believed that. They'd buried a shrunken old lady who had been incontinent and helpless and didn't know who they were and couldn't string a coherent sentence together.

The unctuous vicar had called her Beatrice Connor. It was Beatrice Connor carved on the gravestone and the messages on the wreaths were all commemorating Beatrice or Beattie. But it wasn't Beattie they buried. Not the Beattie that Amy and Connie and Colin and Holly had known. That indomitable lady was sitting up there on a cloud somewhere having a good laugh at them and clucking at their gullibility in assuming that the wretched body in the coffin could possibly have been hers.

That's the way Amy liked to think of Beattie. But she could never talk to Connie about her feelings for her grandmother. She wondered whether Connie even liked to think of Beattie at all, or, if she did, it was from a different perspective. There was something between them that Amy had never been able to fathom, something so deep and hurtful that no amount of cosmetic affection

53

could quite disguise. It was, she always felt, strictly business, between Connie and her mother and the driving force, initially, had been Beattie.

Suddenly she realised that tears were welling up in her eyes and streaking down her cheeks.

At first Lewis didn't notice. When he did he put his arm around her. "It's just delayed shock," he comforted her, misunderstanding. Well, yes, it was, she thought. But not the shock of being threatened by some mindless thugs. It was the shock of comprehending how much she missed Beattie, the real Beattie, after the years of Alzheimer's and her merciful death.

"I want to tell Connie about us," she said finally, when they'd swapped the cab for their parked car and he was nosing it back over the bridge toward the A4 and Richmond.

He didn't answer for a while, making a great play of concentrating on the roundabout and the sparse trickle of traffic approaching from the fly-over. It was now after three, not yet dawn, the quietest of all the unquiet hours in London.

"I wish you wouldn't," he said.

"Why, Lew? It's years since you worked with her."

"For," he corrected her.

She shrugged. "That's immaterial."

"It's the difference between being the boss and being bossed."

"It's still immaterial."

"I know," he agreed. "I'm just putting up an argument. I just don't think it would be a fantastic idea to tell Connie about us."

"Why?"

He ignored the question, ploughing on in the direction they both knew only too well, the direction they'd decided to take when they'd met by chance again at a PR party at the Savoy for the launch of some office computer refinement which had been made obsolete in nine months. That was over a year ago. "We decided it wasn't wise – with Connie in the state she was, grieving

54

over Colin, your grandmother, losing the business. I'd just have been a reminder."

"Lew, that was *then*. She's better now. Oh, a bit eccentric, withdrawn. But she's much more together than she was. I'm trying to persuade her to get about, find something to do. She's not hard up. She'd probably be grateful to have someone like you, someone she knew and could trust, to, well – nudge her along. You know it hasn't been easy, living so close to her, keeping quiet about the man I'm practically living with."

"We're not *living* together, Amy," he said firmly, then, relenting, "yes I know it hasn't been easy."

"You mean you don't want to be tied down." She sounded huffy, hurt.

"No. Yes, I don't want to be tied down. That's part of it."

"And what's the rest of it?"

He opened his mouth as if he'd arrived at a decision. Then he closed it and remained silent.

"So?" Shut up, she told herself. They'd both been so clever with each other up until now, not prodding or prying or talking out of turn.

"Amy," he sighed. "I'm tired. I'm sore. I need this sort of discussion like a ruptured appendix. It's late. I've got an early meeting at the agency tomorrow with some guy who thinks the best way to sell the Grand Canyon to tourists is to have Norman Wisdom fall into it—"

"You're joking . . ." she interrupted his flow with a levity that usually amused him.

"Yes, I'm joking," he replied with exasperating patience. "I *am* joking. But I am not joking about being exhausted. So, please, Amy, give it a rest."

He half-turned toward her with a coaxing smile. "We'll talk some other time."

It was the smile that did it. "I might not be available," she said archly. But, of course, she would.

When he deposited her outside her flat they went their separate ways, but at least they hadn't actually rowed, as

55

Connie would have rowed if placid Sam had given her half a chance.

This urge to confide in Connie about her relationship with Lewis Diamond had been brewing up for some little time, since she'd realised it was no passing fling like all the others. That she should even take seriously anyone in advertising, let alone fall for him, had amazed her. She always regarded advertising as the tinsel that conned the consumer, the glitter that produced nothing but demand. ("And where would any business be without any demand?" Lewis would chide her good-naturedly because he knew and understood her prejudices against anything that struck her as insubstantial, unlike financial solvency and good business management.)

Yet she was always aware that, while you got what you saw with Lewis, what you saw was not quite all the man. There was something extra, a part of himself that carried the warning sign: 'Keep your distance'.

Perhaps Connie had been privy to that missing link, perhaps that's why he hadn't minded that she'd called him 'Little Lew' when he had first come to work for her. But then Connie had always invented nicknames for favoured employees: her factory floor supervisor had been 'red Eddie', not because she had auburn hair or been christened Edwina, but because Connie enjoyed battling with her Bolshie truculence.

Lewis had been fresh out of art college then and brimming with ideas. If he'd noticed Amy it had been only as Connie Remick's serious schoolgirl daughter and if Amy had noticed him it was only as part of the frivolous fringe of CC Connections. It was his age rather than his size (five feet six and every inch a power house of energy) that had prompted her mother's nickname for him.

Connie had known him when; that important 'when' which is the demarcation line between what a person was and what a person becomes. Amy envied her that: knowing Lewis before he'd acquired that veneer of slick and easy charm he used to such profitable effect in his job and which Amy found so offensive when he thought he could get away with using it on her.

"We all have our tricks," he'd laugh. "You, too." "But I know when to leave the tricks in the office." He'd looked sceptical. Maybe she just kidded herself that she left her ploys and techniques for being the best at what she did at the office.

"I can't figure us out," he once ruminated as they treated themselves to a bottle of chablis after an especially satisfying sexual skirmish which had left them pleasantly exhausted. Then, fearing perhaps that she might take it as an invitation to examine their relationship too closely, he had drained his glass, kissed her briefly on the forehead and wriggled into his Levis and sweater. "Must rush," he said as he always said, too quickly, before she could suggest he stay the night. She accepted that, as she accepted the casual rider "I'll call", because he always did and she had learned not to make the mistake of calling him first. She took all this for granted, for she knew if she dwelt on it she would get angry with herself for behaving like any lovesick fool instead of the strong-minded self-assured woman she knew herself to be.

"I can't figure us out, either," she'd called to him as he opened the door. He blew her another kiss and they both smiled, because they understood. They were indeed an odd couple.

He was slight, darkly handsome in a lean and hungry way, with his fierce Jewish drive and volatility, his unshakeable attachment to faith and family upon which no outside relationships or commitments were allowed to intrude. And then there was his code of personal principles that were quite separate from his work. These were the contradictions that she loved in him but was never permitted to be part of. She suspected it was the lack of complexities in their relationship which appealed to him.

By contrast, she was the outwardly reticent, almost forbidding *shiksa*, superficially concerned with appearances above all else, to whom religion was a cursory

57

observance, family a responsibility to be accepted rather than cherished and principles a vague obligation to do the right thing provided it wasn't too inconveniencing.

And while he was attractive to women, she had never been particularly attractive to men. She had unruly mahogany hair already peppered with grey, bold hazel eyes, strong chiselled cheekbones that jutted out almost at right angles to her cheeks. The whole aspect gave her a kind of gaunt grandeur that some found off-putting. Sam had once told her she had the appearance of a primitive sculpture, all angles and bulging eye sockets. Not a pretty young thing – ever.

She wished she had been blessed with her mother's looks. There was a roguish air about Connie, despite the depressions of the last few years. Her feline eyes always seemed to be sizing up a situation and finding it amusing. Her mouth was way too wide and her nose had a crook in it and she often couldn't be bothered to have her hair properly shaped and tinted at the roots when the dye grew out. Her figure had always been too bony and thin. Yet Connie had a way with her that was beyond beauty: a larkishness that Amy envied and Holly had inherited. Part of her success had been due to that beguiling ability to convince people that she was in the business for the fun of it. It was part of her failure, too; only Connie had never understood that.

When Sam had telephoned that morning early with the news of her mother's little "accident" (nicely put, she thought) the day before, she hadn't been particularly surprised, even about the shoes. Nothing Connie had ever done particularly surprised her. Connie, it was agreed, was a character and she always had been, whether she was on a high of success or in the depths of despair.

The sooner you accepted that, the less liable you were to be dazzled or hurt or simply puzzled by her behaviour. Amy felt she had been born with that knowledge about her mother. Holly had learned it along the way without too much emotional damage. It was Colin who had never been able to come to

58

terms with the way Connie was and, in the end, it had destroyed him.

Her thoughts came back to the present, and then she circled her head several times round and round, noting the faint clicks of tension in the muscles of her neck. She wouldn't think of Colin now. If she did she would get angry with herself, Sam and, above all, Connie. And then she would feel put upon for having had to let herself into Connie's flat with her spare key, pack a suitcase and trundle it down to her at Southdean, when she would far rather have spent an extra couple of hours in bed nursing her bruise before keeping her appointment with an especially cussed client in Shoreham.

The car in front of her lurched forward and an officer from a police patrol car was signalling a detour round the crashed vehicles with that pained impatience common to traffic cops coping with the chaos wrought by idiot drivers.

Amy shifted into gear and joined the slow-moving flow. She *would*, she decided, tell Connie about Lewis, despite his objections. She realised she would be taking a risk. But it was a risk worth taking. If there was something she hadn't known about Connie and Lewis then it was better out in the open before she made more of a fool of herself over him than she already had.

Maybe a few days with Sam and Karen would make a world of difference to Connie, she reasoned. Perhaps, unknowingly, that's what her mother had wanted. To come back to Southdean. And the nonsense in the precinct hadn't sounded that serious, although, of course, she would have to behave as if it were. Serious. Her mother would expect her to. Amy was the one who laid down the law and presented all the unpleasant sides of an argument. Amy was the family pill – or pain in the ass, as Holly might say.

She saw a sign to Angmering and the sea, first right past Sainsbury's and a newish maze of bungalow developments. She remembered the holidays they'd used to spend in caravan parks, not in genteel Angmering that frowned on caravan parks, but further down the coast where you didn't have to mind your manners. She supposed they had been hard up then and she wished she could remember that Connie had been more attentive and Sam more assertive and they'd all been one big happy family. But that wasn't the way it had been. Even then there had been a remoteness.

She and Colin had mucked about in the sea and scrounged ice-creams from Beattie, while Sam had smoked his pipe and read a lot and Connie had fretted about her infant business and, one year, the other infant who would become Holly, she was carrying.

Yet she could still feel the sand between her toes and the joy of finding strange things in rock pools and the even greater joy of meeting a snotty nosed girl from Lewisham who used the 'f' word and then proceeded to graphically explain the meaning of it. That evening back at the caravan she had eyed the swelling in her mother's tummy with more interest than usual.

It had all changed quite rapidly after that. When they went on holiday it was to large hotels abroad. Her parents didn't even sell the caravan. They gave it away to the Salvation Army, so they couldn't have needed the money. One of her teachers at school said that Amy must be very proud of her mother and Colin had cried a good deal but no one quite knew why.

The old house, in which for years they had lived like squatters, began to look smarter after an invasion of carpenters, plasterers and decorators.

It still looked smart, Amy thought as she swung into the drive, but cosier, too, a friendly place. She supposed that was due to Karen. And she imagined Connie now having to grit her teeth and be nice to she-who-could-do-no-wrong. The image lifted her spirits and she no longer felt frazzled by the traffic jams.

Connie was sitting on the terrace, taking in the sun, an untroubled expression on her face which was unusual.

Amy dumped the suitcase and bent down to kiss her on the cheek. "Mum! I brought you some things, enough for a couple of days." She noticed the shoes but didn't say anything. Connie seemed to have forgotten all about them.

"I suppose you're cursing me for dragging you down here." Connie looked at her daughter dubiously. You could never be quite sure with Amy.

"No problem. I'm seeing a guy in Shoreham and I'm staying over a couple of days in Brighton anyway. Business," she added, as if it were necessary to establish that she had other reasons than Connie for being there.

"Well?" Her mother sounded defensive.

"Well what?" Well what were you doing trawling for stray infants in Southdean shopping precinct? She almost said it, but stopped herself. Not now. Later.

"Well, get on with it! Tell me off for behaving like a lunatic!"

"Were you?"

"I don't think so. Not much anyway." The tone – soft, reflective – belied the prickly response. Something was different, thought Amy. It was as if her arrival had intruded on a private memory, forcing Connie back into a present that was less agreeable.

"Are you all right?" she asked. Stupidly. Despite the events of the previous day, Connie looked amazingly all right.

To her surprise, Connie got up and put her arms around her daughter, a real Beattie cuddle. "Probably as all right as you are," her mother whispered in her ear. "I won't ask where you got the bruise." (How could she imagine Connie wouldn't notice *that*!) "Thanks for coming, Amy. Really! It's been too long."

Amy shrugged free of her mother's embrace and stared at her, more worried than perplexed.

"Mum! It's been forty-eight hours! At most!"

Connie shook her head earnestly, willing her to

understand, as if she were a child who couldn't quite grasp a simple equation. "No, Amy. It's been half a lifetime."

Chapter Six

"How long has this been going on?"

They were sitting in Sam's study drinking something peculiar that was non-alcoholic and Karen-approved. The fax machine in the corner had just gobbled up his weekly column for a national newspaper and been duly acknowledged. She recognised the expression on his face of contentment at a job done. It didn't have to be well done, just done.

Amy, on the other hand, hadn't even started on her job and she was feeling irritable. She was late for her appointment with the client in Shoreham and she'd detected the note of pleasure in his tone as he assured her unctuously on the phone that it didn't matter one bit. He was brash, shrewd and could be ugly and he hadn't taken kindly to the idea of a woman, especially a young woman, advising him on how to streamline his company and he already regretted being prevailed upon by his partners. Amy's unpunctuality merely confirmed his prejudice against her and female executives in general.

Knowing this made her irritable. But her mother's behaviour made her even more irritable. For the past two years she had been able and prepared to cope with the process of disintegration that had afflicted Connie after Colin's death and the failure of her business. She had got used to the listlessness, the forgetfulness, the aimlessness. She was prepared to make decisions for her mother; in fact it was a lot easier than allowing her to make choices, cleaner, quicker. Her mind could accept the positiveness of the breakdown. The mother who had been so dynamic and certain and wonderfully persuasive

63

was now dependent and weak. There was a logic about that. There was even a logic about asserting Connie was getting better when she knew she wasn't. But listening to her chattering on about how she had been missing out and losing touch, about how she was feeling more responsive and energetic quite suddenly, was perplexing. It demanded a whole new reassessment of Connie and Amy wondered whether she had the time or inclination for that.

She couldn't understand how Sam could seem so placid about the change in his ex-wife. But then he didn't have to assume responsibility for the day-to-day Connie; a responsibility, Amy freely admitted, of her own choosing.

Sam was filling his pipe. A leisurely, rather furtive, process. Although he had sworn off smoking, he felt the resolution somehow didn't apply in this, his inner sanctum. At the same time he had the sense that he was letting Karen down. She hadn't nagged him or ostentatiously opened doors and windows and waved away any smoke that wafted in her direction. If anything she was the reverse of a nag. She was, as with everything else, sweetly reasonable. If Sam got pleasure from his pipe then she would be the last to stop him indulging. It was just, perhaps . . . with the baby coming . . . and all the fuss about passive smoking which she personally felt was nonsense, but maybe there was something in it.

He took a deep, contented puff and felt able to handle his elder daughter's searching question. How long has this been going on? Title of a lovely Gershwin song. He had a mental image of Audrey Hepburn singing it in *Funny Face*. He didn't realise it but he was smiling. They didn't write lyrics like that these days.

"How can you be so complacent, Dad?" There was no mistaking the exasperation in Amy's voice. Under Karen's quietly equable regime he had forgotten how awesome three generations of strong-willed women could be. Beattie, Connie, Amy. He shivered slightly, feeling disloyal.

"I'm not complacent. It's just that I don't see as much of Connie as you do. She was upset yesterday, but this morning—"

Amy interrupted him. Was he being wilfully slow? Was he hiding something? "Christ! It's as if she's seen a vision! The light! Or something nasty in the woodshed!"

"Close!" He took the pipe out of his mouth and pointed the stem at her. It was a gesture that invariably commanded attention. "I think she's seeing herself."

Amy stared at him, not sure he was serious. Then, she punched her clenched fist in the air, half angry, half playful, within inches of her father's chin. "Oh, come *on*! That's mumbo-jumbo. There had to be something."

Sam didn't bother to flinch at the shadow punch. "No, I mean it. I think she's finally taking stock. A bunch of things came together. . . ."

"What things?"

"This surprise urge to visit Southdean. Seeing the town again. There was some child in the precinct who caught her attention for whatever reason. She spoke to Bill Daley. He was lopping a tree in the garden and she didn't know I'd taken him on after he'd been made redundant. So that reminded her of the factory and the girls, Phyllis and Maisie. And then there was the phone call from someone she hadn't seen for . . ."

". . . Half a lifetime?"

"Exactly. A man named David Levitch."

"And who is Mr Levitch?"

"He's the man your mother was in love with. If it hadn't been for Beattie she probably would have married him. Instead she settled for me. On the rebound I believe it's called."

He seemed so serene and unconcerned that, for a moment, Amy could barely believe what he was saying. He could have been relating a rather boring incident of no consequence from someone else's life.

She sat down awkwardly, trying to take it in. "She never said. You never told us," she said, realising

65

instantly how childish that sounded. Why necessarily should her parents have discussed with her something that happened long before she was even born?

"Incidentally," he said, "Con doesn't realise that I knew how involved she was with this chap. If she ever talked about him it was just as an acquaintance; she was friendly with his sister at school. It doesn't matter now. But if she wants to be coy about him that's her business."

"How . . . how did you find out?"

"Not until years later. I'd always assumed we were very much in love when we married. Far too young, I might add. And perhaps in a sense we were. In love. It's awfully easy to convince yourself you're in love when you're too young to know better. Of course, I didn't need any convincing. Con was a dazzler. I couldn't believe my luck at the time. I suppose that should have tipped me off that I was just a second choice. Or maybe not even a choice at all. I was handy and I suspect marrying me so quickly was Con's way of getting back at Beattie."

"What did Grandma have against this Levitch guy?"

"Who knows! I believe he was a bit of a roughneck. But mainly, I think, she had plans for Connie and they didn't include a man who wanted to spirit her away to farm in Illinois. There's a hell of a lot of corn in Illinois to be farmed, I understand. Cattle, too. He had relatives there and wanted to emigrate. The one thing to be said for me was that I was settled. I wasn't likely to up-sticks and take off with her darling daughter. I was, as they say, amenable to reason."

All the time he was speaking he was smiling, which Amy found curiously off-putting as if he couldn't be bothered to associate himself with what he was telling her. Indeed, maybe he didn't. Maybe it was all so long ago and so much had happened since then that he really didn't relate to those youthful happenings any more. Certainly he had another, possibly more fulfilling life with Karen and the prospect of a new baby and the knowledge that, without any particular fuss, he

66

had transformed a gift as a plantsman and landscape gardener into a prestigious money-making career.

"You've never ever spoken like this before," she said, again aware that it was a childish remark.

"Yes, well, we all keep things to ourselves, don't we?" He looked at her rather beadily, she thought, and she wondered whether – and, if so, how – he knew about her and Lewis.

"It was when Beattie's mind started to wander that she confided in me," he went on. "You know how she was. She couldn't grasp everyday things or retain anything you told her from one second to the next. Half the time she couldn't even remember who you were. But the past, the long past, was crystal clear. Sometimes she called me 'Albert'. That was her father's name. It was then that she told me about Con and David Levitch and how she interfered – that was the word she kept using – interfered, with their lives, their plans to set up house, emigrate to America. If she'd been rational and knew who I was I doubt whether she'd have unloaded all that baggage from the past. But all the time I was 'Albert', the father she used to run to with her problems, then it probably seemed only natural. I got the feeling that in her muddled mind she wanted in some way to make amends. Only, of course, it was much too late. Con was coping with the crisis in the business and hardly had time even to visit Beattie."

"And what about you, Dad?" Amy flicked a guilty look at the clock on his desk. She really shouldn't be sitting here listening to her father reminiscing and she felt a fleeting irritation that he should have chosen such an inconvenient time. But part of her was intrigued. Intrigued to know more about a man who had once been the centre of her mother's world. It was a side of Connie she had not conceived possible, for she had never known her when she wasn't formidably self-sufficient and dismissive of women who needed a man to justify their existence. Apart, that is, from the last couple of years when everyone had agreed she 'wasn't herself'.

"The odd thing was that it didn't affect me any more. It should have done, I suppose. I should have minded that maybe during our lives together we had been living a lie." He made a disparaging face. "I sound like someone baring their soul on television to what's the name of the woman? Winford? Winthrop? Winfrey? All the same there's a truth in it. There was nothing spectacularly wrong about it. Not a very huge lie. Just the kind that a lot of couples settle for in marriage, usually for the sake of the children. The realisation that one or both don't care that much. And twenty, even ten years before, I might have minded a great deal. But by then, as you know, Con and I were drifting apart – adrift, you might say. It was Beattie who was doing the suffering. She'd get so agitated when she dragged up the old days."

From the compost heap of memory, he almost added, then decided not to. Much too pretentious and literary. Besides it had a nice horticultural ring to it. He might tuck it away for future use in one of his columns or when he was ruminating on Radio Solent about historic gardens in the home counties.

It reminded him that he really should brush up on the dreaded Jekyll and Sackville-West whom he regarded – sacrilegiously – as rather overrated, although his own private patch outside his window subscribed to the Gertrude Jekyll concept of a wild, cottage garden. But, professionally, his training in the Parks' Department had instilled in him a preference for order, straight lines and plants that knew their place in well-defined limits.

He realised his mind was wandering again and he felt a hypocrite, dividing his attention between poor Beattie's scatty memories and the work in hand. But he had learned early on in his marriage to Connie that it was not only possible, it was necessary, to compartmentalise his mind, otherwise he would have been sucked into her world as inexorably as a fly trapped in a spider's web.

He jerked himself out of his chair violently, scattering a cascade of tobacco ash as he did so. He looked at the mess pensively.

68

"Clumsy!" He took out a handkerchief, knelt down and rubbed the ash into the carpet.

"Now you've got a filthy handkerchief as well as a filthy carpet," she said, not caring about the carpet with its dull, mouse pattern which seemed to absorb the ash gratefully. "How do you suppose this Levitch person tracked her down?"

"Apparently he had recognised her in the precinct and I suppose it didn't take too much ingenuity to trace her after the ruckus in McDonald's. I gather it was all rather public what with the arrival of the ambulance and some concerned citizen or other insisting hanging was too good for her."

"You're exaggerating."

"Yes I am. But not by much. When people haven't got much to do they can make a lot out of a little."

He stood up, stretched rather painfully and leaned on the good hip that hadn't been replaced. "Amy – you'll come back, won't you? After your meeting? I thought we could all go over to Chichester to see Holly at the Minerva. She asked me to hold off until after the first night. But I believe she's quite good. A paragraph in the local and even a mention in the *Sunday Times*."

"I know. I read it. 'Among the bright young talents . . .' I suppose if you're an aspiring actress grudging remarks like that are manna from Heaven. What a stupid profession!"

"That's unfair, Amy. You did what you wanted. Holly's entitled to do what she wants."

"I know. I'm a brute." Why on earth was she going on about Holly like this? She and Holly got on well enough, as well as any sisters who were diametrically opposed in every way except their shared parentage.

Sam looked hurt. Having been robbed of one child he couldn't bear the thought of friction between the others. Harmony! That was his only goal in life. Amy felt guilty that they should all seem to connive at robbing him of that goal. Except Karen. But Karen was different. From another world. The wonder was that she could accept the Remick family she had married along with Sam with such equanimity.

"Dad. Would you mind if I brought someone else. That is – maybe he won't be able to make it. But maybe he will." Having taken the plunge she was rather pleased with herself. Now seemed as good a time as any.

"Someone special?" he asked, with what seemed to her an aggravating knowingness which in fact was not his style. And she knew it. He had in the past been more inclined to ask a direct question and expect a direct answer.

"No . . . no . . . don't get the wrong idea. Just a friend." She cursed herself for sounding flustered and open to suspicion that she was protesting too much.

"Of course, just a friend," he reassured her. "We might even invite the famous Mr Levitch – that is if your mother sees fit."

"Treats!" She mimed exaggerated anticipation, then lapsed into sober reflection. She wasn't sure how she felt about this long-gone assocation between her mother and a David Levitch. As for her parents' relationship, the fact that it had been less than perfect from the beginning came as no surprise.

"By the way," Sam interrupted her train of thought. "It's none of my business, but I don't suppose this just-a-friend had anything to do with that rather noticeable bruise on your chin?" She inferred from his tone that he didn't consider bruised chins a mark of friendship. But it would take too long to explain.

She sighed. She'd have to slap on some more make-up before meeting Genghis Khan in Shoreham. "In a round-about sort of way, but not in the way you're thinking. I'll tell you later. But I really must get going now. Or else the firm will lose one highly delighted pig of a client and I'll lose my Christmas bonus – or worse."

He nodded, puffing at the pipe. It was a hardy old briar now blackened with age which looked revolting. But they'd never been able to displace it in his affections and the smart, pristine birthday pipes they'd habitually given him sat unused in the Edwardian smoking cabinet he'd discovered at a Scouts' jumble sale in Littlehampton.

"I see," he said sagely.

But he probably didn't, she thought. Her work was as much of a mystery to him as potting up gloxinias and cutting back mahonias were to her. ("'Natural wastage', 'skills rebalancing'; it's just another way of saying some poor bugger has lost his job and can't get another," he'd maintain quite amiably, which made it impossible for her to explain that it wasn't that simple because the argument would be lost on him.)

Jagger nosed the door ajar, lumbered into the room and sniffed expectantly around Amy's legs. He gazed up at her, yawned and then settled himself comfortably on a scuffed old bolster cushion by the open fireplace.

"He looks peaky," she observed.

"He's faking. Just begging for attention."

Jagger wheezed plaintively as if denying Sam's diagnosis.

"No, really. Has he seen a vet?"

Sam sighed. "He lives at the vet's. He fools Karen all the time. But you can't fool me, can you, you old fraud?" The dog gave him a loopy look, then ignored the pair of them.

"See?" he said.

"Dad!"

Her tone sounded faintly alarming and Sam wondered what surprise she might be about to spring on him.

"Has she spoken about Colin? She never does to me. Well, maybe once or twice, but then only about something – well, silly. A memory of when we were little. Whether it was me or Holly or Colin who couldn't stand tapioca pudding. Which one of us had chicken pox first and passed it on to the others. You know the sort of thing. But never anything important about him. I don't know whether she's genuinely shut him out of her mind or whether she just can't stand the thought of discussing what happened to him." She stopped abruptly, aware of the lump building up in her throat. "Oh God, I didn't mean to embark on this now!" And she didn't know why it should all pop out just like that from nowhere, except she imagined her brother was never far from Sam's thoughts any more than he was from hers.

To think that dear, gentle Colin should end up being the spectre who couldn't be acknowledged yet couldn't be ignored!

She refused to meet Sam's eyes, half hoping that he would say something light and trivial or, at least, non-committal so that she could forget she'd brought up the subject.

But he considered her question seriously, taking his time before answering.

"Some," he said finally. "Yesterday. I think she really tried. But it was no good. I don't think she's ready for that yet."

She felt a sudden rush of anger. "Ready! How ready does she have to be? I'm tired of being nursemaid to a mother who can't face facts. It'll never be right until she does."

"No – no it won't." He put his arm around her shoulder and could feel the tensed muscles, the banked-up emotion held at bay. "I'm sorry. I'm not much good in that department, am I?"

For a moment she leaned against him gratefully, then pulled herself erect. "You've your own life now."

"So have you."

"Yes, well . . ." She sniffed. "I'd better get on with it."

He heard the front door slam behind her. She hadn't bothered to say goodbye to Connie who was roaming around the house or grounds somewhere.

He knew he'd failed her, just as he felt he'd failed all his children, one way or another. He should have been stronger, tougher, more ready to fill the gap in their lives left by a largely absent mother – absent emotionally if not physically. Perhaps he'd just been too blinkered to even see that there was a gap. In

72

that respect, was he any better than Connie? Provided the children were well fed, well schooled, well catered for, then the prime requisites of parenthood had been met. You enjoyed playing with them when they were little and discussing things seriously with them when they'd matured into interesting adults. But those crucial formative years in between posed too many awkward problems, too many time-consuming worries for which there were no pat solutions to fall back on. And their children had seemed so undemanding that it had been easy for Connie and, to an extent, Sam to convince themselves that there were no problems and worries, that Amy and Colin and Holly had sailed through their teens untroubled by the dramas that afflicted the offspring of their friends and colleagues.

Weren't they the lucky parents! And they honestly thought they were, if they thought about it at all. By the time they'd realised they had been deceiving themselves they had grown so far apart they were incapable of even trying to repair the damage.

"How could you have been so blind, Dad? You and Mum?" That was Holly. Jolly, carefree little Holly who always seemed to be dancing and singing and telling jokes about the house; now sombre and agonisingly truthful. He would never forget that day.

The scarlet Golf convertible Connie had given Colin for his birthday had been discovered in a lay-by near Beachy Head, an embarrassed young policeman had told Sam. It had been vandalised. The paintwork was scarred with livid gashes. The interior upholstery had been ripped to pieces; the windows smashed. There was no sign of Colin and for a few anguished hours they hoped he might have lent the car to someone or even sold it. He hadn't been in touch for months.

Then there came word that his body had been found half hidden in a crevice at the foot of the cliffs.

He'd had such a serene expression on his face when Sam identified him. Just like the old Colin, he'd told Holly, thinking it might console her. But it hadn't.

"How would you or Mum know what the old Colin was like!"

And Connie had sat there not saying a word, already a stranger in the house in which she and Sam had once played happy families.

Chapter Seven

Connie had felt elated after the phone call out of the blue from David Levitch. It had summoned up all the excitement she'd experienced when she had first been introduced into what seemed to her a wonderfully alien world. It was this alien quality that so fascinated her. The Levitches weren't grass roots English. They most certainly weren't Sussex. And they particularly hadn't been to her mother Beattie's liking. Although she didn't actually specify her disapproval she would grumble about "damned Germans we fought two wars against," adding triumphantly "and won!" Winning meant a lot to Beattie.

The fact that the Levitches had been settled in England since 1935 after fleeing from Nazi persecution in their native country was irrelevant. "I don't think you should be spending all your spare time with – with those people," she'd caution. "You must have lots of other nice friends." And she did. But that was the trouble. Nice! The Levitches weren't, in Beattie's sense, what you'd call nice. And to twelve-year-old Connie this merely added to the attraction of David Levitch and his sister Rebecca.

"They're not Germans, they're Jews," Connie would remonstrate during one of her mother's tirades against the Hun. Even a decade or more after the end of the war, memories were still raw. But she didn't feel on very secure ground and didn't pursue the argument. It wasn't that she was ignorant about the precise nature of Judaism. She had read and seen films about the Holocaust and the pogroms in Eastern Europe and she realised it was nothing like being C of E, which was hardly a religion at all and certainly not worth dying for in her estimation. It was just that the subject seldom came up.

Jews were not thick on the ground in the insular semi-rural suburb in which Connie was born and brought up and she doubted whether she had ever actually met one before Becky Levitch arrived on the first day of term at the grammar school.

Both she and Connie were new girls, but that alone would not have drawn them together; it was Becky's irrepressible ability to focus on any cartoonish quirk in their teachers and mimic it with wicked accuracy behind their backs. To Connie, who had been taught not to challenge let alone ridicule authority, this was a splendid act of defiance and one that immediately endeared Becky to her. Later she realised it was Becky's way of facing up to that slightly patronising reserve she encountered as the one Jew in the class, who was allowed special days off and whose brothers and father wore skullcaps when they sat down to eat.

The family, Connie learned, had moved to the area from Whitechapel in the 1950s. Mr Levitch was a traveller of sorts in costume jewellery and leather goods. Rumour had it that he had had a stall in Petticoat Lane. According to your source of gossip and how ill or well disposed you were to the Levitches, he had either been run out of business for sharp practice by rival tradesmen or he had informed on the local heavy mob to the police and been forced to beat a hasty retreat from London's East End for fear of reprisals. One thing was certain: there was no shortage of money.

David Levitch, who was several years older than his sister and consequently a rather godlike figure to both girls, had laughed himself silly when he'd heard what their neighbours were saying about his family's history. But he hadn't actually denied either version, from which Connie deduced there was possibly some germ of truth in the gossip.

She remembered vividly the first time she'd met him.

76

Becky had invited her home to tea after school one day and, while she swallowed a last morsel of apple strudel that tasted nothing like the anaemic imitation they sold at the bakery in the High Street, she heard what sounded like a fearsome row in the kitchen. She'd glanced nervously at Becky who seemed completely unconcerned. "That's just Dave," she said as if that explained everything which, Connie later realised, it did.

"And the next time you needn't look to your father to get you out of it," she heard. It was Mrs Levitch repeating what sounded like an old refrain.

"What have you done this time, Dave?" Becky didn't look up as the door to the kitchen opened.

"None of your business, nosey. What have we here?" It was said in a lordly way which made Connie feel like something the cat had brought in.

"She's my *friend*," said Becky stoutly.

"Hello *friend*," he mimicked his sister. Then he pulled up a chair beside Connie, reached for a slice of strudel and peered provocatively into her face.

He was, she thought later, the handsomest boy she had ever seen, more handsome than Tab Hunter or Elvis, with a lean, chiselled face, dark, curly hair, devilish eyes and eyebrows that peaked in the centre like Satan's in the Sunday school books. He wasn't pimply like most boys of his age whom she knew and, although only sixteen, he seemed to have missed out on the gangly stage in which arms and legs appear to have a separate, clumsy identity. There was nothing remotely awkward about him; he was totally at ease with himself.

"She's pretty," he said approvingly and inched closer to her.

And she knew in that moment that she was smitten. In the years to come she would realise she'd fallen wildly in love over the remains of the apple strudel. But when you were twelve in those days you didn't countenance anything as earth-shattering as that happening to you. At twelve you had 'crushes' and blushed a lot and heeded your mother's warning about what happened to girls who were too free with their feelings, because the alternative was too shaming to contemplate.

"Shy, too," he said. Then he got up as abruptly as he'd sat down and took himself off to another part of the house and another row with someone else.

"He's dreamy," she breathed.

Becky grinned. "He'll probably end up in jail," she said as if she really meant it. "Truly."

This added to the sense of awe with which she regarded the Levitches. They were so open, so extrovert. As she got to know them better there seemed to be dozens of them: sisters, brothers, aunts and distant cousins who were liable to turn up unannounced from nowhere and were fed and housed without any undue fuss. In Connie's experience visitors were planned for weeks in advance and were more honoured in their going than in their coming. 'Glad to see the back of him/her/them' was a phrase that echoed in the households with which she'd hitherto been familiar long after the hapless him, her or them had returned to wherever it was they came from.

The Levitches inhabited a huge, ramshackle house on the outskirts of town, set well away from terraces of neat little homes whose pristine paintwork and symmetrical front gardens seemed to reproach their unruly neighbour. The house had been empty since the war. It had been glancingly damaged by the only bomb dropped in the vicinity which nevertheless caused a bizarre double death. While the elderly owner suffered a heart attack, his equally elderly wife was knocked unconscious by a loose chimney stack. They both died peacefully a few days later in hospital leaving the house to an estranged son who, on being demobbed from the army, declared the place gave off weird vibrations and spent the next few years trying to sell it.

This unwise comment continued to haunt it even after he had spent his demob gratuity money on getting the house done up. Locals whispered darkly about it, children scooted, squealing with delighted terror, past it and prospective buyers, sensing they might be purchasing more than bricks and mortar and an acre of scrubby lawn and tangled trees, shied off long before they reached the firm offer stage.

Over the years the story was embroidered. 'Weird vibrations' grew into 'curses' and 'sightings'. So when Mr Levitch appeared on the horizon with cash in hand, the price was dropped to rock bottom to wrap up a quick sale and the estate agent made very sure no hint of curses and sightings reached the ears of Mr Levitch before contracts were exchanged.

But when he did hear the tale that went with his newly acquired property Mr Levitch dismissed it as a load of codswallop.

"When you've been through what my family has gone through for generations, a friendly ghost or two would be a blessing," he'd say in his thickly accented voice which always sounded as if it were on the verge of telling a joke. Then he pressed a knowing forefinger to one nostril which was supposed to mean something.

It was never made clear why the Levitches should have chosen this fairly remote area of Sussex in which to buy a house, despite a vague suggestion that Mrs Levitch had always fancied the country. As Mrs Levitch constantly complained about the lack of life in this 'God-forsaken hole' and gave absolutely no indication that there was anything about the country that she fancied at all, this, too, was open to question.

To say they lived in the house wouldn't be entirely accurate. Camped was a better word. They appeared to exist in a constant turmoil. The house was a great, untidy confusion of packing cases not quite emptied, books waiting to be arranged on shelves and china, Meissen jumbled together with Woolworths, stacked precariously on sideboards. Even to Connie's untutored eye, much of what they had brought with them was good quality. The furniture was dark, rich and Teutonic looking; the curtains were stiffly elaborate and scalloped ("whore's drawers" was how David rudely described them); the carpets were Persian, and the silver cutlery was heavy with intricately sculpted motifs on the handles.

The garden, all back, front and sides of it, they simply ignored until it got so bad that the entire family was dragooned into service: clearing, cutting, mowing, lopping, weeding and sowing.

But for all the welcome they extended to Connie, she always felt a little of an outsider, not privy to the more subtle jokes and family rituals. "That's because we're Jews," Becky had confided. But it wasn't just that. There was the suspicion that one day they might just up and leave on a whim, as they'd arrived, without even mentioning it to her and she would knock on the door to collect Becky for school and no one would be there.

This bothered her more than she cared to admit. As an only child whose father had died when she was little she secretly regarded them as a surrogate family. Connie wisely kept this sentiment from the overly suspicious Beattie who would have considered it an act of betrayal both to herself and to the man for whom she had little regard in life but considerable respect in death. All the same she could hardly not have been aware that the Levitches had become a fixture in Connie's life which was a cause for concern.

While Connie was still at school, Beattie suffered her daughter's friendship with the Levitches, convincing herself that once she was out in the world and earning a living she'd meet a different sort of people, her own sort. At first, she accepted that the main attraction was probably Becky whom she had to admit was a lively, funny girl and very endearing. Schoolgirl friends were part of the natural order of things and you grew out of them.

But as Connie became older and more conscious of her sexuality it was obvious that David Levitch was increasingly the focus of her fascination with this exotic tribe. Beattie liked him well enough but at a distance, not as a companion, let alone a possible suitor, for her daughter. In any case she was already firmly of the opinion that girls should have a career before they had a husband and babies.

She would have been even more worried if she'd realised how intensely the relationship between Connie and David had developed, at least in Connie's imagination. David treated her with the same flirtatious charm that he used on an endless stream of girlfriends who all seemed to look like Marilyn Monroe. But Connie had no problem convincing herself that that was just his 'way' and that she, above all the others, was special to him. And he didn't disabuse her of what she later saw was a misconception, based on nothing more binding than hopes and hints and some fairly frenzied necking sessions that always stopped short of the point of no return beyond which nice unmarried girls weren't supposed to venture.

In fact, though, it was David not Connie who decided when enough was enough, usually by the time they'd exchanged several moist French kisses and a good deal of indiscriminate groping. She had mixed feelings about this display of restraint on his part. Half of her wanted him to go on and the other half was scared that he might. At such times the vision of an outraged Beattie loomed large.

"You're such an innocent kid," he'd say fondly. She'd wonder what she had done wrong and then they'd buy a couple of cokes and sit on the pier at Southdean watching the waves lashing on the underpinnings of the old Victorian structure that stretched way out to sea. He'd take her home and go off to keep what he invariably described as an important appointment. She tried not to think that the important appointment might be one of those girls who weren't such innocent kids.

From her bedroom window Beattie would watch him zoom off on his motorbike, leaving Connie on the doorstep, hugging herself and looking forlorn and abandoned. She would bite back the angry words of greeting: "Where have you been?" But she couldn't disguise her anger at David Levitch.

That he was several years older than Connie was less off-putting than the fact that he never seemed to be doing anything; at least anything that could be construed as a job.

"He's extremely talented," Connie assured her airily. "They're all talented." It was true; they were. Not just Becky who had had no trouble passing her exams at grammar school, but even plump, florid Mrs Levitch and the Levitch twins who at the age of five could read Grimms' fairy-tales in German and English and do their multiplication tables, and two other brothers, younger than David, who could repair anything mechanical. And they were all great talkers.

Everybody in the extended Levitch family debated everything. They argued about philosophy, music, politics, religions of every persuasion as well as all kinds of trivia. They'd read *Lady Chatterley's Lover* and *Ulysses* in the unexpurgated versions and could discuss the merits as well as the morality of them. They even argued about the sanctity of Israel as the Jewish homeland. It followed, of course, that, should someone outside the family venture an adverse opinion, they closed ranks to present a united front.

According to Mr Levitch, his family had been scholars as well as tradesmen in the old country, persons of substance. He couldn't count how many who had remained behind ended up in the gas chambers, but there still seemed to Connie a lot of Levitches left and their facility with words and acquiring skills made her feel inadequate. The only thing she had any talent with was a sewing machine and that from necessity because Beattie couldn't afford to buy her the fashionable clothes, like those worn by Sandra Dee and Helen Shapiro, that were all the teenage rage at the time.

But David! David was a mystery. When questioned he'd say that he did "a little bit of this and a little bit of that". Sometimes he was on trips with his father. Sometimes he helped a friend who had a bric-à-brac shop in the Lanes in Brighton. Sometimes he worked in

82

a street market in Chichester. Once Connie had seen him in huddled conversation with dubious looking fairground characters who were setting up rides on the sea front at Southdean.

Occasionally when she was at the Levitches there would be a visit from a policeman and then she'd overhear Mr Levitch talking in despairing tones to his wife about "that boy" and how much better it would have been if he'd "gone with the others." She didn't know what he meant by that but assumed it wasn't a reference to the gas chambers. The Levitches were always talking about moving on. "Where to next?" was not an idle fantasy but a serious question, as if they were on an eternal package tour. Particularly among the younger members of the household, there was much loose talk about New York, Tel Aviv, Toronto, Johannesburg and relatives somewhere in the mid-West – anywhere but Munich whence they came originally. It was all part of that air of impermanence which had once so intrigued Connie and was now so worrying.

But nothing could alter her conviction that David Levitch was destined for great things, together with the hope that she would be part of that destiny. He'd said as much in a light-hearted way when he'd given her a gold chain with an amethyst tear-drop pendant on her sixteenth birthday and kissed her so gently and lingeringly that it felt like 'goodbye'.

"You don't want to pay any attention to him," Becky had warned her, realising that that was the last thing her friend wanted to hear. If she had told her he was a brute and a womaniser that wouldn't have mattered so much. According to Connie's reading of the movies, brutes and womanisers could be tamed by the right woman. But dismissing him as not worth paying attention to was altogether too unromantic. "Just forget him, Con. You're such . . ."

"An innocent kid?" said Connie, flushed and angry.

"Well – times are changing, Con. It's the 1960s. You

83

are allowed to question whether mother knows best now and then." (Not my mother, thought Connie.)

Becky fixed those wise, dark eyes, oddly tragic for such a jolly girl, on Connie and registered the stricken look on her face. "Besides . . ." She shook her head. "Just forget him, Con," she repeated.

After that it appeared to Connie there was a more urgent atmosphere of restlessness in the Levitch home. It had always been fairly chaotic but now that chaos seemed to have assumed a sense of direction. For days she didn't see David but there was always a plausible reason. He was helping a friend set up an automobile parts shop up north. He was visiting a relative who had fallen on hard times. He was learning his father's business in order to take over from him when he retired. He was just not available. But it was easy for Connie to practise the self-deception that accepts a lie.

She admitted to herself that everything conspired against any sort of lasting relationship between her and David Levitch. Her mother. His family who, for all their friendliness, believed Jews should not marry outside their faith. But these were hurdles to overcome, the very stuff of popular romantic fiction.

All this she confided at night to her diary, embellished with fevered imaginings culled from the magazines she read and the films she saw.

She would invent an invisible barrier between them behind which she could indulge her longing for him without actually having to do anything about it, a kind of mental masturbation.

She would make up shared yearnings which she considered deliciously provocative.

'I want to make love to you.' Heavy breathing!

'I want to make love to you.' Heavier breathing!

'I suppose I'll just have to quietly explode until the intermission.' Wildly erotic!

Burning looks and passionate sighs exchanged! Assignations planned!

Later she understood what more liberated young people

84

meant when they derisively accused her repressed generation of having sex in the head.

But once it was on paper in her diary it all took on a truth and permanency.

The diary became her comfort, filling the gap left by the absent object of her desire. During her last weeks at school her work was sloppy, her manner was distant and strange and she did poorly in her exams. Her teachers were disappointed. "We always thought she'd do so well," they told Beattie.

It was then that Beattie swallowed her pride and visited the Levitches. When she came home that evening, Connie found her mother sitting at the kitchen table. She looked as if she'd been there a long time, waiting. Her expression was grim, but concerned too.

As Connie entered the room Beattie thrust a book at her, her hands were shaking.

"What's this?" she raged.

"That's my diary. Mum, that's my *diary*! My *property*!" She looked first at the diary then at her mother in horror and tried to grab it.

"Oh no you don't, young lady. You've been sleeping with that boy haven't you?"

"No!"

"It's here!" She waved the book in her face again.

She quoted back at Connie chunks of her fantasies which sounded so childish and silly as they spewed venomously out of Beattie's mouth.

"What intermission? What play? When was that? When they took you to London last Christmas?"

There had been a play. *The Mousetrap*. Mr Levitch knew someone in the management who had given him complimentary seats in the front stalls. Afterwards he'd taken them across the road to the Ivy where the *maître d'* had welcomed him effusively and escorted them to a large table with a commanding view of the star-studded clientele. (Mr Levitch seemed to have legions of such strategically placed acquaintances.) But nothing improper had taken place. She'd sat next to David and they'd held

85

hands. And there had been several other Levitches with them all the time.

But what was the point of telling her mother she'd made up most of the incidents in the diary? Hadn't she ever kept a diary, too?

Seeing her mother so enraged, she suddenly felt very tranquil and expectant. The diary, she suspected, wasn't the whole of it.

From a far distance she heard her mother demanding to know what she had to say about it and then not giving her a chance to answer if she'd wanted to. And she hadn't. She'd never speak to her mother about the Levitches again in her whole life.

Beattie was calmer now, too. "Well, you can forget all about him now," she was saying, just as Becky had said. "He's gone. To America. He was always going to America. Waiting for the right time. He's engaged to marry a Jewish girl out there. A friend of the family. He always was. Oh, don't just take my word for it, miss. Ask your precious Becky. I've been round to see Mr and Mrs Levitch. And they told me. They were very sorry if . . . well . . . they said of course if he had anything to answer for . . ."

"There's nothing to answer for, Mum. Your little virgin isn't pregnant," she said coldly, summoning up a rebellious courage she never knew she had. "How did you find my diary? What right had you to read it?"

Beattie shrugged. "You shouldn't leave it lying around on your dressing table."

"I didn't leave it lying around on my dressing table." And that was the end of it.

For days the feeling of numbness persisted and she was grateful for it. At least she didn't have to feel anything; the misery of that first lost love.

She saw Becky a couple of times after they left school, but they were uneasy with each other, not quite sure what to say.

"Don't judge all Jews by us, Con. We're careless people," Becky had said on the last occasion. Connie

86

couldn't have believed then that, in time, she, too, might become a careless person.

There was an unspoken agreement between Connie and her mother that they wouldn't speak about what had happened. It was the only way they could survive and share the same house. After a while a kind of truce was declared.

During the summer Connie spent her holidays in a grey stone boarding house owned by a second cousin in Freshwater in the Isle of Wight. She surprised herself by having quite a good time. She met a young man named Sam Remick who had just graduated from college and was celebrating with his mates on the island. They swam and fooled around on the beach and bought glass phials of Alum Bay sand and drank shandy outside the pub in the evening. He was taking a job with the council at Southdean. They agreed it was an amazing coincidence. He wanted to know if he could see her when they got back from holiday. She said yes because he was rather slow and pleasant and not the least bit like David Levitch.

When she returned she waited a few days then took herself off to the Levitch house. She wasn't sure why. Unfinished business maybe. She couldn't just pull down the shutters on that part of her girlhood without even a backward glance. But as she walked up the drive and rang the doorbell she knew there would be no reply. She went on ringing all the same, more insistently, until the postman cycled by.

"No use ringing, love, they're gone," he said. "Didn't even leave a forwarding address."

It sounded so final. End of story. In retrospect she realised she had experienced one of those rare moments of truth in which irrevocable changes take place. It was the moment she became a different Constance Connor. No longer pliable, trusting, gullible. No longer nice.

Hearing his voice on the telephone all those years later, the memories began to crowd in again. Perhaps they'd never been far from her consciousness, just suppressed.

87

"You won't remember me," he said with the confidence of someone who is perfectly sure he will be remembered. It was the familiar David.

The years in between were of no account.

She wondered if he even recalled that they had never even said goodbye. That he and all the other Levitches had done what she had always feared: just disappeared.

Eight

She let him talk, not saying much herself, alert for clues as to the man he had become. But nothing much seemed to have changed. His attitude, his manner, his mode of speech, his laugh, even his voice – except it was gruffer with the hint of an accent she couldn't quite identify – were instantly recognisable.

She felt surprisingly composed as he talked, which seemed to have the effect of unnerving him. She noted with satisfaction that the more he rattled on the less sense he made. He was probably already regretting calling her, regretting the extraordinary "God-damnedest luck" that he should have been in the precinct when she passed by. He hadn't been totally sure. But then when he'd seen her taken away in an ambulance he knew for certain she was Connie. The cop had given him her name. Remick. So he figured she was married now. Anyway, on an impulse he looked the name up in the telephone directory. It took him a while to get up the nerve to contact her. A whole night in fact. But at least he could find out how she was. The officer had told him it wasn't serious, but it was better to have the hospital check these concussions. Well, actually there was a whole lot more to it than that. But what was the point of discussing it on the phone? Why couldn't they meet? Maybe at the house? He'd like to see the house.

He didn't appear to notice that she wasn't responding. Maybe that was the kind of man he had become. Someone who didn't notice. Then he said: "Con, I really would like to see you." Sounding as if he genuinely meant it. She felt a sharp stab in the pit of her stomach that was more pleasure than pain. (The stomach had always been a more reliable barometer of emotion for her than the heart and she'd never understood why that particular organ should have such a high profile in matters romantic.) It was that feeling, which she always associated with her innocent adolescence and had never experienced since, that roused her to some kind of reaction. That and his reference to the house. She couldn't bear the thought of him facing Sam who would be polite and hospitable and unaware that he was living in the home that had once belonged to the Levitches.

It had, of course, been years after their departure and the house had gone through several more owners who had proved as restless as the Levitches. "It's a wreck," Sam had joked.

"That's why we can afford it," said Connie, "with a little help from the building society," who hadn't been all that keen about lending money on a rundown Victorian pile. But she'd kept quiet about its history and had cautioned Beattie to be similarly discreet under threat of restricting visiting rights with her grandchildren.

"You'll rue it," Beattie had grumbled but she hadn't let on to Sam. Over the years she and Connie had come to a wary accommodation about the past. All the time they didn't talk about it it didn't interfere with business and business was the one secure bond that united them.

"I'd rather you didn't come to the house," she said brusquely, then realised she no longer had any juris-diction over who visited the house. If Sam was intent on being nice to this old friend of hers and inviting him to dinner it would be very awkward for her to put up an argument. Of course it was all hypothetical. Maybe she wouldn't even discuss the mysterious caller with him. Maybe she'd dismiss him as a terrible bore she wouldn't inflict on anyone least of all herself. But even as these permutations of either/or flashed through her mind she knew without any doubt that David Levitch had insinuated himself back into her life and, by association, Sam's.

"I'm sorry," he apologised, presumably feeling an

apology was called for but not quite sure why. "I shouldn't have sprung this on you." Sprung *you* on me, Connie mentally corrected him. "That's what my wife always said. You go in like a bull chasing a scarlet cape," he went on.

Connie laughed. "Is that what I am? A scarlet cape? Red rag to a bull?"

"That's better." She sensed him relaxing on the other end of the phone and the reference to a wife took the tension out of the call, cutting David Levitch down to ordinary size.

She felt able to be ordinary too. "Actually it's not my house. It's my husband's. My ex-husband. We're divorced."

"Oh?"

"But friendly," she amended hastily, not wanting to give the impression of total breakdown between her and Sam and, thus, some kind of failure on her part. She wasn't prepared to surrender her pride that easily. She wasn't yet sure what tone to adopt with him and sensed he didn't know either. They were circling around, prodding here, nudging there, but not fully acknowledging their roles in a past that perhaps meant different things to each of them. Was she perhaps to him just a girl he'd fooled around with when he was a very young man and didn't know any better? No harm done, good pals, his sister's best friend. Becky! That was a memory to conjure with too. She hadn't wondered what had happened to Becky or, indeed, even thought about her for years.

She considered asking about his family, but perished the thought immediately and, instead, elaborated on how she happened to be in the same house as her divorced husband. She felt on safer ground. "After my – my accident – in the precinct, the hospital got in touch with Sam, my ex, and he collected me. I'm staying for a day or two. Although I'm perfectly all right. Just a fall. A bump on the head."

Just a fall! And the rest! "It's a game." Who had said that? She had a vision of a peaky, clever little face and a child who was undersized and named Victoria and knew a thing or three about life Connie couldn't even comprehend. Why did she keep remembering her? What was so special about a streetwise kid who was probably no different from thousands of other deprived youngsters all over the recession-hit country? If indeed she was deprived. Certainly she wasn't lacking in one department: she was as mentally sharp as a tack. She really must stop dwelling on the whole, silly incident in McDonald's, she told herself, and shook her head vigorously as if trying to rid herself of a worrying gnat.

"Connie! You still with me?" The tone of self-satisfied assurance in his voice grated on her.

"I'm still here," she corrected him. "I was just thinking," she lied. "Wouldn't it be amusing to meet at the pub by the pier. You remember the pub by the pier? Bring your wife. I'd love to meet her." It was a silly, flirty suggestion off the top of her head and she regretted it as soon as she'd made it. Remembering the pub put her at a disadvantage and would give him the edge if he couldn't recall it at all. She realised that constantly having to assess these fine distinctions of one-upmanship would make any reunion a wearing exercise.

But, yes, he assured her, he did recall the pub, although he couldn't exactly pinpoint it. It had been a lot of years. "And, by the way, there isn't any wife. She's dead." He didn't sound too put out and followed that news up with a further admission offered just as baldly. "The first one didn't count."

"Oh!" Now it was her turn to react. The first one! The one that took him to America away from her? Just like that! Of no consequence. And was it just the one or had there been others in between?

"Who's counting?" She replied, flippantly.

He laughed. "Well, actually, my lawyer, my accountant, my kids and the guy who runs the delicatessen downtown and delivers the best bagels in Chicago. C'mon, Con, there's a whole lot to talk about. I'll find the pub. What time do they open these days?" It occurred to her that she hadn't asked and he hadn't volunteered what he was doing back in Southdean anyway.

"It varies – I think. I don't go to pubs much," she confessed. "They've relaxed the licensing laws since you . . ."

"Since I up and left you in the lurch. Right? Right!"

"Wrong!" She said furiously.

"Touchy!"

"I'll see you there at five-thirty."

She slammed down the receiver although not in a spirit of pique, but as part of the game rules he seemed to have laid down in his mocking *resumé* of his marital record. Another game.

She had become adept at these sparring games in the years since he had left. Perhaps if she had been good at them before he might not have left at all. But she refused to speculate about that. For the time being she relished the feeling of renewed excitement his call had generated. It was as if in the past twenty-four hours everything was conspiring to bring her back to life. Meeting David Levitch again was merely a part of it. There were other accounts that had to be settled.

She wondered how she could have allowed herself to stagnate for the past two years, to insulate herself so completely from any emotion that even her family described her as a vegetable, half in jest, but half in earnest. Perhaps the bump on her head had done her a whole favour. But, no, it had started before that – with the tape and the odd shoes and the child.

"You're looking very pleased with yourself, Con."

Sam was standing in the arched doorway between his study and the circular hall. It was the circular hall that had sold him on the house finally, she remembered. That and the acre of garden with its wretched clay soil and unkempt trees that had challenged his gardening expertise – not to mention his patience.

It wasn't his fault that whenever she stood in the circular hall or wandered in the garden she peopled them with all shapes and sizes of Levitches.

93

"He lived here," she blurted out. "That man who called. David Levitch. He lived here. With his family. Before I met you."

He nodded thoughtfully, thrusting his hands into the copious pockets of yet another identical woolly cardigan. "I know."

She stared at him, not sure she'd heard right. "You know *now*. I've just told you."

"I knew some time ago. Beattie told me before she died. We talked a lot about you and her and how she'd buggered up your life. I think she was probably exaggerating. She was confused then and rambling on about any and everything. But I imagine there's some truth in it. You were in love with this David Levitch and she didn't approve and did all she could to prevent you being together."

She continued to stare at him in disbelief. Then she felt an uncontrollable urge to laugh as if at a giant joke whose punchline she only now understood. It started as a smile, which dissolved into a giggle and then erupted into a full-blown hysterical belly laugh. The kind of laugh that isn't sparked off by wit or humour but by a ripe sense of the ridiculous. Because that's what those years of silence between her and Sam had been: ridiculous.

He watched her, at first surprised at her reaction. Then he, too, seemed to see the point of the joke and he found himself chuckling at a situation that need never have arisen if they'd been honest with each other. Perhaps if they'd loved each other enough, although he doubted whether Connie had ever loved him at all.

"It wasn't . . ." She started to speak but the spurts of giggles kept welling up, choking the words in her throat. "It wasn't quite like that," she managed to stutter at last, wiping her eyes. "It's really very, very funny. Don't you think it's funny, Sam?"

"It's good to hear you laugh like that again, Con." But he wasn't smiling any more. "When you think about it it's not all that funny. Just a waste. Why couldn't you have talked to me, Con? Why couldn't you have trusted me to understand? It would have made things so much easier for us, for all of us."

"I know, Sam. At least I know it now." The explosion of laughter had left her feeling limp, but liberated too. There was no longer any need to hold back on her feelings as she had seemed to be doing during all their married life and in the bitter aftermath of divorce. "You see after David Levitch I never really trusted anyone, except in business." She nodded ruefully. "I suppose that was my big mistake, trusting the people who only regarded me as a money-making machine and not trusting the ones who cared about me as a person."

"It's over now, Con. Don't get yourself all worked up about things past." He was looking at her with that concerned expression that, when they were together, she had come to detest and then ignore.

"It's not *over* Sam. Or else why are we standing here discussing some chap I haven't seen for thirty years and the delusions of a dying woman? It wasn't just Beattie, whatever she manufactured in her mind. Although I could never forgive her smothering me with rules and regulations, scaring the shit out of me if I stepped out of line. Go out there and conquer the world, my girl, but never surrender to temptation! So far as Beattie was concerned there was only one temptation: sex. And David Levitch was that in capital letters. I honestly think she would have been more understanding if she'd learned I was a serial killer than if she'd caught me in the sack with David. But the truth is Beattie didn't break us up. He did. He just left. Not a word. Apparently he was engaged to some girl in America. And to be fair he never really gave me a false impression. *I* gave me a false impression. That's a joke, too, Sam."

"Connie, give over—" He raised his hands, whether in a gesture of conciliation or exasperation she wasn't sure.

"No, wait, Sam. What I can't fathom is why you didn't hate me for wanting to live in this house. His family's house. It must have seemed to you as if I wanted to live with a family of ghosts. I mean it's really weird that you

95

shouldn't have minded, shouldn't have felt duped. Tell me, Sam, now that we're finally being honest with each other. Tell me!"

"What's to tell, Con? When we bought the house I didn't know anything about it except that it was several bricks short of a desirable residence but, as the master would say, with capabilities. Then when I did find out about it from poor old Beattie, frankly, Con, I didn't care. We, you and me, just weren't in the picture any more, were we? It was just a question of time before we split. I'd had you up to here, Con." He sliced his hand across his neck.

She smiled nervously. "God, that is *honest!*"

He shrugged. "Honest is what you asked for, remember. I couldn't care less about your sad little past and pathetic romances and dreary little fantasies about living in the house of your lover. Sorry! Would-be lover. If Jack the Ripper had lived in the house I wouldn't have cared. It was a nice house. I, we, had worked hard on it. It was ours now, more mine than yours, nobody else's. Besides it had become part of *my* job. You know. The one that was so much less glamorous and exciting than yours. Digging around in the dirt, planting things that would take years to grow and blossom and bear fruit; writing boring articles and books for boring people who also dug around in the dirt; selling plants and shrubs you couldn't tell from weeds grown in greenhouses you described as aircraft hangars. The only times you ever visited the nursery you complained about getting your shoes muddy."

"You really felt all this? Was I that bad?"

"Maybe not that bad," he relented. "But, Con, have you any idea what it felt like for all of us knowing the only damned thing that mattered to you was improving your market share of the rag trade? CCC! Connie Connors Conniption!"

"What?" She felt another irrational attack of giggles coming on. She should be reeling under the blows to her ego that Sam was aiming at her, not laughing at them.

It was the 'conniption' that did it. He surely must have made it up.

"What what?" He frowned. "Oh! Conniption. It's old American slang for hysteria. Karen used it a lot. Someone blows their top and they're having a conniption. I think she got it from Booth Tarkington or Mark Twain. You really know how to slow a fellow down, don't you Connie? This is supposed to be my great get-it-off-your-chest performance and you trip me up on a comic word." He sounded as irritated as his even temperament allowed him to be.

Booth Tarkington and Mark Twain. Surprising! Connie would never have taken the thoroughly English Karen for an avid reader of American classic fiction.

She looked steadily at Sam, noticing the wavering hand holding the pipe and the mouth twitching, sure signs that he was uncommonly cross. It was a rare sight and she found it rather endearing. In fact she couldn't even remember such a sustained display of fraught emotion on his part before. It made him infinitely more attractive than he'd been as the interminably patient and placid peacemaker who had somehow held their marriage together when by rights it should have disintegrated long before. She began to speculate on the nature of his new marriage and suddenly felt very alone.

She wanted to tell him that she missed him but a sense of discretion, maybe of fairness, prevented her. If she'd overlooked the best of Sam it had been her own bloody fault. She had no right to start stirring it up now.

"I like it. That word! Conniption. What could an advertising agency do with that? I suppose the business *was* my hysteria in a way. But do admit there was a lot of it about in the Eighties, courtesy of Maggie's do now, pay later and pay dearly policies. Still, I was in good company." She shrugged. "What the hell!"

"You didn't come off it too badly, Con," he reminded her.

"Give or take a nervous breakdown," she joked. "No, seriously, Sam, you, being here, it's a tonic. That's what

Beattie always used to say when I was down. You need a tonic! Thick brown stuff from the doctor's. This is a better tonic. Facing things." She mimed a gesture of fearlessness and he half expected her to beat her breast and yodel like Tarzan.

"Facing David Levitch?"

She nodded.

"Facing Colin's death?" He felt he was being brutally blunt but there was no other way to make her confront the trauma that tormented her most.

"That, too."

Her eyes were glistening with the fervour of good intentions and he was worried. It was so typically Con to think problems could be solved with one giddy frontal attack. Sometimes they could be. But if they couldn't he feared she'd sink deeper into the despairing lethargy of the past two years.

"Don't expect too much, Con," he warned.

"What a fusspot you are, Sam. Can I borrow a car?"

He frowned. "Have you got a licence?"

"I think so. Yes, I'm sure so. In my bag." She sighed. "I'm perfectly safe on the road."

"There's Karen's Renault out back. She won't be using it. She prefers the Range Rover. It's a hardy little runner. Not long serviced. You're all right with gears aren't you? It's not automatic."

"Sam!" she screamed in mock fury. "Just give me the keys. I want to go into Southdean."

"They're in the hall table drawer over there. I'd take you in myself but I have to go to the nursery. Karen's probably back. She—"

"*No*, Sam. It's a one-woman show. Sort of rediscovery. If that doesn't sound too fancy."

He looked at her doubtfully.

"Just take it easy, won't you?"

"If you go on any more I promise I'll smash the car and get arrested for . . ." She stopped. That's not funny, she thought. Not funny.

He caught her drift. "Like I said, take it easy. One . . ."

98

". . . Step at a time. I know."

He seemed reluctant to leave her.

When he did, she wandered through the house as if it too needed to be rediscovered.

She paused at the door to Colin's old room. She knew it hadn't been used since he'd died. Like Amy's it was much as he had left it.

For some reason Karen had felt it wouldn't be proper for her, the new wife, to make such a dramatically clean sweep, particularly as the old wife was having so much difficulty coming to terms with his death.

In less charitable moments Connie put a different construction on this preservation order: it was Karen's way of rubbing Connie's nose in the mess she had helped to create. The doggie analogy seemed especially appropriate since Karen had inherited Jagger along with his more anti-social habits.

She took a deep breath and opened the door expecting the room to smell musty, unused. But in fact the air was sweet with the fragrance of freshly picked superstar roses in bowls on the bed table and window ledge. The curtains had been drawn and were newly laundered. Everything was neat – Colin had been neat – but not so pristine that the room looked like a magazine spread. It seemed so lived in that Connie had a momentary feeling that he might actually walk through the door and pick up a book or re-align the mobile that hung over his bed. Not an aeroplane like most boys might favour, but a pattern of intricately entwined metal arms covered in dark felt that looked like the petrified branches of dead trees.

She'd never really looked at it before although she remembered seeing him labouring over the design of it, his fingers sticky with glue, when he was barely out of kindergarten. Sam had helped him shape the metal but Colin, young as he was, had been very particular about how it should look: spare and elegant and somehow menacing. It was as if even then he had had a sense of doom.

She could see this now. Why couldn't she have seen it

then? The answer, she knew, was painfully obvious and very boring. She'd discovered it was quite possible to feel guilty and yet bored by that guilt at the same time.

She went over to his desk, which wasn't really a desk but a small kitchen table, by the window. He hadn't wanted a desk, it reminded him of school and he had hated school. No one seemed to know why but then no one had tried very hard. He hadn't made a production of his unhappiness: no tantrums or temperament or screaming matches when term started. He'd just soldiered on apparently cheerfully, so that when he was asked and he said he hated school it tended to be dismissed as the inevitable plaint of a boy who would rather be doing other things than learning lessons.

She picked up the photograph in its frame on the table. It was a school photograph and it was surprising that he should have kept it, let alone displayed it in a place of some honour.

There were thirty-odd boys aged twelve or thirteen grouped in three rows around a smug-looking man who was clearly pleased with himself. The boys wore blazers with the school crest on the breast pocket and shiny smiles that didn't ring quite true. She found Colin in the second row, half hidden, whether by design or accident, behind a huskier boy in front. He, too, might have been smiling but it was difficult to tell because his face was turned toward the boy beside him who was taller and more powerfully built and patently self-confident.

It must have been taken around 1981, not long after she and Beattie, against all the odds, had successfully negotiated a handsome bank loan to increase the capacity of the factory. She remembered how busy she had been because, although Beattie was nominally a partner, she could no longer rely on her mother to shoulder a work-load that was increasing daily. And Sam was occupied with expanding the nursery and taking on extra staff. She recalled how self-satisfied she had been at achieving so much when others were having such a hard job getting started in a tough financial climate;

how even more self-satisfied she was when the country crawled out of that trough and she was poised to reap the rewards of a burgeoning economy.

But all the time she hadn't heard the cry for help of a boy too shy or too scared to show his face full on for the school photograph.

"Shit!" she cursed and turned the photograph toward the window where she couldn't see it. As she did so she caught sight of Karen standing just inside the door. She looked as if she'd been there for quite a while.

"I wonder why a boy so gifted should have committed suicide?" Karen said with a warm, complacent smile on her apple-cheeked face.

Chapter Nine

Suicide! Her son had committed suicide! Why was it that when Karen articulated that tragic truth she believed her?

She hadn't accepted it from Sam or Amy or Holly or the police or the coroner. She had raged at their stupidity in reaching such a verdict. Any child of hers would never be so gutless as to take his own life. To arrive at such a conclusion was a deliberate slur on her, Constance Remick. The note, stuffed behind the windscreen wiper of his car, had said: 'God Forgive Me.' That was all. It could have meant anything or nothing, she had reasoned over and over to herself.

For two years she had refused to countenance the idea of suicide. She would blame herself for much that had gone wrong in Colin's young life, but not that. That was too damning. Yet, when Karen said it, it suddenly became real, inescapable. And she saw that all her denials had been centred on herself: how *she* felt; how *she* had been hurt. And because of that she couldn't begin to imagine what had driven Colin to the edge and beyond.

"He didn't commit suicide. It was an accident," she said. It's what she always said. But this time it was just a reflex reply, uttered with no conviction. Karen, who read Mark Twain and mucked about in the good earth and was gloriously pregnant with Sam's child, had by some curious osmosis shamed her into seeing clearly at last.

She wondered why this should be so. Far more worldly people than Karen had been unsuccessful, including an expensive psychiatrist. Perhaps it was because Karen had spoken of it so calmly, almost cheerily, as a fact of death.

Perhaps when you have spent your life coping with the contrariness of nature you were unlikely to be put out by the imponderabilities of man and why a bright boy with so much going for him should have been intent on destroying himself.

"Of course if it makes you feel better to delude yourself?" It was said without any irony which made it that much more wounding. And because it was wounding Connie took comfort in feeling angry. What right had this woman who had taken her place to judge her? The fact that she had abdicated that place long ago was beside the point.

"You're so damned cocksure about everything, aren't you?" she rounded on Karen and immediately felt foolish for resorting to a kiddish insult.

But Karen didn't rise to it. She just stood there serenely, a slow, knowing smile playing round her mouth. She had a basket of fresh vegetables on her arm and, Connie noticed, her hands were grimy, with dirt rimming her fingernails. Given half the chance she would fold me in her arms like some gruesome earth mother and tell me to let it out and all would be well, thought Connie.

Instead she put down the basket and sat down heavily on a chair, her belly ballooning out in front of her. She clasped her hands contentedly over her stomach and sighed with satisfaction. Pregnancy suited her. She would probably end up having another dozen, now that she's started, Connie speculated, envying her for enjoying what she had always regarded as the whole messy process.

"You know Connie I've always admired you." Karen beamed placidly, making it clear that nothing Connie could say would make her take offence. "You're so — so tough. When I first came to work for Sam you were such a driving force, doing your own work, organising, bossing people around in such a way that they didn't realise they were being bossed."

Connie grinned. "Oh they did," she corrected her. It

really wasn't possible to remain angry or even mildly annoyed at Karen for long.

Karen ignored the interruption. "I thought you were just about the most spectacular woman I'd ever met. And when things fell apart for you, with the business and so forth, I was sure you'd pick yourself up and – as the song says – start all over again. You could have. You still could. What I never understood is why you just crumpled up underneath it all. Why you just gave up."

"How could you possibly know what it's like to lose your career, your son, your mother and your marriage all at once," Connie challenged her.

"That's poppycock." Karen kept smiling her discomforting smile. "You make it sound as if you were struck by lightning four times out of the blue."

"So?"

"So rubbish! If you'd had any sensitivity you'd have seen it all long before it happened. And don't try to make me feel guilty about marrying Sam because you hadn't cared about him for years." She said it so pleasantly, as if not wanting to risk vexing a difficult child, merely pointing out what was obvious in the most agreeable way possible. "What I realised, Connie. Eventually. What I realised is that aside from all that glitter and intelligence you're dense."

"Dense!" Connie snorted. "Me? Dense!"

"Well, bright people often are. Dense about things that are happening under their noses." For the first time the smile disappeared, a serious expression spread across the rosy face. "Me, for instance."

"You?" What on earth was she driving at now?

"Don't look so surprised. I know you like to think I was just a handy consolation, someone for Sam to turn to when you left him and wasn't it fortunate that we were so compatible, working together? What could be more natural? But it wasn't like that, Connie. Sam and I were lovers years before you divorced him. In fact not long after I joined the staff at the nursery."

104

Connie stared at her. She didn't know whether to feel affronted or amused. For a moment she even thought Karen might be lying but discounted that immediately. Among the many virtues she possessed that were so trying was an inability to lie. To imagine Karen telling even a white one was tantamount to conceiving of the Virgin Mary engaging in sexual intercourse. "You were lovers?" she repeated flatly.

"Of course. We weren't even particularly discreet about it, although we didn't talk about it either. I'm pretty sure Amy guessed. Colin certainly did. Maybe Holly too."

"And they didn't tell me?" She didn't know why she said that. The idea of any of her children confiding to her that their father was having it off with the help was not only absurd but impossible. She realised that she wouldn't have given them the chance; she never had the spare time.

"You were preoccupied. Sam was far more honourable than I was. He wanted to tell you we were having an affair and discuss the prospect of a divorce ages before you walked out. But I talked him out of it. I was quite happy the way things were. For someone like me it was all very exciting. An illicit love affair! I'd always been rather dull, not pretty, no figure to write home about. My brothers used to tease me mercilessly about how I looked. They used to say I was a quiet, retiring girl. That was the expression. Quiet and retiring. I'd never amount to much and it was a blessing I had green fingers and did so well in the horticultural line. At least I could earn a living. I was, you might say, stodgy. That's an awful thing for a girl to be, you know. Even when you feel like a top photographic model with the intellect of a Rhodes scholar underneath, you know you're just plain stodgy to everyone else. So, you see, falling in love with a celebrity like Sam and, even more, knowing he loved *me* – well, that sort of thing didn't happen to stodgy old Karen. Old! That's odd, too. You were almost twice as old as me, but you seemed years younger. You still do in a funny kind of way. Maybe that's why I feel able to talk to you like this. Anyway, now you know."

She stopped talking abruptly, puffed for breath, and eased her ample bottom into a more comfortable angle of the chair. She took a long, deep breath and let it out slowly through her rounded lips. "It's the bulk that bugs you, isn't it?" She blushed at the vulgarism. "Bothers you."

"It all bothered me," said Connie absently. "You'll be all right, though." The subject of pregnancy bored her and she dismissed it from her mind. "Talk about odd," she mused. "I was thinking a moment ago that you never lied."

"I never do."

Connie suppressed a smile. Now that she knew Sam and Karen had been lovers behind her back she realised she didn't mind at all. Perhaps she wouldn't have minded even at the time. "Just economical with the truth."

"I thought you'd be cross, hurt, angry. All those things. The first time we ever get to really talk . . ."

"Well, it's more interesting than swapping recipes and the Latin names for house plants. You're quite a revelation, Karen. You're not stodgy at all. You have the knack of . . ." she searched for an apt expression and settled for ". . . total conviction." But what she really meant was that when Karen, in all her unsophisticated certainty, ventured a direct opinion even a sceptic would feel forced to agree with it. She was like one of those grass-roots politicians who capture the electorate with their refreshingly homespun slant on complex problems that had defeated worldlier minds.

"I'm glad about you and Sam," Connie went on. "Truly. And you're right about Colin. There! That's an admission I've made to no one. Not even myself. Now I'll have to deal with that, won't I?" She was surprised how smoothly it all came out, her submissiveness almost oily in its anxiety to please. There, Karen, I'm really a good person, just a little off the rails now and then and I vow to make amends! She looked at the big, round eyes on the big, round face of the big, round woman and detected the hint of a superior smirk. It was barely there, but it said to Connie clearly: at last I've got you! "I wish I liked you, Karen," she said suddenly.

"I don't." The reply came back smartly as if it had been rehearsed and waiting to erupt. "It's easier if you don't like me. Because I dislike you intensely. Oh I admire you as I said. But that's different. You can't help admiring a foxhound, but you hate what it does to the fox."

Connie felt the colour drain out of her face. She took a step or two backwards as if at the receiving end of a blow. She felt the sharp edge of the table that doubled as a desk dig into her back. There ought to have been something she could have said, something smart and sassy and over Karen's head. But she couldn't think of anything. All she wanted at that moment was to be rid of her, to be alone, to try to convince herself that what Karen thought was completely irrelevant while knowing it was probably spot on.

Karen heaved herself out of the chair, kneading the small of her back with the palms of her hands. "You're a careless woman, Connie." It sounded casual, like an afterthought.

Connie winced. ("We're careless people." That's what Becky had said the last time she'd seen her and it had seemed the most damning thing you could say about anyone.) "And now I'm as bad," she said out loud. She looked over at Karen who was acting as if she had dismissed the entire conversation from her mind. Perhaps she had. Once it was out it was out, there was no retracting what had been spoken. That, thought Connie, would be Karen's way. Stir it up and then forget it. It was an uncharitable assumption but Connie wasn't feeling charitable.

"I was just wondering," said Karen, "if you'd like some lunch. I've made some soup and salad and there's some stone-ground flour bread. Quite delicious. A new

107

recipe." She chuckled. "I forgot. You don't like recipes, do you?" She spoke so amicably as if they were two chummy ladies at a sewing bee.

Well, why not? Two chummy ladies under the same roof. No point in bearing a grudge. It wouldn't be fair on the others, although Connie had never been overly concerned about being fair to others. Besides she wouldn't be here much longer. "No – no thank you. Lunch! I'm sure it *is* delicious. But I've an appointment in town and I'd like to . . . mooch around a bit."

"Here?" Karen's eyes raked the room, Colin's room. "You don't mind?"

"Of course not. It's just . . . maybe, maybe you're not quite up to it."

"I'll soon find out then, won't I? And Karen, thank you for the flowers. In the room."

"It's the least I could do. Poor boy!"

She left Connie seething with frustration. Poor boy! She'd made it sound as if Colin were a waif who had been abandoned on her doorstep. She indulged herself with the luxury of feeling affronted and then admitted to herself that she was simply being paranoid.

The Brummie shrink had warned her about that. Not in so many words, of course. He had never said anything directly. He had wrapped it up in soothing jargon. But she had taken his drift.

She sat down at the table and spread her fingers wide on the mock leather surface in front of her. Colin had painstakingly covered the top of the table with the stuff that he'd bought by the yard from a DIY store. He'd also knocked up a book-shelf from bits of discarded wood from a builder's yard. He had inlaid the sides with chips of tile, arranging them into a decorative pattern. Beattie had taught him to do tapestry work and he had re-covered an old chest he'd found in the attic with a cross-stitch canvas in autumnal shades. There were those who derided it as an odd hobby for a boy of twelve – but not in earshot of Beattie.

"He's good with his hands," Sam had said approvingly,

108

hoping he might have a son who would in time happily join his father in running the nursery.

Beattie had even suggested he might be an asset to Connie's business as a designer.

Connie had thought it would be time enough to make those kinds of decisions when he had graduated from university. She couldn't remember now why she had been so set on him going to university. He had shown no particular academic aptitude. Indeed he had shown no interest in anything very much, apart from a vague artistic leaning. He wasn't good at games and the only time he took the stage at school was, literally, when he took the stage – as a rollicking Falstaff, a crafty Shylock and a wonderfully swashbuckling Mack the Knife.

As she sat looking out of the window Connie realised with a pang that she had never actually seen him act. She had heard about his accomplished performances from others and she had been chuffed when the local paper had reviewed them in glowing terms, but only because all this acclaim for her son proved to be good publicity locally and was partly instrumental in getting her elected as a councillor. It bolstered her image as a family woman as well as a businesswoman and therefore a woman who successfully had it all.

If Colin had been upset by her non-appearance at the school plays he didn't let on. It was understood in the Remick household that Mother was a very busy woman. She made up for it with flamboyant gestures: employing a catering firm to throw an end-of-show party which clashed with the more humble beanfeast the school had planned; sending flowers to the drama teacher and champagne to the cast, most of whom were too young to drink it but did anyway and were paralytic by the end of the evening.

Sam might demur mildly about it all being a bit much for a bunch of school kids, but she would accuse him of being an old spoil-sport in such a way that he seriously wondered if he was.

It was Amy, as usual, who faced her with the damage

her extravagance might do to Colin's woefully inadequate self-esteem. "He hates it, Mum, all of it. If you just turned up once to the plays or the speech days he'd be a lot happier with that than all the parties and champagne."

She'd caught Connie on a bad day. There were more and more of them as the business expanded, it seemed. But the urgency in the girl's voice had forced her to listen. Amy had always appeared to be so much older than her years and she had adopted the role of family mediator as her due.

Connie had listened but she hadn't digested the implications of what Amy was saying. Instead she'd assured her daughter that she had to be imagining things. "*All* boys enjoy kicking over the traces now and then, having a ball, even getting a bit tipsy when you're under-age." She had said this with absolute certainty, because it sounded plausible, so it had to be true. But as Amy was insistent Connie conceded: "I'll talk to him. See what's bothering him. Although I'm sure you're exaggerating."

She had given Amy a quick cuddle. Amy was the easy one. So wise and self-sufficient. Holly, thankfully, was too young to be fractious or awkward. But Colin! Yes, she really would talk to him, make him feel wanted. That settled, she shelved it for future reference in her mind. Perhaps she had been neglectful. And then she had been paged by her secretary to sort out a problem with a manufacturer whose last batch of fabrics hadn't been up to scratch.

"Mum!" Amy had called after her. "You will be careful, won't you? With Colin."

"I will be careful," she'd replied airily, not bothering to enquire what she should be careful about.

It was, she supposed, the close proximity to the things he had left behind that was unleashing this flood of memories. Not even memories, which implied a constant examination of the past. It was more like finding a long forgotten snapshot album in which images, barely registered at the time, were suddenly assuming a vivid clarity.

As she sat at the table, looking out of the window, fingering the paraphernalia of objects he'd seen fit to cherish (Dinky cars already rare, a Victorian pepper mill he'd picked up in a junk shop, a bit of chipped Lalique glass, a Meerschaum pipe Sam had given him), she felt his presence at her side, urging her toward an understanding she had never shown when he was alive. "Now I have you captive," it was whispering in her ear. "Now you must listen, see. Now you must pay attention."

She watched a squirrel burrowing away on the lawn outside with its dainty paws, earthing some titbit it had found round the birdbath. Then it scooted off to another part of the garden and rummaged around there for a while. It was not a splendid red squirrel with a gorgeous brush, but a scrawny grey one. Its movements were quick, jerky and nervous which made it look threatened. She felt sorry for it. It reminded her of Colin. She could feel him gazing out at the same scene, perhaps watching a distant ancestor of the squirrel engaged in the same ritual of hiding its store of goodies.

She was calm now. But she hadn't been calm in the days when it would have helped. She had a vision of herself, all jagged nerves, smart, surface talk, a little too thin, a little too much make-up, a little overdressed and perfumed.

Perhaps he had seen in her bright, insincere smile and constant awareness of time ticking by that her 'little chat' was a duty to be carried off with good but facile grace.

She hadn't known how to begin. It had been so long since she'd discussed anything seriously with him, perhaps as long ago as potty-training when he was a toddler.

"Amy said—" she'd started.

But he'd interrupted her. "What is it, Mum? Did Amy think I needed a good talking to?"

He'd smiled that lazy smile at her and she had realised that he was growing into a striking young man with those strange slanting eyes that owed nothing to Sam or her but bore a remarkable resemblance to Beattie's father who had been half Chinese. It was probably one of the reasons why Beattie was so fond and protective of him because he reminded her of her father.

He was only fifteen, but already tall and rangy. Yet there was a delicate look about him too which made him attractive to girls and a target for tougher boys.

She had observed all this, quite objectively, as if she had nothing to do with the production of this growing child. And, quite objectively, she regarded him as a problem to be solved.

"They tell me you were marvellous in the play. *The Merchant Of Venice*, wasn't it?"

He grinned, not seeming to be plagued by problems. "That was last term. It was *The Importance Of Being Earnest*."

She frowned. "Anyway. I'm sorry I couldn't make it, darling."

He stopped smiling. "Don't call me darling, Mum. You don't mean it and I don't like it."

She opened her mouth and closed it. "Really, I can't think—"

"No, I don't suppose you can, Mum. It's just that 'darling' is such a stupid word. It doesn't mean anything."

She shrugged. "Don't be so judgmental, Colin. And don't be so *serious*!" She squeezed his arm and felt him flinch through the thin stuff of his shirt. "You're young. You should be enjoying yourself."

She shot a quick look at her wrist-watch and remembered she was supposed to be sorting out what was bothering him. It would really be too trivial and probably time-consuming to bring up the champagne and the catered party.

"Are you worried about what you're going to do when you leave school?" Well, that was a start. A direct question deserved a direct answer.

"No." He fiddled with the Lalique scent bottle, scratching the chip on the top with his thumb-nail.

"You know I think you should go to university. And you can decide then. After all, it's not as if now we can't afford—"

"I don't *want* to go to university." He had said it so fiercely that she half expected him to smash the Lalique into the fireplace.

"All right, all right. You don't have to blow your top. Is it the acting? Drama school? For Heaven's sake, Colin, neither your father or I are tyrants. We don't have rigid ideas about what our children should do. We just want you to be happy."

"Happy! You're right, Mum. Acting makes me happy. I'm good at it and . . . well, when I'm acting I can stop being me. But it's not a life. It's a frivolous occupation. I want to do some good. Can't you understand that, Mum?"

"Why, of course, I can, dar . . ." She stopped herself in time. She couldn't remember when she'd got into this stupid 'darling' habit; perhaps when she started to meet so many people whose names she couldn't recall. "And there's so much to do, these days. So many opportunities."

"I don't mean your kind of opportunities, Mum. Making more money than you need, taking out more credit than you can repay, persuading people to buy things they can't afford, selling council homes, the whole capitalist bit. . . . It's rotten, rotten! I don't want to be part of that system. Ever!"

She eyed him coldly. Her son! A bloody little bleeding heart leftie at fifteen! "Then I humbly apologise for giving you a good home, clothes, a fine education, weekly pocket money—"

"Etcetera, etcetera. I know, I know, Mum. I'm as much of a hypocrite as the rest of you." He ran his fingers distractedly through his fine, lank hair.

"*Thank* you," she said crisply. "I think that's quite enough."

She turned to leave but he grasped her hand, pulling her back into the room, forcing her to face him. He was surprisingly strong and perhaps he didn't realise that he was hurting her and she wouldn't give him the satisfaction – or so she thought – of telling him.

"Mum, I want us to talk. I really do. Maybe I don't mean half the things I've said. It's just . . . Please, *please*, stay! Couldn't we, I don't know, have a picnic? Go away for the weekend, like we used to when we were little in the caravan? With Dad and Amy and Holly. All of us."

He sounded so desperate. If she'd thought about it all she might have wondered what torments he had suffered in silence to warrant this outburst. But she hadn't thought beyond the superficial suggestion that a picnic would be nice. She hated picnics. They were a terrible waste of time.

"Of course we'll spend more time together. Just as soon as things sort themselves in the business. You see, everything's going to be wonderful, darling."

He had managed to put on a smile as she left. She had quite forgotten that she had promised not to call him 'darling'.

Chapter Ten

That, she realised, had been the disconcerting thing about Colin even when he was very little. These sudden extremes of emotion. And then, just as suddenly, a smiling calm as if nothing untoward had happened. You wondered if you had imagined the crying jags, the racking sobs, the small, angry fists pummelling whoever was within easiest reach. It was always over so quickly and the aftermath was so reassuringly normal that it became quite possible to dismiss his 'little fits' as the kind of display of temper to which all healthy, cheerful children might be prone.

Hyperactive, that's all he was, she had told herself, confirmed in this by popular child-rearing theories on the subject. She had taken to weeding out the foods with the wrong sort of additives from their diet, until the process got too tedious – and seemingly unproductive, for the occasional outbursts persisted. Their doctor, who was uncomfortable with children and old enough to remember a time when cod liver oil and friar's balsam were the universal cure-alls, said there was a lot of it about and put it down to too much TV. He later retired from his practice in the wake of complaints about negligence in patient care. But by then Colin had seemed to have outgrown whatever it was that ailed him. She supposed she should have understood that what appeared to be normal was a retreat into himself far more damaging than any external tantrum. But what good was that realisation now?

She blinked her eyes fiercely several times to block the flow of tears she felt building up. She wouldn't cry, she determined, because she would be crying for herself not Colin. That she should be capable of this small effort of self-therapy surprised her.

She continued to sit at the table, his table, surrounded by his things, soaking up his atmosphere as she had never taken the trouble to do when he was alive. And, as she did so, the memory of that one crucial day flashed into her mind with great clarity, every detail of it sharply defined.

It was the day when, if she had been half the mother she should have been, she would have paid attention. For, she knew now, it was all he ever wanted of her: attention. He had come trailing into the kitchen and had stood in the doorway, waiting, not speaking.

"Where have you been?" she had said busily, annoyed because the *au pair* was down with flu and she hadn't been able to rustle up any domestic help at short notice. She started to issue directives about wiping feet and washing hands when she had noticed that he was leading by the hand a smaller boy who was staring at her with wide, curious eyes. He couldn't have been more than three. His face was freckled and grimy, his hair vivid carrot and none too clean. He was wearing an assortment of odds and ends, a size too large for him, which were probably hand-me-downs from an older sibling. He looked at first glance like a child from another century, one of those Barnardo orphans transfixed in the camera's eye as a reproachful reminder to future generations of the iniquities of the Victorian age. But then you noticed there was no timidity in him, no awe of authority. If he was a waif, he was a thoroughly modern waif.

"What on earth . . .?" she began to say. But Colin interrupted her in his piping voice, gabbling the words for fear he might not get them out before his mother had time to take charge of the situation he had created.

"I found him on a street corner. He's nowhere to go, nothing to eat. He's poor. We have to look after him," he said breathlessly.

He spoke with a furious intensity, this five-year-old

116

son of hers. He spoke as if driven by demons. But, for a moment, all she could think to say was to question why he was out in the streets anyway. She had told him time and again not to stray from the garden, hadn't she? Heaven knows it was big enough! And then she had pulled her thoughts together and said something foolish like: "Well he can't stay here."

"But he has to," her son had bawled. "He's hungry. He's poor."

Then Sam, who had been working in the greenhouse propagating some exotic strain of hybrid lily, had come in and asked tetchily what all the rumpus was about. He, too, for a moment had seemed at a loss as to what to do about Colin's scruffy stray.

And all the time Colin continued to yell: "He's poor and hungry and Miss Murchison said we had to look after the poor and hungry." Ella Murchison was his nursery school teacher who believed no child was too young to appreciate his responsibility toward those less fortunate than himself. Most of her charges called her Ella, but Colin was a respectful little boy. She remarked upon it to Connie who had replied that she should see him when he was in a paddy.

"So, *that's* it!" said Connie, happily on firmer footing. "Typical! Ella – bloody – Murchison!"

"Con!" warned Sam, flicking his eyes at the children. He turned to the little boy and held out his hand. "Since you're here, you'd better come in." He adopted a jocular tone and the boy toddled into the kitchen as if by right. "I expect you're starving." The boy nodded and stared discontentedly around him as if doubting whether anything interestingly edible could be produced in this sanitised environment.

"Get on to the police," Sam whispered to Connie. "See if they've had a child reported missing."

Damn, damn, damn, she thought, reaching for the phone. Why couldn't she have had all girls. Girls were more predictable. She knew about girls because she had been one herself. Boys were alien creatures. Lumping them all together excluded the necessity of considering her son as a unique individual.

"His name's Barry," Colin volunteered, feeling he had won a point on the feeding front.

"That's a nice name," said Sam absently, slicing bread and spreading it with butter and honey. "Perhaps he'd like to wash his hands," he suggested hopefully. The suggestion wasn't taken up.

The boy sniffed ostentatiously, wiping the snot from his nose on the back of his hand. He seemed supremely in control, judging quite rightly that these odd people were probably a lot more uneasy in his presence than he was in theirs.

He pulled a yucky face at the bread and honey.

"Gotnecrisps?"

Sam found some Twiglets instead and he squatted on the floor cramming the savoury bits into his mouth and crunching noisily. He seemed quite unaware of his saviour, Colin, who was studying him proudly as if he were a specimen under a microscope that he'd discovered and identified.

"He's poor and hungry," he kept repeating doggedly and then had a further astounding thought. "He can sleep with me in my room. I'll look after him," he assured his father. "It won't be like the rabbit or the hamster. I promise."

"They're coming." Connie put down the phone and screwed up her mouth in distaste at the sight of the Twiglet-gorging toddler on the floor. "Honey off, dear?" she mouthed at Sam, mimicking Peter Sellers.

Colin sensed his parents' relief that help was at hand and looked, alarmed, first at his father and then back at his mother. He noted the way they exchanged glances and wouldn't meet his eyes.

"Who's coming?" he shouted urgently. "He hasn't anyone. He's poor and hungry."

Connie knelt down beside him and gritted her teeth. She had to be placid and calm and reasonable, she told herself, but she was seething with irritation inside. She took Colin's clammy little hand in hers, but, sensing he probably wouldn't like what she had to say, he slid it out of her grasp and anchored it firmly behind him out of her reach.

She sighed. "Colin, the little boy has a mummy and daddy too. They'll be concerned about him." That was all right surely, she thought. Right conciliatory tone. Even a five-year-old could understand that.

But Colin stared at her, his lips quivering, biting back the tears. "No, he hasn't. He said not," he lied defiantly.

The child had finished his Twiglets and was throwing the scrunched up cellophane bag in the air, giggling.

Then he jumped up and palmed his hand on the slice of bread, honey side up. This seemed to strike him as the height of hilarity and he ran around the kitchen imitating an aeroplane and smeared the walls with honey. At which point Holly woke up from her morning nap and started to squall, impatient to be fed and watered and changed and generally catered to.

Connie clapped her hands over her ears. "Oh, my God! That wretched Helga and her flu! Who's going to clean up this mess? Not me!"

"Con, don't!"

She had known she was behaving badly. She'd known she should have treated it all as a minor irritation, the kind of things kids did unthinkingly and it all got sorted out without tears and tantrums. And, of course, things did get sorted out with what, in retrospect, seemed a minimum of aggro.

The police eventually arrived, followed shortly by a young, cocksure woman who scooped up her grubby child in a large, loving gesture, while at the same time cuffing the side of his head for causing so much trouble. "I was worried sick, you little bleeder," she said fondly.

She had left him playing while she went to the shops, she said, and he had wandered off on his own. She supposed – grudgingly – that it was lucky Colin had found him, rather than some of the creeps around these days. Terrible what you read in the newspapers. "Wait till I catch that sodding Kev. I'll murder him. I told him to keep an eye out for you." Sodding Kev, it seemed, was two years older than bleeding Barry.

She peered closely at her son's sticky paws. "What's that you've got on your hand?" She looked suspiciously at Sam as if he might turn out to be one of those creeps, after all.

"Honey!" he volunteered sheepishly.

She, like her son, made a face. "Can't stand the stuff," she said with enormous authority. Then she jiggled the boy up and down in her arms by way of compensation for having been force-fed honey.

"Christ, you're filthy!"

She thanked Sam and Connie for looking after him, but not too profusely. And she ignored Colin which wasn't difficult as he was sitting cross-legged and silent under the table. As she left they heard her threatening the offending Barry with a bath and his father's wrath when he got home. Judging by his reaction the bath seemed the more onerous prospect.

They piled into the rusty hatchback in which she had driven to the house. They were both laughing merrily as at some huge shared joke. Connie watched them, feeling herself the butt of their humour. She also felt a twinge of envy. They were completely at ease with each other as she had never been with her children. For a moment she tried to imagine what that closeness might be like and whether perhaps her definition of deprivation – lack of a proper diet, clean, neat clothes, material well-being – wasn't flawed.

But the moment passed and all she could see was a loud, bossy young woman with a snotty-nosed kid and no manners to speak of.

The policeman, who had been treated as imperiously as Connie and Sam, shook his head and muttered something about young Barry having the makings of a future tearaway, then he remembered why he was there and suggested they keep a tighter leash on

Colin and, by implication, his burning urge to do good willy-nilly.

"Well, that's that," said Sam after the police car had driven off. But it wasn't.

She could still hear the scream and feel the chill of it now, years later. Not just a child's howl of temper or frustration or simple bloody-mindedness, but a retching, awful cry that was all the more frightening because there were no tears. It seemed to have been dredged up from the very depths of his being. It was a scream of despair.

Sam attempted to coax the heaving little creature out from under the table with soothing words and the offer of comforting arms. But Colin refused to be consoled.

"I wanted to help him. *Help him!*" he gulped over and over in between fresh outbursts of that terrible scream.

"Of course you did," Sam murmured gently, trying to restrain the squirming boy in his arms. He looked desperately at Connie.

But she just stood there, unable to move, unable to think of a single thing to say, a single gesture to make, that might quiet this disturbed son of hers.

"Connie, do something!" Sam pleaded with her. "He's beside himself."

She remembered waving her hand across her face distractedly. "I can't Sam. I don't know how. You're better with him. I'll see to Holly." She had retreated gratefully to the safety of the nursery and the easier job of settling an infant who was merely demanding the basic necessities and not a commitment of understanding that was beyond her.

As she changed the child's nappy she heard Colin's voice floating plaintively up the stairs. "Mummy!" She felt awful and impotent. But she reassured herself that what she had said to Sam was right: he was better at dealing with the children's dramas than she was. They both agreed that. There was nothing shameful about it. People were good at different things, even if it meant switching the traditional gender roles. She hadn't realised, hadn't wanted to face, that this

121

wasn't just a childish drama. It was something more traumatic.

When she had finished with Holly she came downstairs. Colin was deeply asleep in Sam's arms, a troubled sleep, judging by the way his hands kept grabbing at something invisible and out of reach and his head twitched in irregular spasms. But he was asleep. That had to be a blessing.

"There," she said. "Just temper."

"He's hurting," said Sam simply. Looking back, she understood that things were never quite the same between them after that. If she could identify the time when the slow disintegration of their marriage began it would be that moment when she refused to console the son who needed her so desperately.

They didn't speak of the incident again and, to all intents and purposes, Colin appeared to have forgotten it. He just seemed to withdraw into himself even more; playing solitary games; learning new handicraft skills from his grandmother and spending long hours practising them in his room; begging a tiny plot of garden from his father for planting and tending seeds. He didn't have many little friends or if he did he didn't bring them home.

Although Colin no longer attended the nursery school, Connie had felt obliged to challenge Miss Murchison's opinions on the virtues of doing good which had led to the unfortunate situation involving a cross mother, the police and an apparently kidnapped child. (Maybe it runs in the family, she thought, half smiling, all these years later, the day after she'd been accused of the same innocent crime.)

Being angry with Ella Murchison had seemed an easier option than talking it through with Colin and she could convince herself and Sam, should he raise the subject, that she had actually done something about it.

Miss Murchison had listened to her quietly and then reflected that Mrs Remick didn't appear to know her son very well and that any instinct to help others

122

should be encouraged. She supposed she should have warned against any precipitate action without benefit of parental guidance and she was sorry about the police and the wandering Barry, but no harm had been done and, no doubt, valuable lessons learned. She spoke like that: well-intentioned, but priggish and long-winded with adults who found it hard to believe that this homely, angular girl could be so idolised by her small charges until they actually saw her in close contact with them. Then she was transformed. She really didn't care much for grown-ups.

Connie considered taking the matter of Miss Murchison up with the supervisor of the nursery school, but decided against it, merely making a mental note that Holly wouldn't go there when she was old enough. In the event Miss Murchison disappeared without trace some months later and was only heard of again when her valiant efforts as an aid worker in Somalia were celebrated in a Channel 4 TV documentary.

It took Connie a while to refocus on the present as she sat staring out of the window surrendering herself to all those memories that had somehow got lost in the dusty recesses of her mind. She hadn't thought of Miss Murchison for years or the incident of Colin's doing good and she couldn't imagine how she could have forgotten such a vital turning point in all their lives. She wondered if Sam had forgotten it, too, but she somehow doubted it. Sam, like Colin, was good at keeping things to himself, except, in Colin, that secrecy had become warped and finally insupportable.

She idly opened the drawers beneath the surface of the old kitchen table which had been designed for second best cutlery and cooking implements. Colin had fitted them out in dark green coloured baize to take his exercise books and the usual schoolboy odds and ends of pencils, rubbers, ballpoints, set squares, half-used water colour tubes, compasses, rulers, and other less recognisable items that could only have meant anything to their owner.

The baize inside covering had been neatly executed, the corners precisely cut and fitted together. There were no bubbles of glue rippling the smooth surface. Everything he did, she remembered, had a similar meticulousness about it. It was all part of the self-contained image he presented of himself; an image that ordinarily discouraged investigation. Even she, particularly she, had been fooled by it. The difference between her and the others was that she had been only too relieved to accept this uncomplicated picture of her son.

"He loves you so much, Con, why can't you talk to him?" Sam would say.

"I talk to him – when he wants me to," she'd reply airily and get on with more urgent matters.

And then Beattie would nag her about Colin, too. Only as time went by she didn't pay too much attention to what Beattie said because everyone knew she was becoming forgetful and, worse, repetitive.

The exercise books were piled one on top of the other in strict order by year and subject. The depth of the drawers accommodated six books to a pile and, when one pile was completed, another was started beside it.

It all looked so organised. There was none of that friendly chaos you associate with boys. Even his clothes, those he hadn't taken with him, were carefully hung in wardrobes and folded on the shelves of tallboys. Sam had made the point that nothing had been touched and Connie was sure that Karen would observe this courtesy to the dead.

The writing on the covers of the exercise books, she noticed, was in a thin, almost spidery, copper-plate; the kind which she doubted had been taught in schools since before the war. But it wasn't the same handwriting he used for everyday use and she wondered why he should have affected this strange, outdated style for his school work. She found herself tracing the elaborate loops and curlicues of the letters with her forefinger on the blotter on the table. It was curiously satisfying.

Her search through the drawers, at first an unconsidered exercise, became more agitated. She had to find something that spoke to her of Colin; not objects and lessons, but some statement from him to her. Maybe it wasn't too late – for her, at least.

She found it, as she knew she would. Why else would she have riffled through the drawers so urgently?

It was just a slim volume, stuffed beneath a pile of exercise books. It didn't even look like a diary, but she knew that that's what it was. It had no dates, no gold stamp proclaiming its purpose on the fake leather cover. It was just a book of blank pages with what seemed indiscriminate jottings throughout. Sometimes a page would be missed. Elsewhere one page took in several separate paragraphs. Then there would be whole pages of non-stop narrative. There was no indication of time. It could have covered several years or merely one, maybe even no more than a few months or weeks.

She weighed the book in her hand before studying its contents. As she did so she realised, with a sudden quickening of guilt, that she was acting just as her own mother had acted in stealing her hidden thoughts. Perhaps the spirit of Colin, that unseen presence in this room, would be more forgiving to her than she had been to Beattie.

Chapter Eleven

The inscription on the first page should have alerted her. *'To Whom It May Concern. Joke!'* But the derisive tone was so in keeping with his elusive personality that she didn't see anything especially significant in it.

She debated with herself whether she should continue or stuff the book back in the drawer where she had found it or, better yet, destroy it. But the urge to read on was too insistent and she persuaded herself that it was not only her right but her duty to discover all she could about her son. The irony of a mission of discovery two years too late didn't escape her. But, then, her life, at the moment, seemed riddled with ironies.

'Hub!' The name kept occurring in his jottings. Barely a page missed some reference to 'Hub'. 'Hub' appeared to be the recipient of all Colin's private thoughts.

'Hub says I should strike out on my own, but where to, for what? Funny, I can't talk to her, not really talk and there's so much I want to say. But even if I could, she wouldn't see. It's always things with her.'

'Hub', Connie supposed, was female; some girl, perhaps, he thought he fancied and who was not responding as he hoped she would. Now she came to think of it, there had been a girl. A scruffy, morally righteous teenager who had made Connie feel as if she had committed a mortal sin in devoting her life to business. She wouldn't have remembered her if she hadn't been so forthrightly antagonistic. She could imagine how a girl like that might influence a boy like Colin, but her memory of her didn't square with the idea of someone who couldn't be talked to and wouldn't see.

She went on turning the pages, skipping great diatribes of third hand philosophy about the grim state and probable future of the world. As she did so she realised it was hardly a diary at all. It covered only a few months, during and just after his last term at school where he had acquitted himself so poorly – on purpose, she had suspected – that all thoughts of university had been abandoned. Parts of it she couldn't understand, as if he had deliberately devised a code which would make no sense to anyone except himself and, possibly, the opinionated 'Hub'.

Then something alarming and dramatic would leap off the page. 'It was awful! Hub was splendid, but said it was better not to say anything or it would just get worse.' What could have been so awful and could only get worse? There was so much she didn't know, so much he hadn't let on about. 'I didn't mind the thrashing so much. It was what they said. I felt dirty which was strange, because partly I got thrashed for being too clean. Hub helped. God bless Hub! I think when I finally do a run we might live together.' That, at least, was clear enough, she thought.

And so, too, was the next entry. 'That stupid red car was waiting for me when I got home. She'd promised me it when I passed the test. I wish to hell I hadn't now. I begged her not to. But she wouldn't listen. I said I'd rather have an old banger and give the fifteen grand to the homeless. She swears there aren't any who don't want to be. Thatcher says so. So it must be true. I think I hate her. But then I know I don't. Hub says I probably love her too much. Maybe he's right. Hub's usually right about most things.'

There was nothing coded about that. It was as brutal as an attack with a blunt instrument. Obviously she had been wrong in assuming 'Hub' was a her. It was she, Connie, who was impossible to talk to, who never listened.

She discovered she was shivering, although it wasn't cold. She hunched her shoulders and gripped her arms with her hands, digging her fingers so painfully into the bare flesh that her nails left livid red weals on the skin. She welcomed the pain as a kind of penance for the greater pain she had inflicted.

He was quite right. She recalled now, so vividly, how she had dismissed his protestations that he didn't want a sports car. She was sure when he saw it, in all its gleaming scarlet vulgarity, he would change his mind. But now she saw what a facile supposition that had been. How could she even entertain the idea that Colin would appreciate so ostentatious a gift?

Then she forced herself to go beyond that. "I bought it for him, but I did it for me." She murmured the admission out loud and wondered why it had taken her so long to realise that. A handsome son with a blazing new sports car was as much of an advertisement for Connie Remick as a full page in the local paper or a round of applause at a businesswomen's luncheon at the Savoy. She supposed Sam must have demurred (it was no more in his nature to drive a racy car than it would have been in Colin's), but not positively enough for her to pay any heed. Only Connie had been proud of that damned car which ended up vandalised in a lay-by near Beachy Head.

She flicked through the remainder of the diary. Some of it was revealing, some incomprehensible, some quite dull: arguments with Amy and Holly, crushing condemnations of teachers at school. There was an observation about Sam's new assistant, Karen, who was nice but 'comes on strong'. Karen? Coming on strong? What could he have meant? Had she been too loud, too domineering? Had she tried to seduce him like some temptress in a Schnitzler play? None of these possibilities struck Connie as at all plausible. But then she had to admit she had never really taken Karen very seriously – until, that is, today, when she had learned that Karen and Sam had been lovers long before Connie had been aware that they were remotely interested in each other.

On the last two or three pages of the book the writing changed. The loops and curls became stronger, angrier, as if he had been writing in a great rage. 'She looked glorious in that vivid green that suits her so well. Well, wouldn't she just! How could she? How could she demean herself with that little toad? She was begging him. Actually begging him! And he was telling her it was over and it shouldn't have happened. It wasn't right. And she said who the hell cares about right and stuff like that. They just stood there in the garden and everyone else was knocking back the booze in the lounge and saying how wonderful she was. I thought about coming out of the shrubbery and letting them know I'd seen and heard them. But I didn't. That was it. I've decided.'

The handwriting grew even more erratic. 'Hub says if you write down your feelings as you feel them, it releases you. But it bloody doesn't. End of diary. Boring! Bye, bye! Maybe I'll burn this rubbish before I go.'

But he hadn't burned it, had he? He'd left it – for her. She had the eerie feeling that she was meant to find this chronicle of his after he'd left. She was the one it was supposed to concern. The big joke. Why burn it? Burn her instead. How could he have known that his room and his things would have been kept sacrosanct for all these years? And whose fault was that? Mine, she thought. Sam's. Karen's.

She dropped the book on the table. It seemed to her like an animate object with a poisonous life of its own and she wiped her hands vigorously on her skirt as if to reduce the risk of contamination.

It was a shock to realise what it had all been about! The dreadful row that had resulted in his packing his bags and leaving the house. She'd believed it was a quarrel about his future, his fecklessness in opting for some kind of career. Sam had believed that, too. But that wasn't it at all. It was about her and Lewis Diamond in the garden that summer day when he had told her their affair would have to end.

She had never been sure whether Lewis was uncomfortable about the age gap between them or the fact that they were business associates or just that he didn't care for her any more. It had been a surprise, but not a

129

calamity, really just a blow to her ego. She doubted whether she had begged Lewis, but maybe that was how it would seem to an impressionable teenager. She hadn't loved Lewis, any more than he had loved her. It had been just a pleasant and convenient diversion, more companionable than passionate, and it had lasted only a few weeks. What had mattered was that their professional relationship should remain intact. But, of course, it hadn't. Lewis had left the company soon after that summer day. She had missed his keen expertise in promotion but that was all. Now, she could barely recall that they had been lovers, let alone what they had been like as lovers, and she imagined it was the same for him.

She hadn't felt guilty about Sam. Perhaps, subconsciously, she had realised there was someone else in his life and, if she were honest with herself, it wouldn't have concerned her greatly, even if she had had certain proof of it. Just another case of bruised ego.

It was a matter, when she looked back on it, of absolutely no importance. That it should have had such repercussions seemed almost laughable. But to Colin, she supposed, it must have seemed like a betrayal. If only he hadn't overheard her and Lewis maybe everything would have been different. It was a good, strong, cut and dried conclusion with a satisfying symmetry of logic like those historical speculations that begin 'if only . . .' And even as the thought came into her mind she dismissed it as far too simplistic. What had happened was the culmination of a lifetime of misunderstanding and emotional neglect.

If it hadn't been that ridiculous situation with Lewis it would have been something else, some other undercover excuse for Colin to leave home. And, even now, feeling as she did a shuddering sense of shame at her own behaviour, she couldn't believe there was sufficient cause for her son to just take off. There had to be more. Maybe the ubiquitous 'Hub' would know, if she could only . . . She stared hard at the school photograph, at all those beaming young faces, at first individually and then, finally, focusing on one: the tall, self-assured boy whom her son was looking at instead of at the camera. The name came to her suddenly, as elusive names often do, apparently out of nowhere. Hubbard Crowther!

She remembered Colin introducing him to her on one of those rare occasions when she attended the school speech day. Colin had been so patently anxious that they should like each other, but she had found him cool and distant. His mother was old county gentry, not too well heeled but far too proud to show it. She had bequeathed her maiden name to Hubbard and had been even more patronising than he, giving the distinct impression that she considered Connie and Sam 'trade', an attitude that could still be cutting even if it was ludicrously outdated.

The snub registered with Connie more vividly than the boy or his mother or Colin's pathetic desire to please both her and his friend. Friend! Perhaps there had been a homosexual relationship. Maybe that was part of Colin's problem: that he was gay. It occurred to her that she should have noticed some evidence of that, but then parents were often left in ignorance of their children's sexual proclivities these days – even those parents who prided themselves on being the best of chums with their offspring.

Neither she nor Sam could remotely qualify as 'best of chums' with Colin. She admitted that. But they would certainly have taken a broadminded view if their son had confessed he was gay. Colin could hardly have doubted that. They did, after all, live in the last decade of the twentieth century. Which, alas, raised the corollary spectre of Aids.

But she wouldn't think about that. Her imaginings were just that: imaginings. She would know better when she spoke to Hubbard Crowther, wherever he was. She seemed to recall some split in the Crowther family that had made the local newspaper a few years before, but what it was about escaped her.

She wondered whether the austere Mrs Crowther had ever been called a bitch by her son. Or had he a quite

131

different vocabulary for inflicting pain? 'Bitch!' That was the last word Colin had ever addressed to her. The last word that was meant. Oh, they had heard from him, the odd postcard, the occasional phone call when he was sure it would be answered by Sam or Holly or Beattie, not Connie, a rare lunch with Amy when he was around London, at her expense. At Christmas there was a report, hardly a letter, letting them know he was all right, that he was working for this or that organisation, camping out with travellers, going back to nature in some worthy charitable commune or hacking the tourist route in the Mediterranean during the summer. All calculated to assure them that he needed no help, no money, no concern. Nothing but his freedom from them.

The contentious red car had remained in the garage all that time, until one day Sam discovered that it had been stolen in the night. The garage door hadn't been forced though and Sam had not reported the theft. The assumption was that Colin had taken his own property perhaps to sell to a shady dealer who wasn't too fussy about documents and road tax.

"Why couldn't he have come to me?" worried Sam.

"When did he ever?" replied Connie cruelly, still hurting from a divorce that was too amicable on the surface to be completely without rancour underneath.

She heard the grandfather clock in the hall chime the hour. Three o'clock. She had been rummaging through the past for over an hour. She looked around the room with distaste and her mood of melancholy changed to one of resentment. At Sam and, perhaps more importantly, at Karen for preserving the room as a kind of hallowed place. It was a nice room, well-proportioned, with a good view beyond the garden to the distant Downs. They could surely find a better use for it.

And she doubted whether Colin would have appreciated this shrine to his memory. She remembered that once he had had a heated argument with Amy on the subject of death. He had only been about sixteen at the time but he sounded so untypically certain about what he

132

felt. How when you were dead you were dead and it didn't matter what you'd been in life or who you were. President Kennedy was just as dead as any old bag lady who died of hypothermia in a cardboard box on the Embankment. It had surprised her because Colin had always appeared to be more of a sentimentalist than a realist. What he had said was true enough if you didn't believe in a hereafter, but few people would have expressed themselves quite so brutally. She wondered whether they were his own thoughts or that damned Hub's.

Well, she'd take him at his word anyway.

Greatly daring, she ransacked his wardrobe and packed the best of his clothes into an old suitcae that had been abandoned under his bed. Oxfam. That should please him. He was all for good causes. She pulled herself up sharply. She was thinking about him as if he were still alive. That had to mean something, if only that, conversely, she was coming to terms with his death.

The rest of the clothes, well worn or in need of repair, she bundled up in the corner for a jumble sale. Then she neatly shredded the pages of the diary and dumped them in the waste paper basket. She thought of setting fire to them ceremoniously, but had neither the match nor the courage. Finally, she opened the window, weighed the bit of chipped Lalique in her hand and shied it with satisfying accuracy at the gnarled trunk of the oak. It splintered on contact, splattering shafts of iridescent green and blue crystal on the ground.

That was a start anyway. Karen, she thought gleefully, would probably be appalled. Another example of Connie's incipient madness, she would no doubt warn Sam. Well, it was better than odd shoes, but hardly more rational, Connie conceded.

The question of Hubbard Crowther's whereabouts was more easily solved than she had imagined. Sooner or later, she was sure, she would have tracked him down or, at least, found out what had happened to him after the boys left school. But she had reckoned it would take time and she couldn't shake off the restless feeling

133

that everything had to be resolved in these few days. They were her last chance to redeem herself in her own eyes, her last chance to attain a serenity of mind that might sustain her in the future. Even the unexpected reappearance of David Levitch, that other ghost from her past, pointed in that direction.

Amy would undoubtedly tell her she was being ridiculously melodramatic. There were no sudden cures or redemptions, except in the Bible. It was a matter of highs and lows. Connie was on a high now and the low, that would inevitably follow, would be painful. All this she could understand but she didn't have to believe it if she didn't want to.

She looked round the room once more, taking in the disarray with some satisfaction, and then closed the door firmly behind her. The suitcase was heavy and the catches were none too secure but she managed to trundle it down the stairs. The house was quiet and she supposed Karen was in the garden or deep in some complicated recipe in the kitchen. She opened the drawer of the elegant little rosewood side table, took out the keys of the Renault and eyed the telephone on the inlaid surface.

There was just a chance that Hubbard Crowther might actually be in the telephone directory. Probably his mother would be. She thumbed through the pages of the directory in Sam's study. There were several Crowthers but all of them lived in blocks of seafront flats or council estates except one: Robert Crowther, The Crescent, Southdean. It was one of the choicest addresses in Southdean. Only the great and the good, but not necessarily the wealthy, lived there. From Connie's memory of the mother, it was a suitable residence for the Crowthers.

The voice that answered Sam's extension phone was unmistakably Hubbard Crowther's mother, slightly irritable at having been interrupted in something or other (maybe an afternoon nap?), imperious but not so off-putting that it couldn't immediately switch to honeyed charm if the caller should turn out to be a best friend. It announced itself as Erica Crowther.

134

"You probably won't remember me . . ." Connie began, realising she was echoing David Levitch's introduction on the telephone a few hours before. Well, why should she remember her? Just another awful mum of one of her son's awful friends.

She ploughed on in a rush, the words spilling out, ending, rather lamely: "I'd like to speak to your son, Hubbard. Perhaps you could tell me where he is."

There was a long silence, so long that for a moment Connie thought she had been cut off, then Mrs Crowther spoke, giving her reply the full majesty of her contempt.

"How dare you!"

The response startled Connie. She hadn't expected affability, but she had expected courtesy. It was, after all, a reasonable request.

"Mrs Crowther, I just . . ."

"I don't know where he is," the forbidding voice persisted. But Connie had the feeling she was lying. She decided to grovel, if it would produce results. She debated whether to call her "Erica" but decided that would never do.

"Believe me, Mrs Crowther, I don't wish to pry in any way. But it's very important for me to see him — for my son's sake." The last was a dubious embellishment. Seeing Hubbard Crowther now was a little too late to be of much use to Colin. But it was worth a try.

"I told you I don't know where he is." Connie detected the slightest softening of the tone, a note of irresolution.

"If there's anything you could tell me," she pleaded.

Another silence. Then: "Try the Salvation Army." End of conversation. Connie heard the determined click of the phone at the other end. She looked at the receiver perplexed, as if it might elaborate on the last extraordinary statement of Mrs Crowther.

The Salvation Army! Could it be possible? Hubbard Crowther, that smooth, supercilious, assured boy seemed an unlikely candidate to join that selfless organisation.

135

And, if he had, could that really be the reason for his mother's outright rejection of him?

As she left Sam's study she found Karen standing in the hall. In her hand were several slivers of the Lalique crystal. Her expression was one of extreme puzzlement, anger struggling with curiosity. If Connie hadn't been so fired with excitement at actually getting a lead on the famous 'Hub' with such comparative ease, she might have felt guilty all over again. Guilty at upsetting Karen in her delicate condition; guilty at destroying the Lalique; guilty at rummaging around in Colin's memories. But she felt no guilt, only a sense of triumph that she was conquering the inertia that had afflicted her over the last two years.

Karen looked at the broken pieces in her hand and then at Connie. If she wanted to say something stronger she obviously thought better of it and merely commented: "I thought I heard something breaking."

Connie smiled. "You did, Karen, you did. More than you know."

She picked up the suitcase with some effort and heaved it toward the front door.

"What's in that?" said Karen suspiciously.

"The past," Connie replied.

Chapter Twelve

At first the name of Hubbard Crowther got a blank response at the Salvation Army centre in Southdean. It was only when Connie used the diminutive 'Hub' that the penny dropped. Yes, he had come by regularly for a while. He had even talked about volunteering to join the Army. Then he had drifted away. He hadn't seemed in any particular need of counselling or care or material support. Which had been surprising.

Why surprising? she had asked. Because he had, they explained, just been released from prison. They thought she knew that or else they wouldn't have volunteered the information.

Hub! Prison! She thought of that elegant, confident, rather patronising older boy whom Colin had obviously idolised. She thought of his immaculate manners and breeding and the air of privilege that would surely have opened doors for him in whatever career he had chosen. And for a moment Connie wondered whether they were talking at cross purposes about two different Hubbard Crowthers. If, indeed, there could possibly be two people with a name like that.

But no. He was described to her as she remembered him more or less, allowing for the passing of years.

She was given an address, but warned that it wasn't an up-to-date one and quite possibly had just been a temporary flop house. She thanked the cheerful soldier for Christ who filled out her Army uniform plumply and asked to be remembered to Hub when Connie contacted him. "Tell him to drop by any time," she shrilled, as she accepted the suitcase full of Colin's good clothes that

Connie decided might be just as useful to the Salvation Army as to Oxfam.

Even without looking it up on the Southdean and district street map Connie realised that the address she had been given, Rookshaven Lane, was located in a neighbourhood that tended to be avoided whenever possible. She sat in the car for a few moments, digesting the idea that the famous Hub was an ex-prisoner and wondering whether on the whole it mattered all that much whether she found him or not. He had probably lost touch with Colin after they left school and he might not be at the unsalubrious address anyway.

She'd promised to meet David Levitch in a little over an hour so she hadn't much time. And what kind of fool would she look scouring the seedier side of Southdean for a young man who could easily be oceans away by now?

Besides, she forced herself to admit, the prospect that she might actually meet him and the worse prospect of what state he might be in when she did were hardly tempting.

Then she mentally rapped herself on the knuckles. No good, Connie girl! That's cheating. Making excuses, like all the other excuses you've invented to shield yourself from unpalatable truths.

She released the handbrake purposefully, put the car into gear and nosed the Renault through the traffic in search of Hubbard Crowther.

It took her through streets of Southdean that never figured in the visitors' brochures. Past the untidy sprawl of the industrial site with its factory units, some boarded up, backing on to the ripely malodorous refuse tip. Past the estate of council semis most of which had been bought by their tenants in the halcyon days of easy mortgages before the downside of a property owning democracy became evident. Past pockets of what had once been the old village of Southdean dating back to the seventeenth century, the odd remaining cottages of flint and rubble walls and clay tiled roofs and the much restored parish church with its commanding spire now looking forlornly out of place in a hostile environment.

Connie could not recall ever venturing or indeed needing to venture beyond this last token survival of Southdean's distant past. Beyond it, she had been dimly aware, was the slummy bit where the streets were badly lit and the terraces of Victorian labourers' dwellings had never attracted the intensive gentrification that had been lavished on similarly depressed areas in neighbouring towns. By the time the estate agents and developers had cottoned on to the money-making potential of transforming Southdean's slum row into desirable residences for upwardly mobile young couples, the recession had hit, the money had dried up and the mobility of many of the targeted young couples had taken a downward turn.

Rookshaven Lane belied its name. It sounded quaintly rural, but was in fact a bleak, snaking thoroughfare, faced on either side with pock-marked houses, mostly sub-divided into bed-sitters and flats, and walls daubed with graffiti, some of it political, some of it personal and all of it obscene.

Tacked on at the end of the Lane in an apparently haphazard fashion was the gaunt detached house Connie was looking for, although it seemed intent on disguising the fact, shielding the numbers on the porch under a cascade of dark, fetid ivy. It was only by a process of deduction – counting forward from the few houses that bothered to keep their numbered address prominently displayed – that she decided she had found Hubbard Crowther's hiding place. At least, she assumed it was a hiding place; certainly it was a far cry from the tasteful home in which he had been reared by the indomitable Erica.

She parked the car a few doors away, locked it ostentatiously and debated whether to tip the sullen boy who was inspecting it suspiciously fifty pence to keep an eye on it for her. The Renault wasn't in the best of nick but it was decidedly more spruce than the dented

139

battle wagons that lined the Lane and she didn't think she could face Karen's noble forbearance if she had to tell her it had been damaged or pinched. The boy sniffed at the fifty pence, argued for a fiver and settled for two quid, one on deposit and one on Connie's return.

Instantly two other boys of the same age – maybe eight – materialised as if out of nowhere and discussed with their mate the shrewdness of the deal, given that anyone who was prepared to pay two quid for a favour would almost certainly double that under pressure.

She heard them wrangling behind her. She turned round. "You will . . ." she started to say, but already they were scarpering up the Lane as a youngish man, with a large beer belly escaping from a skimpy vest and low-slung jeans, emerged from a house shouting abuse and making threatening gestures after them. He rounded on Connie. She realised, with surprise, that underneath the flab and the florid complexion were the makings of a good-looking man.

"Give that lying little scrounger Clint a back'ander and you're asking for it," he growled. He didn't specify what and she didn't dare ask. He smiled, an awesome sight revealing a gappy and chipped set of teeth through which a restless tongue kept protruding and licking his lips. "Who you looking for?" he said agreeably.

Well, why not? Maybe he *would* know. "Hubbard . . ." she began, then changed it to, "Hub. Hub Crowther. Do you know him? They told me at the Salvation Army that he lived around here."

"'Ub!" He laughed, a rather nice laugh, not at, but with. "Everyone knows 'Ub round here." He jerked his thumb in the direction of the end house Connie had figured was the right one. "Probably out back with the kids," he volunteered.

"Shouldn't they be in school?" Connie said and regretted it immediately. It was such a prim, middle-class remark. She felt like some lady of the manor checking up on the peasants.

But he didn't take it amiss. She supposed he felt it

140

was only to be expected from a middle-aged woman, neatly turned out and obviously reasonably well heeled who was concerned enough about her car to stupidly give a lying little scrounger like Clint a sweetener to look after it.

"School!" he sniffed. "You a social worker or wot!" It wasn't a question and it didn't require an answer. Presumably if Connie had been from round here she'd know why kids played truant and no one paid too much attention to it.

"Well, thanks for your help," she said.

He sized her up approvingly. Nice figure. On the skinny side. And a look about her. Larky, he thought, not realising he was echoing Amy's assessment of her mother. He nodded at the car. "I'll see nothing 'appens to it."

"Bri!" A woman's voice called from inside, then, "Brainless wonder!"

"Thanks," Connie repeated, conscious that he was watching her bottom as she strode out toward Hub's place and unconsciously tightening her tummy muscles so that her rear looked good. For whom? Brainless Bri! Jesus, she thought, what's happening to me?

She noticed that some humorist had hammered a sign into the concrete plinth that supported a chipped bird bath in the front garden. 'Heaven's Gate' it said and, underneath, 'Everybody Welcome'. Connie assumed it was Hub's idea of a joke. A funny kind of Heaven. It was probably what Bri meant when he said everyone around there knew Hub.

A chorus of whooping screams and oaths came from somewhere to the rear of the house. Outside a crocodile of shabbily dressed and variously infirm senior citizens were being shepherded into a minibus by a young woman and two younger helpers whom she ordered around with a bossy air of authority. "Not *that* way, dummy! *Under* the armpits!" She elbowed one of the helpers aside and demonstrated the most efficient way of steering a fractious old woman up the steps of the bus.

141

"I'd rather be dead," grumbled the old woman.

"You will be soon," retorted bossy-boots and they both chuckled at this graveyard repartee which was obviously a ritual part of their relationship.

Connie approached the organiser of the outing with some trepidation and an uneasy feeling that she recognised her from somewhere.

"Excuse me," she ventured.

"No time. Buzz off."

The brusque reply gave Connie a vital injection of anger. Right miss! Two can play at that game. "I'm simply asking a civil question," she persisted irritably.

"I just want to know where I can find . . ." Her voice trailed away. "Hubbard Crowther," she finished faintly.

The young woman had turned toward her with a boldly cynical expression on what remained of her face. A deep scar slashed down one cheek from the corner of the eyebrow to the jaw. The skin around it was puckered and puffy as if she hadn't had the benefit of expert medical attention in time. One side of her mouth was dragged down giving her a permanently disagreeable scowl. The deformity was all the more disturbing because the face on which it had been inflicted was quite beautiful in a brutal kind of way. There had never been anything soft or pleasingly feminine about it. It must always have been a challenging, angry face. But beautiful. And Connie was even more convinced she'd known it once when it was whole and undamaged.

The girl, for in Connie's eyes she was barely more than that, saved her the trouble of racking her memory for some clue as to where and how they'd met.

"You're Constance Remick, aren't you?" she said, with disconcerting directness. "*You* haven't changed much. Well – not a lot." All the time she was talking she was monitoring the progress of the elderlies into the minibus. "Have a care, Beanie," she reprimanded one of the helpers who was rough-handling a slow mover. "They're not cattle. They're people. Show a little respect. And don't you ever forget it."

142

Her assertive air was as impressive as the undoubted humanity that powered it. She didn't seem to notice the old, rancid smells of her charges and the grouchy rebuffs that were their only defence against a largely uncaring world: any more than they seemed to remark, on her disfigured face.

"I'm sorry. I can't seem to recall . . ."

"Dede Crowther. Hub's sister. I came to your house a couple of times, yonks ago."

"Oh!" Of course, the scruffy, rebellious, teenager! Connie wondered whether she dared ask what had happened to her face, but the expression on it clearly discouraged any such enquiry.

"I knew your son." She peered inside the bus, counting heads. "All aboard? Everyone comfy?"

There was a rumble of grudging assent that everyone was comfy.

"Can't talk now," she dismissed Connie. "Off to the pictures. That's the great thing about this generation. They're all movie buffs. Anything from high tech special effects to sex and violence and Disney cartoons. All except artsy fartsy cult films. Hub's out back."

With that she climbed into the driver's seat, revved up noisily and set off down Rookshaven Lane with a handful of octogenarian movie buffs to dreamland.

"You won't put one over her." The helper who had come in for the rough edge of Dede Crowther's tongue watched the minibus disappear round the bend admiringly.

"I hadn't intended to," said Connie, not realising he was simply stating a fact not warning her off. She nodded toward the open front door. "Is it all right if I . . .?"

"Course." He sounded amazed that she should even ask. Presumably 'Everybody Welcome' meant what it said.

She entered the narrow, gloomy hallway, its peeling walls plastered with scribbled or printed notices, personal messages and cautionary notes about drugs, drink, glue-sniffing, fire and – surprisingly – flood. (Apparently the

143

small stream that bordered Rookshaven Lane had a habit of growing into a raging and invasive torrent during heavy rainfalls.) The hall was obviously strictly functional. The manure brown paintwork looked as if it might very well date back to Victorian times, as did the bare flagstone tiles on the floor and the leaded light porch windows that were encrusted with grime and shut out what little light was available. A single electric bulb dangled from the centre of the ceiling. Although it was switched on it shed only a dim beam, sufficient perhaps to stop you falling arse over head on the uneven flags.

Upstairs, some sort of rumpus was going on, followed by a scuffle. Then a reed-thin youth with straggly shoulder length hair and a pasty complexion shot down the stairs in two mighty leaps, yelling highly inventive abuse at someone on the upper floor who hurled it back with interest.

He caught Connie's eye and paused in mid-flight. "Seen enough?" he barked, then pushed past her and out of the front door.

"Griff!" The voice came from behind Connie. "*Griff!*" it repeated more urgently but with no effect. "Oh, Gawd! That's the last we'll see of him until he's pissed or pinched." Then the voice took note of a visitor and enquired courteously: "Can I help you?"

Connie faced a tall man in a T-shirt, jogging pants and trainers. He was sweating profusely and cradling a football under his arm. His looks had matured and there was a generally unkempt air about him which hadn't been there before, as if he were far too busy for the niceties of grooming. But he still bore himself with that same aggressive self-assurance, only now it seemed to be channelled in other directions than merely self-advertisement. He was undeniably Hubbard Crowther.

Now she had finally met him again Connie was unsure how to proceed. What, in fact, did she want from him? Tell me all you can about Colin? How did he die? Why did he die?

Instead she lamely introduced herself. "I saw your sister outside."

"With her golden oldies." He smiled, the same attractive smile, but she noticed it defined more acutely the deep lines around his mouth and eyes. It couldn't have been more than six or seven years that she had seen him last but it seemed much, much longer than that.

"What do you want, Mrs Remick?"

His keen eyes made her feel uncomfortable, insecure. "I suppose this must seem – well, silly."

"Try me!"

She took a deep breath. "I want to talk."

He nodded as if she'd said what he had been expecting. "About Colin. Finally." The 'finally' had a critical edge to it that found its mark.

"Finally," she agreed. "Can you spare a little time?"

"There's never any time to spare here."

A couple of boys, wearing acid green back to front baseball caps, about the age of those who were failing to watch her Renault erupted into the hall from the rear. They were as sweaty as Hub and their faces were streaked with dirt. "Gis the ball," panted one, lugging at the football under Hub's arm. The other one dragged on his T-shirt, urging him out back again.

"Give over," he told them, not taking his eyes off Connie. His tone was markedly more coarse and authoritarian and it had its effect. The boys instantly stopped fooling around, looking up at him apprehensively.

"Go on. Back into the yard. Practise dribbling. I'll be with you in a few minutes. And if there're any punch-ups you'll get a punch-up from me."

The boys sloped off with the football.

Connie stared at him, not sure whether to be appalled, alarmed or approving.

"Don't worry," he laughed. "I wasn't going to belt them. They know that. But they know I won't stand any old nonsense either."

"What *is* this place?" she gasped. "Pensioners, children, that chap upstairs!"

145

"You saw the sign. Heaven's Gate."

"A man down the Lane said everyone around here knew you. What do you *do*?"

"Search me." He smiled that attractive smile again.

"Be serious," she said.

"Help. However I can."

"You could help those boys by insisting they go to school instead of playing truant," she sniffed.

"No I couldn't. I couldn't *insist* anything." He sounded angry. "Do you know what the percentage of truancy is in this area? I tried talking to the kids and their parents about the benefits of a good education and bettering themselves. But why would they pay attention to me? What did a good education do for me? An ex-con. Look around you woman. It's all about you. Hard, bloody times don't make for noble citizens. These people have sod all."

"There's social security . . ." Connie began parrott-fashion.

"And no hope. No jobs. Do you know what no hope is like? It's like a corrosive disease that saps your will, flattens all your decent instincts. You get just enough money to exist and sometimes not even that. Pensioners who are scared to turn on the gas fire because of the fuel bill. Men who have forgotten what it's like to bring home a wage packet. And they're the lucky ones. At least they've got some sort of crumbling roof over their heads. How do you think they feel when they see and read how the other half lives? Are they supposed to be grateful for being alive? The kids here are tougher and stronger than the grown-ups. They see the resignation in their mothers and fathers and don't want any part of it. And the next easiest step in the world for them is crime. A lot, lot easier than school."

He stopped and suddenly his body went limp. He ran his hands through his hair in a gesture of frustration. "I'm sorry. I didn't mean to lay all this on you. It's just – sometimes. There are so many good, nice people who just don't understand. Those kids! If they run themselves ragged playing football maybe they won't have the energy to mug old ladies or rob Asian shopkeepers."

"They're so *young*," breathed Connie.

"They *are* young," said Hub. "You should study the crime statistics." She felt the full force of his critical gaze on her again. "But you probably do. Only your answer would be the cat-o'-nine-tails."

She ignored the rebuke.

"That was unfair," he conceded. "I don't know you. Maybe deep down you're a great humanitarian. Although I'd always figured you as the sort of person who would choose 'My way' and 'Je ne regrette rien' to be cast away with on a desert island. Dead selfish!"

She ignored that, too. "How did this . . ." she looked helplessly around her — "all this come about?"

She had come to find out about Colin. Instead here she was listening to the rantings of a rabid do-gooder and accepting his gratuitous insults as part of the price she had to pay for his time. She must be out of her mind. Whoops! Too near the knuckle!

"You mean how did I become a wildly over the top champion of the poor and dispossessed? Prison, Mrs Remick, is a great leveller." He froze as one piercing scream after another came from the general direction of the rear of the house. Then, even more ominously, silence. "Fucking kids!" he murmured. "I'll have to sort them out."

He thrust out his large, capable hand and shook hers. "I've given you a rough time. Come back Monday morning. It'll be quieter then." She felt it was a grudging invitation, offered with no great warmth.

"Can't we . . .?" She really didn't want to hang around Southdean that long. On the other hand, why not? What else had her empty life to offer?

"No. The weekend's hell. Open house. Ex-cons, walking wounded. Monday."

"Half the time I can't make out what you're talking about," she said irritably. "Ex-cons, walking wounded!

147

All right, all right. Monday." She'd grit her teeth and sit it out.

"See you!" That smile, that Hub smile. "By the way," he said over his shoulder, "the kids will be back at school. It's half-term this week." And she heard him laughing at her expense as he set about sorting out the ruffians in the back yard. He probably thought her a sanctimonious cow and, at that precise moment, she couldn't honestly blame him.

Chapter Thirteen

The Renault seemed intact when Connie returned to it, apart from a trail of bilious slime on the roof thoughtfully deposited by some diarrhoeic pigeon.

Bri was leaning on his broken gate with a coke can in his hand and a cigarette end clamped in the corner of his mouth. He beamed at the car and her as if he had appointed himself personal minder to both. She wondered in passing what he ever did, beyond observing what went on in the Lane.

He jerked his thumb toward 'Heaven's Gate'.

"Nutters! 'im and 'er!"

But she felt too choked off to put up with any light banter about the Crowther siblings he might have in mind. Instead she nodded, with what she hoped was polite good grace, and gratefully bade farewell for the time being to Rookshaven Lane.

She had, she realised, been brushed off by both Hub and his sister as an irrelevance. A woman of absolutely no importance, a parasite from a society they had, for some reason, rejected. Whatever they had to tell her about Colin would have to be paid for in pride and penitence. She decided that, for all his worthy works and charm of manner when it suited him, Hub Crowther was still a fairly insufferable prig, no less arrogant in his new found role in life than he had been as a lordly head boy at school, apparently worshipped by the littler likes of Colin.

It was, she noted, past the time when she was supposed to have met David Levitch at the pub by the pier. But she couldn't face another possibly unnerving encounter until

149

she had regained a semblance of composure. And if he couldn't be bothered to wait for her then the meeting was probably never destined to be a howling success anyway. All the same, pity, she thought.

She parked in front of the municipal bowling green and realised that part of her problem was hunger. A mouthful of muesli that morning was all she had had since Karen's appetising but carefully calorie-controlled meal the previous evening.

She bought herself a pallid looking hot dog from an open-sided van, doused it with ketchup and sat in a deckchair munching the livid confection with surprising relish. The dog and ketchup filled a hole; not Karen-nourishing but, in lieu of anything better, Connie-nourishing.

Two teams of well-padded women in whites were coaxing their woods toward the jack across the immaculate green with fanatical precision.

"Good girl!" One ample player complimented her partner whose wood came to rest an inch from its target, nudging a rival bowl into second place. From the surrounding deck chairs a round of discreet applause disturbed the majesterial concentration on the green, then subsided.

Connie felt herself unwinding. How easy it would be to forget that the slums around Rookshaven Lane even existed! How easy to convince yourself that there was no seedy side to Southdean! And she realised she was remembering herself once upon a time when, because things were going well for her and hers, there was no such thing as an under-class and, if there were, they probably had brought it on themselves. They didn't belong in self-satisfied, affluent Southdean.

The trouble was she not only recognised the woman she used to be, part of her still was that woman. This sudden burst of self-knowledge may have diagnosed her deficiencies but it didn't provide a cure for them. She knew she could never muster the evangelical passion of Hub and Dede to *do* something for the

150

unwashed, unlovely and probably ungrateful transients of Rookshaven Lane.

Still musing, she bit into her hot dog. The fat and the ketchup were congealing and it didn't taste nearly so acceptable.

"That must be revolting." It was an echo of her own thoughts. The follow-up jolted her out of her reflective mood. "Let me buy you a decent dinner. You look as if you could do with fattening up."

"I know that voice," she said, without twisting round. Soft, courtly, round vowels, clipped consonants. A dapper voice, like its owner. "It's Andy. Andrew Deeley, isn't it?" She felt and sounded pleased at the intrusion.

Even in his late sixties – Connie calculated quickly – Andrew Deeley was an attractive man. 'Fanciable' was the current expression that came to mind. And, while he had probably enjoyed being fancied in theory, his fidelity to his wife Edith had never been in question. "I'm a monogamous man," he would proclaim proudly to the embarrassment of starchier acquaintances who considered this was not a fit subject for mixed company.

He lifted his trilby to Connie. He was practically bald now but it suited him as did the trim, grey beard that was new. At least to Connie. His corduroy trousers and sports jacket were probably quite elderly but they had the look of clothes that had just reached a satisfying maturity, like the highly polished leather shoes. He handled his walking stick as if it were merely decoration, although, she suspected, it possibly served a useful purpose. He levered himself into the deckchair beside her. "You don't mind?" he asked.

"Andy!" She smiled. "I like the beard. Suits you."

"Well, well, Connie Remick! Constance Remick!" He swivelled round sideways and studied her intently as if searching for clues to her identity. "Funny! I never thought to see you down here again."

"Am I in *that* bad odour?"

"I didn't mean that. And you know it." He patted her hand. He had chubby craftsman's fingers but the nails were impeccably manicured. He lifted his face and sniffed the early evening air appreciatively. His skin looked baked hard as if it had been left out in the sun to dry too long.

"I missed you, Connie Remick. Liked your spirit. Shook up a lot of fuddy-duddies around here. Me, too, I'll admit."

She smiled. "I used to think someone like me would be anathema to someone like you. Old family business, well established, properly cautious. For how many years?"

"Well over a hundred. Started by my great-grandfather. Cabinet-makers they used to be called then. Hand crafted fine furniture for discerning people. First premises smack in the middle of the High Street. It's a Woolworths now."

He chuckled, remembering. "It all sounds pretty silly now, I suppose. But even as a lad I was proud to be a Deeley. A cabinet-maker! What a lovely ring to it. Now it's just furniture, plywood and plastic and foam rubber upholstery – fire resistant, of course – mass produced in great barns of assembly plants."

"You always did like to exaggerate, as I recall."

"It's one of the pleasures left to me. One of the pleasures they've left to me." She didn't immediately catch the subtle difference. "You're quite right. They build some very good furniture these days to suit the pockets of people. Not a lot of style or originality, unless you call that ghastly minimal modern stuff stylish and original."

"Oh *you*! You don't think anything's been bettered since Chippendale."

He laughed. "Absolutely! But what about you, Connie Remick? What are you doing down here?"

"I was hoping you wouldn't ask," she sighed. "I don't know, Andy. Trying to pick up the pieces. Trying to *find* the pieces. I didn't realise that was what I was doing, but I guess I am. Made a fool of myself in the precinct yesterday. Almost got myself arrested." She looked into his canny, curious eyes. "I've made an awful mess of things over the past two years, Andy, since the business folded up. I should have paid more attention to you during those chamber of trade and commerce meetings we used to have. 'You're not over-reaching yourself, are you?' you said time and again. And I told you, but not in so many words, to mind your own business."

"You were very polite about it. And quite a bobby-dazzler. There, that's an expression for you. Almost as old-fashioned as cabinet-maker. But then, that's me, old-fashioned. Oh, nicely placed, madam!" he cried in a carrying voice.

The complimented bowler looked angrily over her shoulder then, seeing Andrew Deeley, smiled and curtsied to another round of applause. Such levity was unusual during a bowls tournament, but no less welcome.

Andrew acknowledged her curtsey and tipped his hat as he had to Connie. Old world, she thought. But lovely old world. Not mean-minded, puritanical, hypocritical old world.

"You know there was a time when, if it hadn't been for Edie, I could really have fallen for you. That's what my generation did. Fall!" he reminisced.

"You could have fooled me," she joked. "You always treated me with the utmost propriety. How is Edith?"

"Edie? Edie died. Must have been about the time you left Southdean. Quite quick. Mercifully. Cancer. But *compos mentis* to the last."

He sounded resigned to the death of the woman he had wed and loved for forty years and Connie supposed it was the knowledge of having enjoyed that perfect love which made it easier to accept her passing. "How could I complain?" he added as if sensing her thought. "We'd had so much together, more than most people. And we all have to die sometime."

"How comforting!" said Connie. "To have your peace of mind."

"You'll get there. But you have to work at it."

"I'm sorry. About Edie. She was . . ."

"I know, I know, you don't have to tell me." He

153

cleared his throat noisily, wiping his mouth with a crisply laundered linen handkerchief, at the same time discreetly wiping away a tear that was making slow progress down the side of his bony, patrician nose. Connie averted her eyes as he completed the mopping up operation.

"You mustn't blame yourself, too much, Connie. About the way things turned out," he said, abruptly changing the subject. "It was the times. The propaganda of the times. At your age you would have had to have been iron-willed and probably completely unambitious not to heed the siren call of market forces. With us it was different. We were already there. But *you* had to get there, grab it while it was on offer. And even we had our sticky times. Tempting propositions to go public, merge with bigger manufacturers, expand beyond our capacity. Even some of the family wanted to go that way."

"But you refused to heed the siren call," she quoted back at him.

He nodded with a touch of pride. "I did. Comes with being a forceful chairman."

"Bully for you."

"Sam's doing well. Read him everywhere and occasionally see him on the box. Wouldn't put a spade into the soil without first getting the nod from the expert."

"You never put a spade into the soil in your life," she ribbed him.

"True! I won't ask what you've been doing lately. Nothing useful by the look of it. Waste! Terrible waste!"

She preferred not to comment on that.

"And Deeley's?" she asked.

"Successful. So far as I know."

"Of course you know. Every last digit on the balance sheet."

"Not any more. The old man's been put out to grass. The general concensus was that I was too set in my ways to adapt to contemporary demand. Probably right. They put it very nicely: well earned rest, all that guff, devote more time to my miniatures, take a trip round the world which I did, spend the winter in the Bahamas which I

154

also did. Hated every minute of it, except the miniatures. Anyway. All water under the bridge. And in the long run, best thing that could have happened to me."

Connie was amazed that he didn't seem particularly bitter at being ousted presumably by his own sons. "How could they do that to you? Your family? Deeley's was your baby." But even as she asked the question she knew the answer. Andrew Deeley had been deemed past his sell-by date, and there was little room for sentiment in business these days.

"Well, it's their baby now. They do me the courtesy of discussing new lines with me now and then and I've a sort of honorary title of consultant which means bugger all – if you'll pardon the expression. But we're still a close family, get to see the grandchildren a lot. One's a dab hand at carpentry. Girl. Sally. If she'll only stick to the *craft* and not get caught up in the flim-flam. I think she has the makings of a really gifted cabinet-maker. Early days. But she's a bright girl. Girls are, I find. Probably making up for all the centuries when they weren't supposed to be bright."

His eyes were suddenly bright with excitement as he pounded a fist into the palm of the other hand. "You see, Connie, in the end everything comes down to the skill, the satisfaction of creating something – even if it's only a better mousetrap. All the marketing in the world won't sell an inferior product."

He caught her dubious expression and nodded ruefully. "Well that's what I tell myself and my young people. I know it's not true. But at least it's a principle worth hanging on to. Everyone talks money these days as if it's something of value in itself. Money's just manure as the man said. Some playwright or other."

"'To help make little things grow.' Thornton Wilder," she prompted him.

"If you say so." He looked at her sideways. "You think I'm hopelessly out of date, don't you? Quite right I should have been invited to stand down."

She chose her words carefully, not wanting to offend

155

him, but also half wanting to believe in his Utopian ideals. "I think," she said, "you can't put the clock back. Those days are long gone. It's a whole other world, Andy. If it exists at all it can only be supported and afforded by the fiendishly rich who have probably made their money in just the manner you despise – playing the market, stripping assets."

"I know you can't put the clock back," he said irritably. "I'm not a fool. Foolish, but not a fool." Then he gripped her hand so tightly with such a tense expression on his face that she felt for a horrifying second that he might be about to have a stroke. "I'd like you to visit me, Connie. I've something to show you. I think it would prove to you I'm not entirely wrong."

"I've seen your miniatures, Andy," she began to say, recalling the exquisite doll's house size replicas of classical furniture that he fashioned to scale in his spare time. "They're lovely, but—"

"I'm not talking about a hobby, Connie. I'm talking about a working craft complex, a dozen or so workshops under one umbrella."

"It's a fine idea, Andy." An aimless old man's idea, she thought.

"Not just an idea, Connie. It's up and doing." He nodded his head vigorously several times anticipating her surprise.

And she was, surprised. "How do you mean? Up and doing?"

Satisfied at her response, he settled back into his deckchair, one leather shoe tapping rhythmically on the paved surround of the bowling green.

"Do you mind!" hissed a supporter of the winning side, keenly observing the action a few feet away.

"My apologies madam!" He rewarded her with a smile to melt the most intransigent temper and stopped tapping. "Dedicated lot! Bowlers! Like golfers! Tried golf?"

"No." She was beginning to find the disjointed conversation trying and her appointment with David Levitch was starting to weigh heavily on her conscience. "Andy—"

156

"I did. Waste of time. Better off going for a brisk walk over the Downs. Now bowls. You can see the logic to that."

"Andy!"

"Got your attention, haven't I?" He looked mightily pleased with himself.

"No, losing it." She made a move to get out of the deckchair. She seriously wondered whether first impressions were false, whether Andrew Deeley, the once decisive Andrew Deeley, really was approaching the dotage that apparently lost him the chairmanship of his family firm. She felt his restraining hand on her arm.

"Just a couple of minutes, Connie. I know I ramble a lot. Comes of spending too much time alone. Except for Mrs Battleaxe. My housekeeper. Wonderful woman. Tremendous cook. Great organiser. A treasure, my sons keep telling me. Bloody awful woman! That's why I call her Mrs Battleaxe. Can't bring myself to call her by her real name. Lillian. Lillian Biggs. I asked her once if she were related to the ~~bank~~ robber and where she'd stashed her ill-gotten gains. Didn't take kindly to that. No sense of humour. Left in very high dudgeon. But Peter, my son, insisted on coaxing her back. God knows how. Probably told her I was soft in the head and not responsible. We have a sort of armed truce. Works well enough – I suppose."

He pondered the tribulations of his armed truce with the humourless Lillian Biggs for a second or two, then heaved a deep, shuddering sigh, as if shaking himself free of her memory, and got down to business.

"When I first retired I was all at sixes and sevens. I had plenty of money. And I know what you're dying to say. Money's only unimportant to those who have it. When you don't it's a nightmare. But I suddenly realised I was just wasting what I had on pointless things – long, stupid holidays, rattling around in a house far too big for me, spending lavishly keeping up with friends and colleagues with whom I no longer had much in common.

157

And when I say wasting what I had, I don't just mean money, I mean myself.

"I don't suppose I'd ever have thought how I could put myself to use if I hadn't met this young couple in Brighton. Churchill Square. You know it. Bleak concrete barracks. Shops. Street entertainers. Agitators. They were squatting on the pavement, scrofulous-looking pair, matted hair, knees poking out of their jeans, the usual. But laid out in front of them was a display of quite remarkable jewellery, medallions, necklets, belts, using Mayan motifs. They weren't pushing it, didn't seem especially interested in selling it. They had a whole batch of pamphlets about Third World exploitation by the West which they shoved into the hands of passers-by who mostly put them straight into a litter bin or just dropped them on the ground. Then a copper came by. Very polite. He had a word with them. I suppose it was probably something to do with trading without a licence or obstructing the free passage of pedestrians or whatever counts as a misdemeanour these days. They didn't argue. They got up and started to box up the jewellery and it was then I plucked up the courage to speak to them. They weren't yobbos at all, obviously decently educated. I don't know why I should have been surprised, but I was. Appearances, you know."

Despite herself, Connie was interested but determined not to be drawn into any more tales of woe. "I suppose the story has a punch line," she suggested.

"Quite right! Rambling again. The long and the short of it was I discovered they were art students until they dropped out of college. They produced this lovely stuff but they hadn't the slightest idea how to present it, let alone sell it. They'd canvassed a few regular outlets without any luck and, frankly, if I'd been in business I'd have thought them a very dubious couple. And it occurred to me that what they needed was a little guidance, if they were prepared to accept it, and maybe a proper place to work. Apparently they lived in some squat in Brighton."

158

Connie found she was ahead of him, way ahead. "So you set them up in a proper place to work and then decided if you could do it for them, you could do it for others." Of course! That's the way Andrew Deeley's old-fashioned, philanthropic mind would work.

"Bingo! A complex of craft units, workshops. Maybe just one or two person outfits of small businesses employing an extra couple of trainee workers. Once I got the idea it was amazing how it took off. Through Ben and Ilsa – that's the couple I met first – I got to know others and so on and so on. I found the premises, fitted it out, pressured some contacts in local government I knew to support it and got a small Government subsidy – with great difficulty, I might add. We have textile and ceramic designers, weavers, potters, wood workers, poster illustrators, painters, even a candlestick-maker."

She shook her head, partly in wonderment and partly with incredulity at the boldness of the task he'd under-taken and the alarming possibilities for failure. "It must have cost a fortune to set up."

"I *have* a fortune. A small one. But adequate for the time being, until some of them start to break even from orders. We're doing all right, with specialist sales through the advertisement columns and some shops and buyers have been very helpful. But we have to do much better if we're to survive. Connie – we could do with someone like you."

"Me! You have to be joking." Although she feared he wasn't.

He pondered that for a moment. "It was just seeing you here today. So unexpectedly. It seemed fortuitous. I'm sorry. You've obviously other things to think about."

She wasn't sure whether to be relieved or upset at his sudden retreat. "I suppose I could advise them what not to do," she laughed nervously.

He considered that quite seriously. "Just as useful as telling them what they *should* do, maybe more so. You have to learn to use failure, make it work for you. It's my guess you've spent the past two years convincing

159

yourself you're worthless. And that's damned easy. Proving you're not is hard. Maybe you're not up to it yet. I heard about Colin and your . . ." He stopped, deliberately groping for a word which she supplied to save him the discomfort of uttering it.

"Breakdown. I think that's what they call it in polite circles. Off her rocker, bonkers, not quite herself – that's the gracious expression! However you look at it, I don't think I'm in any fit state to start all over again."

"It wouldn't be starting all over again. Any more than it was for me. Not precisely. We're both past that. But experience has to count for something. And there's a hell of a lot of business expertise, hard earned expertise, locked up in that noddle of yours just asking to be liberated. These young people. They have the skills, they're producing beautiful objects. What they don't have is the guile, the cunning if you like, to cope with the nuts and bolts of creating a business, however limited, out of a talent. And they're getting precious little help from the Government."

"You sound positively poetic, Andy. But it's all really pie in the sky, isn't it? Now I really have to keep this date – that is if I still *have* a date." She sounded regretful, despising herself for puncturing his enthusiasm.

"You're a hard woman, Connie Remick. But then, in your way, you always were. Just call me. Better yet, come round to see me. You'll know the address. I'm there most days for a while, even weekends. Since Edie died, it keeps me occupied."

"I hope this Ben – and – what was her name . . .?"

"Ilsa."

"Ilsa. Appreciate what you're doing for them."

"It's a two-way traffic. *I* appreciate what they're doing for me. A co-operative! That's how they describe our adventure. A co-operative adventure."

"A co-operative," she echoed. "I didn't take you for a closet Marxist, Andy."

"Don't think I am. I approve of the 'adventure', but I prefer to call it a friendly society."

"A rose by any other name." She shrugged. "I think your Ben and Ilsa are taking you for a ride."

She expected him to protest, but he didn't.

"A little, perhaps," he said. "Youngsters like that! They wouldn't be human if they didn't regard me as a bit of an old sucker. Which I probably am. But, Connie, what if I'm *enjoying* the ride? Is it so bad then? Here!"

He handed her a vividly multi-coloured calling card which, she judged, would never have been his choice, but had probably been designed and printed by one of his lame ducks.

He grimaced, but with amusement not distaste. "I'm told it's eye-catching," he said.

"That it is," she agreed.

She glanced at it and then studied it more closely with surprise.

"I told you you'd know the address," he said.

It was the site of the first factory in Southdean which she and Beattie had leased with a loan from the bank as the premises for CC Connections. A million years ago.

Chapter Fourteen

The pub by the pier had changed its name since she'd last been there. No longer The Bo'sun's Mate but The Pink Flamingo which had an exotic, if misplaced, ring to it. It was in keeping with the glitzier appearance Southdean had striven to adopt in the Seventies and Eighties to combat the lure of package tours abroad. ("Keeping up with the Costas," she remembered someone joking and then she recalled the joker had been Lewis Diamond who was renowned for puncturing pretentions in private while catering to it in public.)

The old cockles and whelks and milk stout image which had survived into the post-war years no longer appealed to younger holiday-makers. Families still took possession of the safe, sandy beaches in high summer, but there were no concert parties or Punch and Judy shows or donkey rides and all the deckchair attendants and ice-cream pedlars had become traffic wardens.

The pier was still operating and video games had revived the fortunes of the amusement arcade. There were still people who went for bracing walks up the boardwalk to the end, leant on the railing, sniffed the spray from the breaking waves and persuaded themselves that filling your lungs with salty, chilly, English sea air was far better for you than grilling yourself topless on some crowded foreign shore. But they were mostly on the elderly side. The little, stucco theatre, nestling at the entrance to the pier, still did good business, but only with pop stars, smutty TV comedians and Hollywood legends who were well past their prime.

Fashion, which had overtaken the town, had now

passed it by. There was no point in keeping up with the Costas, because the Costas were out of favour and it was almost as cheap to go to Disney World. To Connie's eyes the new Southdean, as a resort town, looked even more faded than the old Southdean of her childhood and teenage memory ever did.

The Pink Flamingo looked strangely quiet. Pubs were usually bustling about this time. It was then she realised it wasn't a pub at all any longer. It was a bar and disco which obviously wouldn't start popping until much later. She should have checked first. Almost everything else in Southdean had altered. Why should she have imagined the pub by the pier would be the same?

She pushed open the swinging door with no great expectation of finding David Levitch patiently waiting in solitary state for a woman who was an hour and a half overdue. An anorexic nymph in a body stocking and Doc Martens was half-heartedly polishing the tables in the bar area.

"Not open," she said without looking up.

"I didn't—"

"Outside. The notice. Eight o'clock."

Connie stood there, feeling foolish and bereft. She realised that the thought of seeing him had buoyed her up even as she convinced herself she didn't care whether he kept the appointment or not. She supposed she should at least enquire whether anyone had been around earlier asking for her.

The girl looked up from her absorbing task. A frown that just might be the beginning of a thought wrinkled her porcelain forehead.

"You're not looking for some guy or other? Yank?"

Connie nodded, relieved, and was rewarded with the girl's undivided attention. A flicker of genuine curiosity flitted across her flawless face.

She pointed a long purple fingernail into the dim recesses of the disco. The place had a still, gloomy air about it, waiting for the people and the strobe lighting and the music to give it life.

163

He was sitting on a stool, propped up by the bar in deep conversation with the bartender who was hanging on to his words as if they were Holy Writ. He looked large and prosperous and bursting with vitality, a man who had lived the better part of his life in a big country. It was a look defined by landscape and territory.

"David," she whispered. "David Levitch?"

She had spoken so quietly but his antennae had obviously been primed to catch the sound of her voice even at a distance. As he turned she could see traces of the dark, handsome boy with those daring eyes she had fallen in love with, but they were overlaid by this new, expansive persona. No wonder she hadn't recognised him fleetingly in the record store the previous morning, just that flash of familiarity which could as easily have meant a TV personality who appeared so regularly on the screen you thought you knew them.

She walked unsteadily toward him. The girl with the angel face and the black boots watched with interest. She was young enough to be intrigued by the possibility, improbable as it seemed, of a more than strictly boring relationship between two middle-aged people. The bartender started polishing glasses and holding them up to the light in search of the odd smear. From long experience he knew that discretion was the better part of bartending.

"I'm desperately sorry I'm so late. I didn't think you'd still be here. It was just one thing after another. You know how it is some days. I got caught up with this and that and I met Andrew Deeley – you remember Deeley's – on the way here and I just couldn't get away." Why am I doing this, rattling on like a silly schoolgirl covering her confusion? I'm a mature woman who has lived a varied, even extraordinary, life since you dumped me just like that all those years ago. I don't have to be confused or apologetic about anything. You've waited ninety minutes for me. That's a fleabite compared to the time I waited for you. But none of it helped. She felt exactly as she had when she had been sitting in the

164

Levitches' dining-room with Becky and first glimpsed her godlike brother.

"Slow down. No sweat." He looked amused, this large, American man. And she knew with absolute certainty that he hadn't the slightest idea what he and his departure had meant to her. With that knowledge the nervousness suddenly drained out of her. She could relax, face him on equal terms, as old friends renewing an acquaintance. I'm a whole other person, just like you!

"You're looking good, Connie. Thin!"

"You're looking good, too, David. Fat!"

He patted a midriff that was a little too ample to look merely comfortable.

"The good life." He laughed quite loudly. "I keep threatening to take up jogging and go on a diet. But I never get around to it. Just a little light work-out in the gym." He laughed again. He was laughing a lot. Also he was just the slightest bit tipsy. Nothing serious. He didn't seem like someone who just let go that freely. Probably prided himself on being able to hold his liquor. All the same she wondered how many of whatever it was in the tumbler in front of him he'd drunk while waiting for her.

"What'll you have?" He stared boldly into her eyes just as he used to. She realised now it was a trick, a theatrical trick, signifying nothing. She speculated about how many other women he had used it on and wished it didn't have such an unsettling effect even when you knew it was phoney.

The dry white wine wasn't chilled so she settled for fruit juice and felt insufferably prim as if reproaching him for not remaining entirely sober. "And vodka," she added. Well, why not? It had been a day. And it was far from being over.

The thin nymph lost interest and returned to her tables. Just another boring couple having a night out, getting sloshed.

Connie glanced at the clock on the wall and grimaced. After seven. She had to give him A for staying power. "I hope you weren't too punctual."

"I told you. No sweat. Mack here," he nodded at the bartender, "Mack and I were partners in crime way back. Recognised him straight away. We used to call him Mack the Knife." More laughter. Why did he find everything so funny?

Mack-here proudly acknowledged his tired nickname and the longevity of his relationship by grinning broadly and growling: "Those were the days!" Connie suspected it was probably better not to enquire as to the nature of those days, although she had the feeling Mack was rather hoping she would.

"One of the great villains, Mack!" exclaimed David with a show of admiration. She could see he was deliberately lubricating the ego of the old buddy and was good at it. No sweat!

It was clear that this was a milieu to which he was no longer accustomed, however chummy he might once have been with the dubious Mack. America had turned him into a man of substance; a transformation of which his father would have approved. Yet he had about him an ease of manner that could adapt to any company, even an amiable reprobate from his past working in a seedy seaside disco. What's more he could give the appearance of generous enjoyment. Perhaps it was part of his job, she thought.

"What do you do?" she asked directly.

He seemed to catch her drift. "I butter up rich old widows with too much money and not enough sense and persuade them to trust me to invest the fortunes that their husband died – usually of fatal heart attacks – in the process of making."

"Of course. I should have guessed. A con man." But she was mildly shocked.

This time he didn't laugh, but smiled at his own shameless explanation of his work and her gullibility in swallowing it. He put on a but-seriously expression for her benefit.

"I deal in stocks and shares. I'm a broker. In Chicago. I'm also very responsible about other people's money.

166

And fairly respectable if you don't examine my private life too closely. Most people prefer to think we're greedy bastards who really do con old ladies out of their savings. And a few do that. Some of them end up in jail."

"But not you." She was beginning to feel uncomfortable again. He'd always been so clever at putting her on the defensive, except when she was a young girl she had at least the excuse of ignorance. At her age she should have been quicker trading banter with banter. And usually she was. It seemed that only with David Levitch did she revert back to the *naïveté* of her youth.

"Disappointed?" He grimaced, then: "You were always such an innocent, Connie." He said it so softly, almost caressingly, as if he were conveying a compliment and perhaps, looking back from this distance in his life, it was.

Innocent! But not for long, she reflected.

Giving it away with a packet of Persil! That's how Beattie had reacted when rumours of Connie's flighty behaviour had reached her through the grapevine of considerate neighbours ever anxious to be the harbingers of bad news.

Who would have thought it of that nice, well-behaved, obedient girl? What could have happened to have effected such a change? Tight-lipped, Beattie would dismiss the rumours as rubbish. Privately she condemned Connie crudely to her face as no better than a tart, as if the very vulgarity of the abuse would shame her daughter into reclaiming her virtuous reputation. If she suspected that the transformation in Connie was related in some way to David Levitch's sudden departure she kept quiet about it. Neither she nor Connie ever mentioned his name to each other after that last wretched confrontation. It was as if he had never existed.

But he did still exist, his after-effect more powerful than his actual presence. He was there in Connie's truculent rebellion, in her insolent refusal to care about or even listen to her mother's lectures on morality. After David Levitch had left, taking with him her belief in the

167

value of her precious virginity, she had surrendered it with defiant abandon to the first man to ask her a direct question. (After all, she reasoned, what good was hanging on to a cause that had lost her David Levitch? She wouldn't countenance the possibility that she had never had him in the first place.)

She couldn't recall much about her first lover, except that he looked like Albert Finney, was under-manager at the local Odeon and was later sacked for propositioning the female patrons. He had also been surprisingly considerate of her inexperience about sex, so that she had quickly got the hang of it and proceeded to enjoy it on a regular basis with other partners, before Sam had brought a stabilising influence into her life. She supposed Sam had been aware of her rumoured promiscuity, but he had never broached the subject and neither had she. It was the Sixties, wasn't it? It was practically a bounden duty for young people to be reckless.

"Do you want to stay?" His voice seemed to come from a far off place.

"Sorry?" She snapped back to the here and now. Had he even a clue how he had affected her young life?

"You seem preoccupied. Perhaps it's this place."

She looked around her as if surprised to find herself there. The disco was beginning to gear up. A disc jockey was fiddling with electronic equipment on a small raised stage. The girl with the face and the boots had changed into a hip-hugging leather short skirt, spangled top and four inch heels. She was picking at her teeth and staring at them, glassily, swaying slightly as if she might have had a fix of some sort.

"She'll have to go," said Mack. "You can't mix business with pleasure." Then he thought about what he was saying. "Not, of course, that we have any truck with *that* here. Very strict." He nodded toward the door where two muscle-bound bouncers were standing guard. They looked in as much of a trance as the girl.

Connie made a face. "If it's all right with you," she said. "Gives me the creeps, this place."

David Levitch put his finger to his lips, shooshing her. "Don't want to hurt his feelings," he whispered in her ear.

Good God, she thought, since when did you become so particular? And then she remembered it had been thirty years; a long time in which to become particular. "I understand," she assured him. "It would never do to hurt some old chum's feelings, would it?"

He ignored the irony in her tone. It probably didn't sit with his memory of her accursed innocence. "It's all so changed. Do you remember there used to be a stall outside where they sold little brown shrimps and winkles in pots for a tanner? A pin for the winkles was a ha'penny extra," he recalled cheerfully. As he spoke of the past the acquired American accent − more Harvard business school than a distinct transatlantic twang − became less marked and he started to lapse into the lingo of his youth.

"Are you . . . have you . . .? I mean is it important for you to get back soon?" He actually seemed less sure of himself. It struck her as rather endearing, a chink in that seemingly impenetrable armour of avuncular charm.

"No, not especially." She supposed Sam might wonder. Perhaps she should give him a call for courtesy sake.

"I simply asked because I sort of got the impression you weren't a free agent. Well, not quite a free agent. . . . You see, when you didn't turn up I'm afraid I called the house. In case you'd suffered any repercussions. After yesterday, I mean." He was studying her anxiously as if waiting for an explosion. Perhaps one of his Lord-knew-how-many wives or girlfriends had been the explosive type.

"Oh!" She was rather enjoying his discomfort.

"Not good?"

She flipped her hand from side to side. Maybe so. Maybe not. Let him sweat a little.

"A very nice lady answered. She sounded quite worried. Said you'd gone off in her car that afternoon. That's why I was quite relieved when you arrived."

"What did she think I'd do? Top myself?"

"That's acid," he reproached her.

"No *that's* acid." She jerked her head back at the girl who was still gazing vacantly into the middle distance.

"Kids! Probably just a joint." He obviously regarded the possibility of a drug culture in Southdean as too risible to be discussed. "When I gave my name she invited me over. To the house. Sometime."

"That ever so nice lady!"

"Yes, that nice lady! I won't go if you don't want me to." He seemed angry now. Angry with her, maybe with himself, too, for getting drawn into whatever strange situation existed between Connie and the lady of the house.

"No, I'd like it. If I'm still around. It's just I didn't think Karen would take it on herself to hand out invitations to *my* friends." Christ, how petty she sounded! "I don't *live* there, you know. Not any more."

"OK. So who's Karen?" he sighed.

I'm losing him, she thought. Just as I lost him all those years ago. As if it mattered. "Karen's the new wife of my ex-husband."

"And you don't like her."

"Not really. She certainly doesn't like me," she chuckled, finding it suddenly quite funny. "She's a wonderful woman. Everyone says so. She bakes her own bread, doesn't mind getting her hands dirty, cares about the environment, is a considerate stepmother and will almost certainly be a perfect mother of many. The first is imminent. She loves Sam. Sam loves her. And she thinks I'm a piece of shit for buggering up my own life and my son's life and anyone else's you care to name."

He stared at her for quite some time and then burst out laughing. "You really *don't* like her, do you? Come on." He took her arm. "I'll take you to dinner and you can tell me all about it. And then I can tell you all about me. And then . . ."

"And then?"

170

"I don't know. Maybe get a room in a hotel and find out what we missed when we were kids."

His suggestion winded her, the sheer effrontery of it, the gall! Coming back into her life just like that and proposing a one night stand as if she were some hooker he had picked up off the streets. She was working up to a fine display of being mortally offended when she realised how absurd that would be. And in truth she didn't really feel offended when she thought about it. It was indeed quite pleasurable to have a man desiring her again, even if that desire was hardly overpowering as it patently wasn't. Over the past few years she had written herself off or maybe she had willed herself not to notice any expression of male admiration. There hadn't been any room in that pit of depression and guilt for anything resembling enjoyment.

So, instead of rebuking him, she mildly put forward the observation that they weren't kids any more.

He nodded. "All the better."

"I haven't agreed," she said.

"I wouldn't expect you to. Not until after I've plied you with champagne and lobster thermidor like the wicked squire in a Victorian melodrama."

She allowed herself to be propelled to the door of the disco. "You find this all very amusing, don't you?"

"I find *life* very amusing, Connie. I always have. Otherwise it would be too sad to contemplate. You never understood that about me, did you? Pity!" And she realised he was more perceptive about their relationship than she had imagined.

"I doubt whether you'll find much in the way of lobster thermidor in Southdean."

"Then we'll try Brighton. English's. That's still there, isn't it? You can drive. That nice lady's car. A dirty night out in Brighton."

Don't push it, she thought. When I come down to earth I don't want to land with a thundering bump. And there will be a coming down to earth. God surely wouldn't allow her life to change that dramatically over the course

171

of forty eight hours. And there was still so much to know, to find out, to reconcile to. There was still Colin.

"David!"

"Save it, Con," he said sternly.

The disco was filling up with youngsters in war paint and an assortment of bizarre outfits, most of which looked as if they'd been picked up in thrift shops, mixed and matched with the odd bit of hippie glitter and ethnic homespun. It seemed to Connie like fancy dress and then she realised that's what it was supposed to be. The disco, so the sign at the door said, was having a Sixties night.

"Did *we* look like that then?" she asked David.

"God knows! But we sure as hell don't now. I feel like Methuselah."

He waved at Mack who was too busy to respond. Now that the serious business of the evening was getting under way he was less hospitable, eyeing his erstwhile buddy with caution.

"That's better," said David, when they got outside. "By the way. I lied." It came out quite spontaneously and for a moment she didn't catch what he said.

"Come again?"

"Lied. I lied. A little. I know more about you than I told you on the phone. It was true about seeing you in the precinct and the ambulance. I was waiting for my niece – Becky's daughter – and her little girl. That's how I happened to be there. She wanted . . ."

". . . a hamburger at McDonald's." It came to her in a flash of understanding as if she'd known it all along but hadn't been prepared to admit it. "That young mother and her child – the one I was supposed to be kidnapping? Becky? And you?" She shook her head. "Funny! I should at least be surprised. But I'm not. I don't know what to say."

"Well – 'it's a small world' might do for starters. Or you could say it was a strange coincidence. Or fate. Vicky was full of it. She seemed to think you were a load of laughs, good at games."

172

"Oh yes. We played a good game. Staring each other out. Until . . . I sensed that child wasn't just any child. Just as I recognised your face but couldn't place it when I saw you in the record store." She felt his eyes scrutinising her, demanding more and more from her and suddenly she resented this intrusion. What's more, she didn't have to put up with it.

"David! I don't think I want to go on with this. I want to go home. Sam's home. Pack my bag and go back to my flat."

"And give up."

"That's right. Give up."

"Crawl back into your hole."

"Stop it! What right do you have? You're not allowed to know that much about me. Not after all these years. *I* won't allow it."

She put out her hands and pushed forward with her palms as if warding off some kind of physical attack, averting her face as she did so.

He grasped her wrists tightly and shook her so hard that she felt she was losing balance. "OK. If that's what you want. Leave me here. You go off. Forget about me and Beck and that son of yours you're supposed to have ruined. It's easy. All you have to do is switch off. Is that what you want? Just to switch off, Con?"

She steadied herself against a lamppost and then, pacing carefully, walked toward a bench on the promenade and sat down. In the distance she could hear the waves softly pounding the shore for it was a still balmy evening, but for the relentless beat of the disco music. Something she recognised, from the Beatles. Well, it was a Sixties night.

She felt his hand gently pressing on the back of her neck. "Put your head between your knees and breathe deeply."

She did as she was told, aware that she was the centre of some attention.

"Drunk!" A couple of girls giggled, but not maliciously, on their way into the disco.

173

"Don't mind them," he said. "Kids!"

After a bit, she pulled herself up, feeling not too bad. "I'm better now. Sorry for the spectacle. I seem to be famous for spectacles lately."

"Well?"

He wasn't giving up on her yet, which, despite her outburst to the contrary, was oddly consoling.

She smiled weakly. "I thought you promised you were going to ply me with champagne and lobster thermidor. Although frankly, right now, I'd rather settle for a cup of tea."

Chapter Fifteen

He was a good listener; not overly sympathetic (that would have been demeaning), but attentive. She hadn't remembered that about him. But then listening was an acquired skill. When you were young, which was her only memory of him, there was neither the time nor the inclination for listening.

Even as she talked about the highs and lows of her life with an honesty she had never vouchsafed her family or the shrink she hadn't liked, she could still quite dispassionately weigh up his attributes. The look of him. The manner of him. What might be genuine and what bogus about him. That which had been exceptional in him as a boy was now set in the mould of a middle-aged man, no longer outstanding but part of a whole.

His spoken responses were minimal. He barely uttered as she told him about her marriage to Sam, her children, Colin's suicide which she had not accepted until now, even the discovery of his diary and her search for Hub. It seemed important to leave nothing out, nothing but the hurt he had inflicted on her. She made a joke about her breakdown and he laughed dutifully. She was more serious about her failure as a businesswoman and he found that funny, too.

"It happened all over," he said.

"That doesn't make it any easier."

"You have funny priorities, Con. I'd have thought a nervous breakdown and the loss of a son were more devastating than the collapse of a company. After all, you can always start over again. Hundreds do."

"That's the second time today someone's said that

– well, not precisely, but very like." She remembered old Andy Deeley proposing she contribute her business acumen to the running of his workshops.

She crumbled a poppadum and scooped up a mouthful, thoughtfully.

She hadn't felt up to English's or the drive to Brighton and they'd found a friendly little Indian restaurant, incongruously named The Cottage Tandoori, near the railway station, which was patronised more for its take-away. The 'Cottage' bit amused David, as did the 'take-away' ("to go, you mean"; which made her realise how long he'd been away).

They had the dining area to themselves, apart from one other couple who were too deep in each other to bother much about what they were eating, let alone anyone else in the restaurant.

She toyed with the chicken Vindaloo and wished she'd ordered something milder. Then she wished they weren't there at all. It suddenly mattered a great deal to her the impression – a shady disco, a down market curry place – he would be taking away of the town he had once regarded as home. Except, of course, the Levitches had never seemed to regard anywhere as home. And she realised she hadn't asked him about his family at all. She hadn't even asked him about himself and why he was in Southdean.

"This must seem very small town to you." She stabbed a piece of chicken with her fork, bit into it, gasped and put out the fire with half a tumbler of water. "Hot!" she panted.

"Evidently," he said. He'd ordered the cool Korma.

He watched her with that amused smile of his which kept sending confusing signals. Was he genuinely interested in her or just curious?

"I thought – that is I understood – you were farming in America."

"That's what the dragon lady told you?"

"Dragon lady?" But she knew perfectly well to whom he was referring.

"Your mother. Whatever happened to her?"

"She died."

"A slow and lingering death, I hope." Then he realised his mistake and laughed apologetically. "Sorry!"

She looked at him coldly. Whatever he felt about Beattie's disapproval of his association with her she had felt far more and more intensely, but he hadn't the right to express it.

"Don't be," she said. "As a matter of fact she did. Die a slow and lingering death."

He lifted his shoulders and spread his hands. "I'm not really that callous, Con. It's just that in the grand scheme of things your mother was not one of my major concerns."

"You're lucky. She was one of mine," she said wryly. "And what about your family? We never did know why they left Southdean so suddenly."

"They moved up north – Liverpool. A little local difficulty they thought they'd left behind in London caught up with them – accidentally, so to speak."

"You mean they really were on the run? Just as people thought?"

"Sort of."

"Good God! From whom?" He was right. In the grand scheme of things Beattie Connor would not have seemed a major threat.

"In a sudden rush of civic-mindedness – which, I might add, he later regretted – Dad volunteered information that put away a couple of small-time crooks who'd been putting pressure on local traders. Quite brave, really. But it was no big deal, he thought. There were dozens of bully boys in the East End then making an easy buck where they could find it. The police promised to keep Dad's name out of it and the poor sucker believed them. He honestly believed he could settle in an out of the way seaside town and no one would ever be the wiser. The guys were sent down for five years, three with good behaviour. And the word went out to get Dad. Eye for an eye. Law of the jungle. Just like the movies.

177

Dad packed up the family and disappeared again on the tip-off from a shopkeeper who owed him a favour back in Whitechapel." He grinned. "Colourful lot, the Levitches!"

"And your parents?"

"They intended to follow me to the States. But they never got around to it. They were killed in a car crash." He was talking very deliberately, very calmly, and she suspected he was trying to keep his emotions under control. For all his apparent unconcern he had a strong sense of family. He would never have described his father as a "poor sucker" if he hadn't wanted to prevent his feeling for him spilling over into maudlin sentimentality.

"That's awful!" She put out her hand and rested it on his. He didn't respond and she withdrew it, feeling she'd overstepped some nicety of behaviour she didn't even know about.

"Yes it is," he said. "And don't ask me if it was an accident because I don't know and nobody ever took the trouble to find out."

The couple who had been so absorbed in each other now appeared more interested in overhearing tales of East End crooks and protection rackets and tip-offs and car crashes that might not have been accidents.

Connie was uncomfortably aware of their attention, but David didn't seem to care. He had lost the middle class English habit of discretion – if, indeed, he had ever had it – and his carrying voice made no distinction between everyday pleasantries and family secrets.

"The rest of the family went missing," he continued. "Scattered. Some of them went to Israel. My brothers went to Germany – crazy! I'm afraid I lost touch."

"It gets to be a habit, losing touch," said Connie, glaring at the couple who whispered to each other and then attacked their cold curry with furious concentration. Maybe, she thought, I look tougher than I feel.

"You think that too, Con? I sort of sensed you would. You go through life shedding the people who are no longer important to you at that precise moment. And it's only later that you start clocking up the cost in lost relationships. At the time I guess I just didn't want to know any more. About my family. Our roots. Everything I'd left behind here. Except for Beck. Beck and I were always the closest."

As he mentioned his sister she felt a stab of regret. Not merely that she hadn't seen her in so many years but that she hadn't thought about her. Oh, maybe in passing. But not in any real sense of the word: remembering. Remembering the friendship they had had, the confidences they'd shared, the growing up together with all the confusions and sillinesses of adolescence.

"I missed her. Becky. For a while. She never wrote. Not a word. A message. Anything." Her tone clearly implied: it wasn't my fault, it was hers.

"I guess for a while it was better no one here knew where they'd moved to. In case anyone asked."

She knew that was logical, given the need for the Levitches to keep not just a low profile but a non-existent one. But she still felt aggrieved. "No one asked. And she didn't have to give me her address. Just a nod."

"Did it matter that much?"

"Probably not. After a bit," she conceded. "I hated you all for quite a long time, until I was too busy to bother."

He nodded. "Becky guessed that. When she returned to Southdean she tried to contact you a couple of times, but you didn't reply." He volunteered the information as if it could hardly have mattered less. Calls that weren't returned were just part of the infuriating pattern of life. No big deal, he would probably say – and did. "No big deal."

He seemed surprised that Connie should look so startled.

"I didn't know," she whispered. Did she? She tried to recall.

"It was a few years ago, I gather, when you were quite a big wheel down here. Maybe it was just some dopey

179

secretary. Or you didn't catch on that it was Becky. It was a different surname. Howard."

"I – I always seemed to be so, so all over the place then."

"That's what she figured."

"You're staying with her?"

"For a few days. Like I said, I've always kept in touch with Beck. She worked abroad. Mostly in Brussels. As a secretary with a law firm. Then as a translator with the EEC. That's where she met her husband. In Brussels."

"Clever Becky. She was always good at languages." She smiled. "I was a terrible duffer. She used to help me with my French grammar. But she could never do anything about my accent. 'You're so *English*!' she used to say. As if she weren't. But I suppose if you're Jewish, being a Jew comes first."

"Typical gentile prejudice! Next step: being a Jew means being different and being different means being dangerous and—"

"That's not fair," she said angrily. "Next thing you'll be calling me a Fascist."

He threw back his head and laughed loudly. The only other couple in the restaurant looked at him with some alarm, gathered up their belongings and signalled for the bill. Connie noticed that they weren't young at all as she'd supposed, but middle-aged and rather drab and possibly having an assignation somewhere that they wouldn't be seen by anyone who knew them. She wished she hadn't glared at them so coldly and tried to make up for it with a tentative smile, but they weren't having any and swept past them hurriedly as if fearing further contamination from this loud Yank and his equally strange companion.

He was still laughing which surprised her. She hadn't seriously considered he was implying she was a Fascist but it wasn't all that funny, either.

"Oh Con, Con, Con! Lighten up! You always did take everything so damned literally. Maybe that's why Becky

180

was so fond of you. She said she felt as though you needed protection."

"Funny!" said Connie. "I always used to think I was protecting her. You know how school kids can be making someone feel an outsider. Parroting anti-Semitic remarks they'd heard at home about Jews and kosher food and skullcaps."

"Yarmulka! If you're going to say it, say it right. A skullcap is a Yarmulka!"

"Patronising bastard!" Now she laughed. And they both felt easier. "So, when did Becky marry this Mr Howard?"

"*Sir* Edwin Howard, if you please!" He sounded quite smug as if publicly conveying that he was not in the least over-awed by the title while being privately rather impressed by it.

"So, Becky's a Lady! Well, well!"

"Not that Beck would let you know it. I guess she's the most down to earth person I know. It was no love match. She married Howard because she felt sorry for him. He was a diplomat of the old school and he just couldn't adapt to the new Europe."

"Not much of a basis for a marriage. Pity!"

"I don't know. Maybe it's as good a basis as any. He was a good deal older than her and he worshipped her. He was a widower and his kids thought he was mad to marry so late in life. But Becky probably gave him the happiest years before he died. And in her way she was fond of him. I suppose you could say she married well. He left her comfortably off. Enough money to travel if she wished. To buy this big, architectural freak of a house a few miles along the coast. It's on a headland overlooking the bay and it looks like a giant liner with its bow facing the sea. You get the feeling it's going to take off at any minute, ploughing into the waves. It's the first time I've visited her there and I just love it. What is it, Con?"

She was looking up at him, puzzled by this description of Becky's handsome life-style. "It's just . . . I'm surprised. That young mother and the kiddy in

181

McDonald's. They struck me as, well, rather deprived. Under-privileged."

"I suppose you could say that. Kit – Catherine – was a classic drop-out. For a time she hated Becky and she certainly hated poor old Edwin. She got into drugs, married some no good guy and had Vicky. When he walked out Becky took her and the little girl to live with her. They're not a happy family, but things are getting better. Becky's more patient than I am. I just can't figure how someone who had all the advantages can just go off the rails."

"I can," said Connie so quietly he probably didn't hear her. She thought of Colin and she thought of Hub and his sister.

"It was partly because of them I'm sure that she came back to Southdean. She remembered it as stable and respectable. The sort of place in which to be at peace. She thought it would do Kit good to get away from all the rotten influences."

"And has it? Done her good?"

"Well, Southdean isn't what it used to be, is it? But I know how Becky remembered it and how she felt about getting back to it."

"Even if it hasn't come up to expectations?"

He shrugged. "So, what does come up to expectations? I sometimes think I'd give anything to just slow down. Then I tell myself I'd die of boredom."

"A low threshold?"

"You could say. I thought when I went out to Illinois and married Anna I'd be happy to settle down with her family as a farmer. They owned quite a bit of land near Galesburg. Something of a curiosity. There aren't too many Jewish farming families in Illinois. Lots of Scandinavians. Not many Jews. Anna was a sweet girl and they were sweet people. But it wasn't long before I figured that the company that bought the crop made more money than the farmers who sold it and the guy who traded in the crop made even more money. That's when my marriage broke up. We divorced.

"I went to Chicago, worked at anything during the day and studied at night. Got my qualifications, talked my way into a job with a small brokerage business. . . . Well, typical Horatio Alger success story, that's me! But sometimes I think: whatever happened to happy? A big apartment overlooking Lake Michigan. Two kids – both boys – who called me 'sir' up to their bar mitzvah. They're so well brought up, private schools and all the rest, that they couldn't even bring themselves to call me 'Dad'.

"Their mother was a real Jewish princess: rich, classy, on the board of all the best charities, gave dinner parties to die for an invitation to. You know something I wouldn't tell another soul but Beck? I laid siege to that woman like Hitler laid siege to Leningrad." ("Oh – and you could, you could," she remembered with a twinge.) "From the moment I first met her through her father I made up my mind to marry her. And I didn't even have Beck's excuse: pity. I wanted her for her position, her money, her breeding and somehow or other I got her.

"I was outrageously unfaithful until she died, but she refused to see it. Her code. Her ridiculously outmoded, old-fashioned code wouldn't allow it. She was a helluva lot kinder to me than I deserved. A bit like your Sam, I guess. Maybe we deserve each other, Con." This time he reached out and touched her hand and this time it was she who didn't respond.

It was too soon, far too soon, she thought. There was much about him which she found distasteful, not least his confident assumptions about her. Although even now she knew that he could still make her love him. Perhaps that's the way he had always been, except when she was sixteen she was too dense and certainly too inexperienced to see it.

"You know the States?" He took a mouthful of iced tea which she'd insisted on ordering to cool the curry and grimaced. "Yuk!"

"A little," she replied. "A couple of nights in New York, Los Angeles, when the company was thriving. Breakfast meetings with business executives who were

183

running late for their next appointment. The usual run-around. A trip to Disney World with the children. No, I don't *know* the States. Like most tourists, I've flirted with it."

"You should come, Con. It would give you a whole new perspective."

She studied his face for clues to some underlying motive to the suggestion. But his expression gave nothing away as if he were waiting for her to provoke a reaction.

"I think I'm still trying to deal with the old perspective."

He looked back at her thoughtfully. "I'd like to have known you when you were on top – the business, I mean. It's like nothing I imagined for you. Who'd have thought? Little Connie Connor!"

Indeed, she reflected, who'd have thought? Except, in a sense, he should, if he'd been paying attention.

She remembered Beattie's surprise at Connie's sudden and diligent interest in the money-making potential of her mother's sideline: the bit she made from dress-making to supplement the small income from the savings her husband had prudently put by while he was alive. Running up outfits for special occasions for neighbours whose budgets couldn't run to the prices asked in the shops had started as a hobby and become a treadmill – at least to Connie who was expected to help out on the finishing and buttonholes and trimmings.

"You mean she only charges cost?" David Levitch, young, arrogant, know-it-all David Levitch, had said in disbelief.

"What's cost?" echoed Connie.

"Cost of fabric, patterns . . ."

"Well, they're friends." She said it positively, persuading herself it was a true and logical reason for expecting something for nothing very much.

"Too right, they must be," he'd laughed. "Running up couture copies for friendship! Your mother must be mad."

She hadn't relaid ^(relayed) this comment exactly to her mother but she did start to question the sense of spending all that time and effort on a special frock for hardly any recompense. "Just cost."

"What do you know about cost?" her mother had asked sharply, probably guessing it hadn't been her daughter's original thought.

"Nothing," mumbled Connie and got on with her homework. But she could tell Beattie had taken it on board. The next time a neighbour popped around to ask her to do a 'little favour', Beattie spun a plausible hard luck story, together with the veiled threat that she might have to give up dress-making for other people if she couldn't see a little profit in it.

Listening to Beattie through a crack in the door Connie had been quite proud of her mother who sounded purposeful and businesslike and very much as if she knew what her work was worth. And far from losing custom, Beattie found she was being swamped with orders. So much so that Connie grudgingly gave up more of her time to readying the garments for the final fittings, negotiating a five percent deal on profit over and above cost for herself – on the urging of David Levitch who seemed to know a lot about the rag trade. But then he seemed to know a lot about everything. It had been Connie's first lesson in never undervaluing your talent or underestimating the price people might pay for it.

Beattie didn't mind. She was only too pleased to see her daughter developing an astute nose for business and in the long hours she spent huddled over her Singer sewing machine she began to envisage a future that might prove very lucrative for both of them.

When Connie told David all about this, he had merely smiled that superior smile and said he'd told her so.

She became aware that this middle-aged David Levitch who was almost a stranger was waving his hand in front of her.

She shook herself briskly. "Miles away."

"Where?"

185

"Just – away – then!"

"Ah, then!" he said as if it explained everything. "What about that hotel?"

"Not right now, David."

"You mean some other time?"

"I mean – not right now. Just that. But I would like to see Becky."

He nodded, resigning himself presumably to a lonely night. Or maybe not? he wondered. "I'll pick you up tomorrow morning if you're free. Take you to see her. She'd like that."

"You don't mind? About tonight?" Damn it, why should he mind? What did she owe him? "No, of course you don't," she answered herself, forestalling some snappy reply from him. "How will you get back?"

"I've a hire car parked in one of those streets off the promenade."

She frowned. "Will you be all right?"

"For Christ's sake, Con, I've been drinking fucking *tea* for the past two hours." The attentive Indian proprietor, who was laboriously making out their bill, shot a pained look in his direction which clearly signalled his opinion that expletives should be deleted.

She chuckled, not for effect, but because he suddenly struck her as rather funny – an aspect of him she'd never noticed before. "What a waste of your time, David. How would you calculate that in financial consultancy fees? Let's see – two, three, perhaps five hundred dollars an hour?"

He took her hand and squeezed it. This time she didn't pull away.

"OK. Funny lady."

"Funny man."

"You've never really forgiven me, have you, Con?" he said quietly. And this unexpected perception of the gulf between them took her by surprise.

"I thought I had," she replied as directly as he had challenged her. "Now – now I'm just not sure."

186

Chapter Sixteen

Sam was standing in the porch when she got back. It was dark but the light from the open front door silhouetted his unmistakable shaggy shape and curls of equally unmistakable pipe tobacco smoke eddied around in the night breeze. At the sight of him she felt a prick of guilt. She should, she supposed, have telephoned – at least to let him know that she hadn't wrecked Karen's car or got herself arrested for some fool thing or other.

He would say he was just taking the air. But he was, she knew, waiting for her and the pretence of trying to be unobtrusive would make his patience seem positively obtrusive. As long as she was under his roof she would have to get used to the fact that she was also under his care.

"Con!" he called, affecting surprise, although he had probably heard the Renault enter the drive. "I was just taking the air."

She remembered the tone of voice so well, the measured calm. Even when they'd divorced he had assured her that she could always rely on him; just because two people no longer wished to live together didn't mean that they couldn't behave like civilised, caring human beings. Needless to say it was a sentiment with which Karen heartily concurred.

Connie should have been grateful, but she hadn't been. She'd have preferred a bitter, name-calling divorce, so acrid with abuse that they could both convince themselves it was the only sensible solution. But Sam's sense of decency wouldn't allow it. And she shuddered as she recalled the time when she had need of that decency,

187

that reliability, when it was Sam who was called upon to pick up the pieces when the great black hole swallowed her up.

Her memory of her disintegration was faulty. She could pinpoint the casual effects, but not the actual experience of falling apart: how it felt, what she did, how other people reacted. For months she had lived in a kind of daze, dependent on the anti-depressants and the ministerings of others: Sam, Amy. Not Holly. And after those months, when she began to emerge from that limbo of nothingness, his voice would always seem to be whispering in her ear. "You'll be fine, Con, just fine."

It was only later that she had learned how he had funded her care in a sympathetic and fiendishly expensive nursing home, organised her future and her finances, helped pick the cheerful flat in Richmond, near enough to Amy to be handy but not so near that Connie would feel stifled and spied upon. It wasn't his fault that she had defaulted on her consultations with the unlikable psychotherapist he had urged her to see.

Oh yes, she had had need of Sam. She just wished she had been more gracious about admitting it. After all, she was no longer his responsibility. Maybe if she had stuck with the shrink he would have weaned her off her compulsion to be such a shrew to Sam. Maybe David Levitch had been right: self-absorbed and careless, they deserved each other and had no right to marry nice, kind spouses.

"Con? That *is* you?" She could hear the apprehension in his voice even though it was carefully controlled, the what-state-is-she-in-now? tone.

"Of course it's me. Who else would it be?" she muttered to herself.

Irritated at his concern, she butted her head lightly down onto the steering wheel. Then, arranging a broad smile on her face as precisely as she would a bunch of daffodils in a vase, she opened the car door.

He looked so relieved she wasn't sure whether to hug him or hit him.

"Sorry I'm so late, Sam. You must have wondered."

"I did. A bit. Karen, too." Underlying the casual response he was really saying: "You could have phoned. I've been worried out of my wits. And you've upset Karen who can do without this sort of unnecessary anxiety at this late date in her pregnancy. Why couldn't you have a little more thought for other people?" And she rightly understood this hidden message.

As he understood her hidden message when she chirped gaily: "Fuss! fuss!" – as in "For Heaven's sake, Sam, you never did know how to lose your temper and have a good, knock-down-drag-out row. And you haven't changed."

"Have you eaten?"

"A curry."

"Lousy?"

She pulled a face. "So-so."

"Nightcap?"

"Am I allowed?"

"If you've been good." He sounded as suggestive as Sam, in his goodness, ever could.

She smiled, linking her arm through his. "Well I'm here, aren't I? So I suppose I must have been good."

He took her into the study where he could smoke his pipe in comfort and not disturb Karen. "She went up early. Tired." He poured her a weak malt whisky and drenched it with water. "She said you cleared out Colin's room," he said mildly as if merely querying the daily routine of the cleaning lady.

She sipped the whisky. "When you say weak, you mean it, don't you?"

He topped it up. "Better?"

She sipped again and nodded. "Not exactly cleared it out. I just thought maybe it wasn't such a good idea keeping it as a shrine."

He frowned. "Is that how it struck you? A shrine? It wasn't meant to."

"No, of course I don't mean a shrine. That's just me exaggerating. It's only that keeping everything pretty

189

much as he left it doesn't seem all that – well, healthy."
When she said it, she had the grace to blush. Who was
she to pontificate about what was emotionally healthy
and what wasn't?

"I'm sorry you felt that, Con. It was really on your
account that Karen insisted on leaving things undisturbed.
But if that's how you feel . . ."

"It would make a pretty nursery."

"We've already planned the nursery," he reproached
her, perhaps for not asking about their nursery plans
before as any other maternal woman might.

"Well, it would make a nice playroom. Or a second
nursery for the next little Remick. I assume this is the
start of a football team!"

He looked up at her while continuing to tap the old ash
into a blackened enamel tray, refill the pipe with fresh
tobacco, put it down evenly into the bowl and light it;
an exercise that appeared to give him more satisfaction
than the actual process of smoking.

She realised he was using the time to think of a suitable
reply and also to allow her to feel reasonably ashamed
for being so flip about Karen's approaching motherhood.
"That was silly," she apologised.

"Yes it was. You know I'm more of a cricket man."

She laughed. "Well, either way, I'm sure they'll all
play for England, girls as well."

"Damned good cricketers, the girls. Won the tro-
phy last year. Better show than most of the male
sportsmen."

"Bully for them!" She clapped her hands together
slowly.

"You should be proud. Strong feminist like you."

"Am I? Was I? A strong feminist, Sam? What was
it Amy used to say when she was arguing with Holly?
'I'm a feminist for me.' Maybe we have – had – that
in common."

She snuggled down into the deep armchair. The whisky
was having its effect, not a massive jolt, just a gentle
glow. She caught sight of herself in a photograph frame

190

on his desk. One of several, but quite prominently displayed; Karen's was fractionally to the fore. The fact that he should still keep her likeness near him when he was writing his handy hints for hardy gardeners pleased her more than she expected it would. At least he must have some good memories of their life together.

He followed the direction of her eye-line, picked up the photograph and scrutinised it; a gesture that seemed natural to him as if he did it many times, perhaps searching for the woman he must have loved once. "We had happy times, too, Con," he said.

"As well as the rest, you mean."

"How was your David Levitch?"

She started to compose a fairly bland reply and then realised that wouldn't do. He expected more because he knew more.

"How long did you know about David Levitch?" she blurted out suddenly, amazed that she should have been so dense all these years, just because they had barely talked about him.

"Beattie told me before she died."

"And?"

"And what? I never really imagined you were pure as the driven snow when we married. I honestly don't think I cared. When you want someone or something, come to that, badly enough you don't waste time weighing up the pros and cons."

"Con's pros and cons. Now I am being stupid. Not even a *good* schoolboy pun."

"Well, it's all in the past." He puffed away for a few seconds. "So how was he?"

"Affluent, very American, probably a bastard but charming with it. Not very different, except older. Like me. He's taking me to see his sister, Becky, tomorrow morning. We were great friends at school."

"I don't recall you mentioning her."

"No, I don't suppose I did. Sam!" Her tone indicated a change of subject. She didn't want to talk to Sam about this confident stranger from across the

191

Atlantic. They belonged to two different compartments of her life.

"I'd still like to meet him," he persisted.

"I imagine you will, if you're around tomorrow," she snapped. "That is if you don't mind me staying over the weekend. There are a couple of things—"

"As long as you like. You know that. I've spoken to Holly about going to see her at the Minerva, Saturday. It'll be fun. Amy, too. She may be bringing someone. You could invite—"

"Oh, I don't know, Sam." She shook her head.

"Scared?"

"Yes." It was true, she realised. She was scared of too close an association with him. She knew she couldn't cope with being let down twice by the same man and she hadn't the slightest doubt that he would be capable of disappearing from her life just as suddenly a second time as he had before.

"Sam. What do you think about me going back into business? Not actually into business. But – well, getting my feet wet again or maybe getting back up on the horse again would be a more appropriate metaphor. Gracious, how literary! It must be the whisky."

"A good malt will do it every time. Not with this man, Connie? Surely." He didn't bother to disguise his surprise.

"No, of course not. I met Andrew Deeley by the bowling green."

"Andy. Good grief! Poor old Andy!"

"He didn't strike me as poor old Andy. He was quite chipper. Told me about being ousted from the firm by his lovely family. . . ."

". . . It wasn't like that at all. . . ."

". . . Comes to the same thing. He was full of this new enterprise of his. The workshops, helping young craftsmen, giving them a place to work and an incentive to market their product. He asked me – just tentatively – if I'd like to give them the benefit of my business expertise, as he put it. The nice thing was he didn't regard me as a totally spent force: once a failure, always a no-hoper. He seemed to think I could really contribute to something worthwhile."

"What did you say to him?" He sounded unusually guarded for Sam who, if he couldn't be completely open, preferred not to speak at all.

"Nothing really. I vaguely promised to visit the workshops, meet the people. He's leased the site of the old CCC factory. I'd like to see the old place. I did tend to dismiss the idea at first. But you know, Sam, talking to him I felt – I really began to feel the old adrenalin starting to flow again. If Andy could do it, why not me? What do you think, Sam? Honestly?"

The 'honestly?' obviously rankled and she felt contrite. Sam didn't lie. He didn't answer her for what seemed an age, but kept fiddling with the pipe, peering into the bowl, studying the stem, taking an occasional puff.

"I really should give this up," he said finally. "I don't really like it any more. Habit!"

"Sam!" She heard herself shouting as she used to shout when he put up a diversion to deflect discussion of an awkward question or subject. He placed the pipe on the ash-grimed tray and sighed the sigh of a man who accepts that the awkwardness isn't going to go away of its own volition.

"You don't want to get too involved, Connie. With old Andy."

"Don't keep saying *old*! He's not yet seventy and a good deal spryer than a lot of your stodgy friends in Southdean. Why not? Why shouldn't I get involved?"

He recognised the edge of truculence in her voice which used to preface a stubborn refusal to see something that he thought eminently reasonable. It took him back to the years of contention between them that had worn them both down; contention on Connie's part and silent dismay on Sam's.

But he ploughed on, probably because he realised it no longer mattered. They were two separate people, different people, now, and keeping the peace was no longer an imperative.

"He's made himself a bit of a laughing stock – with his crackpot schemes – since he retired. Probably misses Edie. That's understandable. Felt he needed a new purpose in life. But there were plenty of causes he could have taken up. Activities. And he's still a consultant at Deeley's."

"Technically." She glared at him for putting up an argument she had initially been inclined to put to herself before dismissing it.

"All right. Technically. But his sons acted out of consideration for him, not out of spite."

"How? Just tell me how!"

"He was getting out of touch with modern methods of manufacture. It was becoming difficult. I know one of his sons quite well. William. He told me." For the first time that she could remember he seemed to be on the defensive. Maybe deep down he, too, felt Andrew Deeley had had a raw deal from his family.

"William! *That* young fogey!"

He ignored her interruption. "Bill serves on the same fund-raising committee to preserve what's left of the Downs from development, trunk roads," he explained as if that might make their relationship more palatable to Connie.

"You mean you throw yourselves in front of the bulldozers!" The very idea of Sam and the stuffy William Deeley breaking the law and doing battle with beefy contract labourers and heavy duty machinery struck her as irresistibly amusing and also quite brave.

He looked shocked. "Good lord, no! We're not in favour of militancy. We lobby the right people. That's the way to influence policy. And, of course, paying for consultants and lawyers to argue the case."

Jagger ambled into the study, cross at being disturbed and curious to see who was making all that noise at this time of night. He yawned pointedly and crooked his chin on Connie's lap, looking up at her with his bleary,

194

yearning eyes. "Poor old thing!" she murmured, fondling his loppy ears. "You still haven't told me what's so terrible about Andrew's new project and why I shouldn't 'get involved'." She quoted his warning back at him.

"Apparently – according to Bill – they're very concerned about him and the kind of people he's supporting. Hardly better than layabouts, spongers. Some of them even stay in his house. Of course it's his money and he can do what he likes with it. And he's even managed to get some council funding. But they – Bill and the others – can't help feeling he's losing his grip."

Connie sighed. Was *that* all? A family spat over money. Or, rather, when you got right down to it, the inheritance after Andrew died.

She was conscious of Jagger snoring peacefully on her lap. They'd never been great friends when she'd lived in the house. But now, she realised, she quite missed him.

"You do see, don't you Connie, how unwise it would be to mess around in something as – as peculiar as Andy's project? I mean, there are plenty of schemes these days for getting people back into the work place."

"I suppose it depends on the quality of the work. Andy seemed to be talking about craft not just labour."

Irritated, Sam kicked a dead log in the fireplace. The noise stirred Jagger who eyed him reproachfully and let out a single, plaintive bark.

"Now look what you've done," said Connie, rather enjoying the spectacle of Sam being cross.

"Can't you hear what I'm saying, Con? He's been got at. I'm sure of it." He stopped. "Well – Bill's sure of it anyway. It just takes a plausible bounder like Hubbard Crowther to exert influence over a lonely old man and—"

"What did you say?" she said abruptly. She had been listening sleepily to Sam's droning recital of William Deeley's complaints about his father's eccentric way of spending his retirement and, more important, a good deal of money besides without paying too much attention until now. "What do you know about Hubbard Crowther?"

"I could hardly *not* know about Hubbard Crowther. I was there at the annual Conservative dinner when he poured a bottle of vintage port over the sitting MP." Whether it was the fate of the vintage port or the discomfiture of the sitting MP, he was clearly outraged. "The Crowthers – John and Erica – were appalled. And who could blame them? They'd stood by him loyally when he'd been sent to prison and then when he's released, *that's* how he behaves!"

Her curiosity got the better of her urge to giggle at the thought of a port-soaked Tory MP trying to rescue his dignity in a deplorable situation. "Why had he been sent to prison?"

"Reckless driving. Worse. He'd been over the limit and killed a boy on a cycle. I suppose he got off quite lightly. Two years. Although he was out in a little over a year. He could have taken up a decent career after that. It wasn't too late. But he was totally changed. He quite alienated his parents and just about everybody else. The last straw was when he picketed a Save The Downs meeting, parading a poster outside saying: 'Sod The Downs! Save The People!'" Even Sam couldn't keep the hint of a chuckle out of his voice, although he was a deeply serious conservationist. "Cheeky bugger!"

"That sounds about right," said Connie thoughtfully. "I met him today. At least I met him *again* today. You *do* know he was a friend of Colin's? Maybe more than a friend?"

Sam looked puzzled. "I remember he'd been here a couple of times. Same school. Nothing more."

"Well, I guess there was a lot more. Colin's full of him in those strange diaries he wrote. But then I suppose you never read them. Up in his room."

Sam sat down heavily. "No," he said faintly. "I never read them. It didn't seem – well, quite right."

"I know. I didn't feel it was quite right, either. But I couldn't help myself. He – Hub – is running some kind of shelter for kids, ex-convicts, derelicts, right out over in Rookshaven Lane. He and his sister."

"Deirdre! That was another bone of contention with the Crowthers. They felt it was through him that she . . ." He paused.

"Went to the bad?" Connie grimaced. "I'm sure that's how Erica Crowther would express it."

"Don't be so snide, Con," he said softly. "It's hard for parents, when both your children just don't want to know you."

"One is bad enough? Eh, Sam?"

He nodded, without indicating that he shared her guilt. "I'm surprised if you had such a long chat with Andrew that he didn't tell you about his association with Hubbard."

"I'm surprised, too," she admitted. "Or maybe I just wasn't in the mood to make the connection." She massaged her forehead vigorously as if trying to ease the throb of a headache. But it wasn't a headache that was troubling her. "Oh Sam, Sam, what a tangled web – as the man said."

"Webs usually are. Tangled."

The fresh voice startled them. Karen was standing in the doorway. They hadn't heard her coming. She was good at silence, thought Connie. She was wearing a voluminous nightgown, the pregnant bulge clearly visible underneath, and no dressing gown. Her feet were bare. Her unruly hair looked as if it had been thrashing around on a pillow, which it probably had. But her rosy, outdoors face was serene and peaceful. How lovely, Connie speculated, to feel that secure in yourself.

"I'm glad you got back safely, Connie," said Karen. "Are you coming up, Sam!" Not a question, a request. Then, as suddenly as she had put in an appearance, she turned round and disappeared like some ethereal white-robed ghost, gliding into the hall and up the stairs.

197

Chapter Seventeen

"So this is where you live!"

Amy Remick wrinkled her nose with disapproval and immediately regretted it. What right had she to question where her sister Holly should choose to live? On the other hand, in the whole of pretty Chichester there had to be something better than this bijou wreck. The only things to be said for it were that it was close to the environs of the Festival Theatre and it was in such a disreputable state that the extra chaos Holly and her fellow young trainee actors, who rented it for the season, introduced could hardly make much difference.

"I mean," she added hastily, "it's different."

"What you *mean*," said her sister pointedly, "is that you can't imagine any civilised person wanting to camp here even for the night, let alone take a summer lease."

"Are you short of money? If you are . . ."

"Not especially. We get paid peanuts, but that's all right – just watching Alec McCowan and Judi Dench from the wings is worth a week's hard slog. And there's the income from the bit Beattie left me which you cleverly advised me how to invest. And if the bailiffs were at the door I know Sam would help out. I'm one of the lucky ones. That's half the trouble. As Nye says: I'm not hungry enough. Don't you Nye?"

A large lumpy girl was stirring a saucepan of something that looked sinister but smelt rather good on the hob of the cooker in the cluttered kitchen. Under her loose cotton top her heavy breasts swung around like small sacks of nutty slack. She wielded the wooden spoon with a flourish, licking it every so often and dipping a none too clean forefinger into the concoction for no discernible reason except perhaps the gratification she got from seeing Amy's expression of distaste.

"Not hungry and not talented. You've two strikes against you, kid."

"See?" Holly sounded positively pleased at this damning assessment of her chances in the theatrical profession, until Amy realised they were speaking in a kind of code in which abuse is a compliment and intended to be totally incomprehensible to the outsider.

She was, she saw, being set up. It was only to be expected. She hadn't been able to have a sensible conversation with Holly for years, long before Colin died. She had the feeling that Holly had secrets she would guard with her life. And she wondered, as she had over and over again, as she drove back to London and decided to break her journey in Chichester, why she was putting herself through this. The meeting with the client in Shoreham had been traumatic enough and the confrontation she intended to have with Lewis in London would probably be even more difficult. What was the point in adding another aggravation to her day?

The 'Nye' girl wiped her hands on a dish towel and waddled – it was the only word for the curious way her heavy body rotated as she put one foot in front of the other – over to Amy.

"Naomi O'Dowd." She had an Irish accent, softly Southern. "I've heard about you. Big wheel in the city. Holly here says."

"Hardly that," said Amy, chuffed that Holly should even have mentioned her.

"Well, no. But then Holly here exaggerates. It comes with not being hungry or talented."

Holly-here punched the big girl in the small of the back quite hard, but Naomi O'Dowd seemed to be used to it. "A natural-born punching bag, me."

"*Hag*! Punching hag!"

"Oh, ha, ha! Have you seen this one in the revue at the Minerva?" Nye asked Amy. The Minerva was the small theatre attached to the Festival Theatre where young players in the company sometimes had the chance of showing off their ability in experimental work that often won praise from the critics.

"Not yet," she admitted. "Dad did say—"

"Saturday night," said Holly, as if through gritted teeth. "The whole bang shoot. Him, that Karen, you, Mum. Uncle Tom Cobleigh and all."

"The theatre's going to be filled with Remicks. Treats!"

"Bugger off, Nye. I expect Amy's got something to tell, else she wouldn't be here."

Nye was not to be dismissed that easily. "If you blink you'll miss her. She plays 'Atam Irah'. Actually she's not bad for a no-hoper."

"What's 'Atam Irah'? It sounds like a Pakistani fast bowler."

"Very good! It's an anagram for Mata Hari," Holly sighed. "The show's a sort of pageant with music of twentieth century icons. Nye's Mae West." She caught Amy's start of surprise. "Truly!"

"I read a review. They mentioned you, but not 'Atam Irah'." Amy laughed. How absurd these theatricals were: so deadly serious about their work and so frivolous about everything else. Well almost everything else. They seemed to get incredibly worked up about minority causes.

"What about my stew?" said Nye.

"I'll watch it."

"No you won't, you'll let it burn."

"So, all right, we'll go into the other room. C'mon."

She beckoned Amy out of the kitchen into an even more cluttered sitting-room, filled with shaggy armchairs, the stuffing spilling out of the tattered upholstery, small tables, their surfaces patterned with heat rings from carelessly deposited coffee mugs, and books, scripts, papers, cassettes strewn over every spare space.

Holly swept a half-eaten pizza on a cardboard plate onto the floor and made a hole in a settee for Amy. Amy lowered herself carefully into the cushion which sagged alarmingly, mindful of the pale coffee-coloured Armani trousers she was wearing.

Holly, she thought, in her ghastly kimono, sashed at the waist with a length of old curtain rope, looked wonderful. Her great bush of frizzled chestnut hair actually suited her. She wore no make-up, as many actresses didn't on their days off to give their faces a rest from the heavy greasepaint, and her unvarnished complexion was the sort that might grace the cover of a woman's magazine. Although she would hate to admit, even contemplate, it, she had the look of a modern, younger Connie.

"I suppose it's nice being in repertory. Not on call all the time," volunteered Amy for want of something to say that wasn't completely crass.

"When you phoned I turned down an invitation to sit in on a rehearsal of *King Lear* – all the cream at work." She didn't sound reproachful, merely stating a fact. Although clearly watching how the 'cream' coped with the majestic intricacies and tragedy of *Lear* would have been preferable to having a nice chat with her sister.

"I'm sorry. I just thought." She sank down deeper into the spongy cushion. "I don't know what I thought, Holly. Some sort of moral support, I suppose. I hoped, but then we never did have much in common, did we?"

Holly blushed. She was still young enough to blush; the toughness of the profession she had embraced hadn't yet eroded her capacity for such naïve responses to emotional situations. She brushed her cheek as if trying to erase the revealing colour.

"There's a lot you don't talk about. To us. Isn't there, Holly?" Amy persisted. Then she put up her hand, warding off a confession. "I don't want to know what you don't want to tell me. But I just felt you should know about Mum. When was the last time you saw her?"

Holly screwed up her mouth, perhaps trying to remember or, more likely, trying to forget. "I don't know. Is there any point?"

"There is now. She's changed, Holly. I've only seen

her fleetingly. Yesterday – at the house. With Sam. I brought her down a suitcase of clothes."

"And lots of shoes, I hope." Holly giggled. "Dad told me some garbled yarn about her being nicked in the shopping precinct wearing odd shoes."

"It's not *funny!*" From Amy's tone of voice Holly realised humour was not in the best taste. This was serious stuff.

"It just struck me as funny. I don't suppose it was. So, what's new then? Mum acting peculiarly. Same story."

"No it's not. It's like – it's like she's suddenly come out of a long tunnel. She's taking an interest."

"It's a little late for that." There was only a trace of reproach in Holly's voice. She hadn't the knack for sustained bitterness. Life was too short and too busy.

"I think she probably realises that. When I spoke to Dad early this morning he told me she had cleared out Colin's room and was looking up an old friend of his from school. She's even come to terms with the fact that he actually committed suicide. She'd never admitted that before. Never even mentioned it."

"Never even cared more like." It sounded callous, but she was thinking of something quite else which escaped Amy.

"How can we know, Holly, what goes on in people's minds when they're – when they're not responsible for how they are, what they do?"

"You've changed too, Amy. I know you've been great with Mum. A better daughter than I ever could be, or want to be. But you were always so, I don't know, cool about it – almost martyr-like. As if it were a duty. Not out of any kind of love or affection or even sympathy."

Amy nodded. She realised Holly had accurately gauged her own altered attitude toward her mother, which she could barely explain to herself. "I'm worried for her. But happy for her, too. There's some man she knew, was in love with I think, donkey's years ago before marrying Dad. He turned up suddenly from America and she started acting as skittish as a teenager."

"Great!" Holly whooped.

"What I'm trying to say Holly is: be careful tomorrow. Don't – well, just *don't*."

"Don't what? Upset the apple-cart? Cross my heart and hope to die. I'll be perfection. Promise."

"Don't make promises you can't keep, kid!"

Did everyone call everyone kid around here? wondered Amy. (All the fault of the *Casablanca* cult, she supposed. "Here's looking at you, kid!") She looked up at a very tall, very thin, very striking West Indian with a short back and sides hair-cut and the most mesmeric eyes she had ever seen. People just seemed to come and go with no thought of privacy. But if Amy minded, Holly didn't. She got up, hugged him and put up her face for a kiss.

"This," she said. "Is John. John Branco."

Holly didn't attempt to still the excitement in her voice. She's in love, thought Amy. And, what's more, judging by the glow in those incredible eyes, he's in love with her. Fancy! Her little sister! Not that she had ever assumed a big sister role with Holly, any more than Holly invited it. Still it was a revelation and, of course, her surprise had nothing to do with the fact that John Branco was black. At least that's what she told herself and firmly believed it.

"Funny kid!" he said fondly, ruffling Holly's already well ruffled hair.

"And you are in the show Mr . . ." – then, thinking better of it – "John?"

She was appalled at hearing her own voice and realising how priggish she sounded. Like Lady Bracknell. Perhaps he was an embryo star and she really should know who John Branco was.

"Why, lordy, Miz Scarlett, I's jes a po' ole scene-shifter!"

Ouch! Now it was she who blushed and she knew for a fact that she hadn't done that since she'd accidentally dropped her knickers on stage during a school play; the drama teacher could never get her on a stage again, even just carrying a spear in Shakespeare.

203

Amazingly, it was the love-struck Holly who reprimanded him. "You don't have to come the old chip-on-the-shoulder with my sister. She only asked."

He didn't seem to mind being ticked off, either. They were all so free with each other, Amy marvelled, assuming that these three were typical of the whole bunch who were rooming together.

"You're absolutely right, kiddo. My week for chips on the shoulder was last week. This week I'm forever grateful to the boss man for giving me my big break and inviting me to sit at his table." He grinned hugely at that. "Nice to meet you Amy Remick." He, too, had obviously heard of her from Holly.

"John is one of the ASMs in the Festival Theatre. But he's really a fine musician," said Holly helpfully.

He was easier to talk to after that. But not very easy and it was partly her, Amy's, fault, for she had no idea what to say to him. And it had nothing to do with his colour or race. It was his profession.

She really didn't feel comfortable around show business people. They talked in a language she could barely understand about things of which she had no knowledge. It occurred to her that it would be nice if just now and then they could drop their arrogant guard and try to find common ground with *her* – like what is the newest thinking on Systems Development and how do you arrive at the best way to motivate resources in the competitive market-place? She could rattle away quite cheerfully for hours on those absorbing topics; she could even be scintillating and witty about them.

Lewis had the knack. He could converse about anything to anyone. She could hear him telling her, as he often did: "Loosen up, Amy!" And she realised how much she longed to be with him.

She was glad to escape from that odd house. Probably too hastily. Almost rude. Although she doubted whether Nye or John or even Holly would be overly bothered about rude.

She would have been surprised to learn that rude, in fact, was being much discussed behind her back.

"Why did you have to be so rude to her?"

"Was I? I thought I was like I always am." He grinned again, confident in his ability to make people take him as he was or not at all.

"Yes, you were. But Amy doesn't understand that. She's a bit – well, she's not like us."

"Uptight?"

She nodded.

"And your mother? Is she uptight, too? You best let me know so I can behave – how was it you said – perfectly, tomorrow."

"No she's not uptight. Just peculiar. You'll probably love her to death."

"I'd rather love you to life." He turned her to face him and started massaging her hips and buttocks with his long, sensitive hands. She closed her eyes dreamily and wrapped her arms around him in anticipation. But he didn't respond. Instead he slid his hands up the sides of her body, over her shoulders and under her chin.

She felt the pressure of his fingers as they kneaded the soft flesh of her neck. It was a tender, rather than a sensual, gesture. All the men, boys, she had known before (not that many, but a liberal cross section) would have had her stripped and rolling around on the floor by now. But not John. With him it had to be slow and suitable. He had, as he rather primly lectured her, standards, instilled in him by a matriarchal Jamaican mother and a strict father whom he still revered even though they were four thousand miles away in Kingston. She suspected that he faintly disapproved of the free and easy life-style of the whites with whom he associated. He disapproved even more strongly of their assumption that because he was young and West Indian he should be randy, Rastafarian and into all night rave-ups and reggae music. He was also sternly opposed to the use of drugs and was known by the company as 'the Professor'.

"Why don't you give your mama a break?" he whispered in her ear. He'd obviously been thinking about it during all that massaging and kneading.

She opened her eyes, stared at him for a moment, half baffled by his sudden train of thought and half angry that he should take it upon himself to bring up the subject. She pulled herself away from him roughly.

"What business is that of yours?" A lame response, but the only one that came to mind.

"None," he admitted. "But maybe she's hurting more than you think. Of course, I only know what you've told me—"

"That's right! And more fool me."

"I was just thinking, Holly, maybe you'd be a happier person if you sort of gave a little. You know?" He kept fixing her with those eyes and she wished he wouldn't. They were like a cat's eyes. You couldn't look away.

"I *am* happy," she said. "And giving a little is a two-way passage. How about her giving me a little?" And she knew what he would reply when he was in his reasonable mood, which he clearly was now.

"You could try her. Don't you think she at least deserves to know that she has a grandson?" He said it so quietly, calmly, he could have been commenting on something quite trivial and, just for a second, he made it seem almost trivial. But only for a second.

She opened her mouth, not speaking, just hoping that the right words might form themselves into a coherent response without any conscious effort on her part. He waited. He and his cat's eyes.

"How do you know about that?" she said finally, faintly. "I never told you or Nye or anyone, not even Amy or Dad. I promised . . . I promised someone."

"The funny girl with the scar? Holly, Holly, how do you *think* I knew? I've been living with you for the past three months. Those regular visits to Southdean! You didn't go to see your father, so who did you go to see? Then a couple of times you brought them back here – the girl and the kid. Friends, you said. Honey, that was no friendship. That was love. The kind of love that makes a family. That dear octopus!" He quoted the familiar phrase as if he'd freshly minted it.

"That dreaded tarantula! You and your flipping reverence for family!"

"Either way. It locks you in. He wasn't just a nice little boy to you. He was much more than that. I could see it in your eyes. He was your brother's child. I don't know what promise you gave to the kid's mother. But maybe it's time you broke it."

She sank down limply into one of the spongy armchairs and picked at the frayed upholstery. What was the use of denial? She should have known that John was too bright not to deduce the relationship between her and Dede and little Colin.

"I'll think about it," she said weakly. She wanted to please him, show him she could be mature and sensible, but her long-held conviction that a woman had a right to silence, as well as a whole barrel of other rights, was against it. It was the sort of damnable conflict that came with being in love and, just briefly, she cursed herself for falling victim to that old trap. And she looked forward to the gathering of the clan the next day with more anxiety than the simple actor's worry that she might not be at her best on stage that night.

"Do I have to?" Lewis Diamond glanced at his watch, trying not to do it conspicuously, but Amy noticed it all the same, as she tended to notice everything about him as if she were studying a subject for an important thesis. He gave a slight shrug of irritation as he noticed her noticing his surreptitious time check.

She managed to catch him between meetings and they had agreed to a late lunch at some nondescript Italian restaurant near his office.

"No," she said, sipping her wine and barely tasting it although it was rather good. He was meticulous about wine.

"Then I want to." Why not? Even though he had

deliberately avoided it before he now realised it was time he saw Connie again and he felt a little shamefaced that he had never made the effort when she was suffering her breakdown. She'd often told him to his face that he was a self-centred bastard and he supposed he was. But she had accepted it and, despite being briefly lovers, they had also been chums. Associates and chums. He feared that her daughter Amy was a different proposition. With Amy it was all or nothing. And it was up to him to make that choice. "I'd be glad to see Holly at the Minerva. And Connie. And Sam. I'll look forward to it. We could all go out to supper afterwards. On me. Don't look so surprised. I pulled off a big one yesterday." He had, too. It was a sort of farewell gift to the agency, he'd figured.

"You're so contrary. Just like . . ." She had a mental image of that thin, tall, challenging West Indian who loved her sister Holly. No, not just like. All too clearly she could see that Lewis was not in love with her and never would be.

"Who? Who am I just like?"

"Nobody. Somebody you don't know. But you will, you will," she sighed. "I have a terrible feeling of fate ordering everything just now."

"Why so low?" He reached out his hand and grasped hers across the table. Now that he knew what had to be done he felt quite protective about her and memories of much that was good between them reinforced that feeling.

"I don't know. Seeing mother like that. It was a sort of shock. And then there was this shitty meeting with the clients at Shoreham. Well, one, the senior partner. They've got a nice little computer software company, innovative ideas, doing well in Europe. They just needed a little guidance, maximising assets, cutting out non-profitable areas, better auditing. Their workshop contravenes God knows how many Factory Acts, but that's easily rectified. And they were all receptive to suggestions, except this one guy. A real, hard, dyed-in-the-wool reactionary, male chauvinist, hanging and flogging, back to the days of the workhouse and, probably, transportation for felons for all I know. I did the unforgivable. Had a dreadful stand-up row with him about how the sale of council properties has helped create a homeless sub-society."

"Good for you!" Though sympathetic, Lewis was hardly serious.

"*No.* Bad for me. It was so unprofessional. I could have kicked myself."

"But it was all right in the end."

"I suppose so. The other guys were quite amused, I might say. Apparently they all think of him as a political fuddy-duddy. Unfortunately, he's a brilliant administrator and it was he who had the vision to start the business in the first place. You can't argue with that. Politics, yes. But success in business, no."

"So, your job's not on the line for that one indiscretion." He brought her down to earth with a bump.

"Naturally not." She straightened her back and smoothed her hair. Just talking about her job, even the down side of it, made her feel sleek and efficient and in control. She chewed thoughtfully on a lettuce leaf, ignoring the congealing pasta.

"Amy!" And she knew from the tone of his voice, kind, conciliatory, that she wasn't going to like what he had to say. "Amy, I'm leaving."

"You mean, going back to the office." She didn't know why she was so determined to draw out the agony! She was perfectly well aware that going back to the office was the least of it.

"I'm leaving London. I've been offered a job in an agency in Stuttgart. And I've accepted."

"Just like that? Overnight?"

"Not quite. It's been on the cards."

"You never said."

"No. I wish I had." And he realised he genuinely did wish he had. This wasn't fair to her. Here in a public place. The end of the affair. Easier for him, lousy for her. "I'm sorry, Amy."

"You'll hate Germany. All those neo-Nazis."

"Maybe. It's a good offer, though."

"And a good way of letting me down – well, I suppose you could call it lightly."

She looked at him so frankly that he couldn't lie. "Yes. That, too. You know I'll always . . ."

She put up her hand. "Don't! Don't! Just let's leave it at that, shall we? What about your family?"

"I'll be back often. Weekends. We could . . ."

"No, we couldn't," she silenced him. "Clean break." She wondered if he knew what all this stiff-upper-lip common sense would cost her in private pain and lonely, sleepless nights. Probably not.

"I'd still like to come tomorrow."

She'd forgotten tomorrow. Hell! "Of course. You're invited," she said with a brittle brightness that apparently fooled him for he repeated how much he'd look forward to it.

They left the restaurant arm in arm, but she refused to share a taxi. The sooner she started adjusting to a life without Lewis the better and no one who saw her striding down Regent Street would have guessed there was a small, miserable creature hiding inside her who wasn't being brave at all.

Chapter Eighteen

Through her binoculars Rebecca Howard watched the muscular boy and the matchstick thin girl step gingerly over the pebbles to the firm sand by the breakwater. They spread two striped towels on the sand, anchored them with bulging Tesco bags and stripped down to bathing trunks and bikini. In their semi-nakedness the boy looked even huskier and the girl more skeletal. Then they ran hand in hand down to the sea. The tide was out and when the tide was out on the coast around Southdean it was truly out. They had a long way to run.

They didn't speak to each other or laugh or seem to communicate in any way, intent simply on their headlong rush to full immersion, unconcerned that Southdean's famous tonic sea had failed to meet EC regulations. The sea was the sea. It was free and wet and a degree or two above freezing. It was the paradoxical nature of the sea − constantly changing and forever unchanged − that appealed to Rebecca Howard and perhaps, without them even considering it, to the two lone bathers on the beach.

The girl squealed coyly as she breasted a wave and the boy plunged into it masterfully. Despite all their faults, the British, thought Rebecca, were a hardy race. If the calendar told you it was summer, then that was when you swam in the sea even if you froze in the process.

A shy sun peeped through a break in the overcast sky. It was a typical dull, dreary day in midsummer at the British seaside.

She had always been surprised at how nostalgic she used to get about just such a sight when she lived with

211

Edwin abroad and in the house in London. It wasn't as if she'd spent all that much time living near the sea. Just a few early, but she supposed impressionable, years. Edwin had never been able to understand her longing to smell that salty, sewagey odour thrown up by the spray and the seaweed; to shiver in a biting east wind from off the channel; to look at the grey horizon and the occasional grey tanker ploughing its way between ports.

In his later, less adventurous years, Edwin liked Nice and Cannes, where the sun shone brighter, the sand was yellower, the hotels were grander, the service more obsequious and there were friends and colleagues to offer hospitality on the sparkling yachts that cruised the Mediterranean and moored off-shore. Once a year they stayed at the family home in Scotland where his elder brother and his tyrannical wife played hosts to an enormous brood of relatives. Only the severest illness or crisis could possibly be accepted as adequate excuse for evading this annual duty – and, even then, not without strenuous argument. One gallant daughter-in-law had insisted on making the journey with a ruptured appendix which earned her a revered place in the Howard hall of fame, an accolade enhanced by the fact that the poor girl died in great pain two days later.

Recalling those obligatory weeks of torment Rebecca felt she knew what it might have been like to be Princess Diana or the Duchess of York up for royal inspection on a visit to Balmoral and found wanting.

It's true her sister-in-law had said at Edwin's funeral that marrying her, Rebecca, was probably the smartest thing he had ever done, then adding, after pausing for effect, "But Edwin was always a stupid man."

Privately Rebecca agreed that Edwin had not been the brightest of men and probably if he hadn't caught her on the rebound from a disastrous affair with a randy, penniless and utterly charming Spanish painter she would not have taken his proposal of marriage seriously. Apart from the fact that she felt she was not cut out to be the wife of a diplomat, even a fairly undistinguished and low profile one, she knew he was regarded as just a 'nice old buffer' in need of care and protection and company and she wasn't sure she wanted to spend her life cherishing any old buffer. There had to be something more exciting than this! And she was still nursing those reservations as they made their vows at a discreet register office ceremony which his family, including the offspring from his first marriage, pointedly boycotted.

But in the event it had been a contented marriage, if not a happy one.

She had taken her vows seriously, had come to some kind of accommodation with his disapproving relatives and had ignored the subtle whiffs of anti-Semitism that occasionally surfaced. She had little doubt that there was a good deal more ingrained prejudice buried underneath that surface, but she had never been overly sensitive on that score. The Levitches' philosophy had always been based on the sticks-and-stones theory and, having suffered the sticks and stones of Fascism, which many of them had, they weren't about to be hurt by such relatively mild persecution as they experienced in Britain.

Her one bitter regret was that in devoting so much care to Edwin she hadn't been sufficiently alert to see what was happening to her daughter, Kit. (The girl had rejected her given name, Catherine, as far too fancy, from an early age; which should have prepared Rebecca for the mutinous streak in her daughter that would cause so much damage later.) Because she felt it herself, she understood Kit's rebelliousness against the stuffy conventions of Edwin's family and, understanding it, she hadn't attempted to curb it until it had developed far beyond a simple revolt against social propriety.

Poor, bewildered Edwin had always regarded Kit with a kind of bemused annoyance as if being born should have been sufficient for her, without upsetting the family apple-cart as well. He had been a remote father to his first brood and the arrival at his late age of another small creature to disrupt his comfortable routine and the full-time attention of his second wife did nothing to bring

213

out any latent paternal love. In fact he actively loathed, if not the child, the idea of the child, although he was far too well-mannered to make this loathing evident.

Fortunately both he and Kit, who caught on quickly that so far as he was concerned she was *persona non grata*, learned to keep their distance and he had died before she had managed to scandalise the family and feature in the tabloids by becoming a junkie, a battered wife and a single parent living in a squat. ('Dead Diplomat's Druggie Daughter Discovered Living In Squalor' the *Sun* revealed in a fairly restrained – by its own standards – and damningly truthful report.)

"Well at least I've rescued her from that," Rebecca would console herself. But she realised it wasn't much of a consolation for all the years when she might have been more supportive, before Kit shut her out of her life completely. And she wasn't complacent. Even though Kit and her daughter Vicky were now living under her roof, she had been warned by experts that there was no happy-ever-after guarantee. Kit might seem cured of her addiction, but she could as easily succumb again, both to the drugs and the attraction of brutal, worthless men.

As for Vicky! The child was an animal. Shrewd, quick, predatory and wonderfully likeable when she wanted to be. Rebecca had only met her father twice. Once when he had tried to pressure her into paying him in exchange for keeping his distance from Kit. The second time when her solicitor and a private detective had convinced him that that was not only a bad idea but also a criminal one. Even in these disadvantageous circumstances she could see the seductiveness of the man, how a girl born into a stiflingly conventional family might very well be drawn to the danger and the excitement he generated. There was, Rebecca conceded, probably something of him in Vicky, although the child never spoke of him, as if she had wiped him out of her memory entirely. At first Rebecca had wondered whether perhaps he had abused her, but apparently not; according to Kit the only person upon whom he had vented his violence was herself. He had been an OK father whenever he could be bothered to stick around which was so seldom that it probably accounted for Vicky's non-recall of him.

How strange that it should have been Vicky who had caught the attention of Connie Connor that morning in the precinct. More than a coincidence. Almost as if it were meant; a means of reuniting two old school friends. She shivered. It smacked too cosily of Angela Brazil and all those jolly hockey sticks heroines who vowed to be best friends forever.

However close she and Connie had been as girls it had never been that kind of complacent, open relationship. It had been far more complex; there had been barriers between them, secrets unshared, thoughts undivulged.

From what she had heard about her behaviour on that morning, she wondered if Connie had become another basket case and she didn't feel she could cope with another such lost soul. Kit was her priority.

She realised that she wasn't at all sure she wanted to see Connie now. She had when she had first moved down here, but when Connie hadn't returned her calls she had considered it an omen that they weren't to meet. She wished that David hadn't extended the invitation. She had understood him wanting to see Connie, indeed she had urged it. But he had no right to include her, she thought irritably. But, then, that was David. He'd been away too long. He thought just by lending his presence to an occasion it would make it all right, but he would never be around to have to bother about the repercussions. She loved her brother, but she knew his faults and increasingly wasn't averse to lecturing him about them.

He would laugh and tell her that she had become autocratic and he was probably right; something of the Howards had rubbed off on her after all.

The two bathers were emerging, shivering, from the sea. She could almost see the goose pimples and suddenly felt awkward at observing them so closely without their knowing, as if she were a hidden camera on the lookout

215

for shoplifters in a supermarket. She unhooked the strap of the binoculars and stuffed them into their case. The bathers receded into tiny pinpoints on the beach, still just barely visible from her vantage spot in the garden high on the cliff overlooking the shore.

She turned toward the house, admiring it as she always did when it caught her unawares, with its great white stucco bow arching forward to the cliff edge. Windows looked out onto a railed-in deck that surrounded the upper level of the house and, above that, there was a circular room, like a look-out. It did, indeed, resemble a ship. When she'd first bought it she had merrily considered running a flag up a mast. But, being merry hadn't lasted very long. And the relief of never having to be polite to Edwin's family ever again after his death had been replaced by concern for Kit and Vicky.

Edwin would have considered the house "a bit over the top, old girl," meaning a lot over the top. A house was a house. And a ship was a ship. To build one in the likeness of the other was as absurd as those art deco Twenties teapots modelled in the shape of motor cars and omnibuses. Why she should have taken to it immediately she hadn't understood at all; it wasn't in her temperament to be so impulsive or to feel drawn to anything quite so ostentatious. It was as mysterious as her decision to return to Southdean. And she could only put it down to a sense of liberation, a need to make a gesture of defiance at odds with her own nature and the previous tenor of her life.

A helpful architectural historian had informed Rebecca that she was living in one of the few true follies to which the town could lay claim. An equally helpful surveyor had told her the whole structure of 'The Headland' as the house was named, was suffering from subsidence and would probably slide into the sea before the turn of the millenium. Oddly, that very impermanence appealed to Rebecca. It confirmed her hope and belief that there was an end to everything: the good as well as the bad, the best of times as well as the worst.

She felt a tug at the strap of the binoculars and instinctively tightened her grip on it.

"I want that," shrilled a small, aggrieved voice.

Rebecca looked down at the indignant little creature raring for a fight. She stood four square, legs apart, arms held stiffly away from her body, the hands curled into fists. She was wearing a mini-bikini and dripping water into puddles around her from the indoor swimming pool that was one of The Headland's prize features.

"Well, that's just too bad, Vicky," Rebecca said coolly. "You can't have it. It's for grown-ups. I'll get you a pair of binoculars for little girls sometime."

The child returned her level gaze. "I don't like you Grandma."

"I'm not overly fond of you." It wasn't strictly true. She supposed she should feel a pang of something or other, failing to win the affection of her only grandchild. But children were not her speciality. However, Vicky seemed more like a small adult with an adult's wiles and motives. And on those terms – woman to woman – they got along rather well. They had established a wary, feisty sort of relationship which was beyond the comprehension of her daughter, Kit.

"I want to go home."

"This is your home."

"No it isn't. It's Plum Close," the piercing voice persisted.

"You haven't lived in Plum Close for two years. You know that very well, Vicky," Rebecca replied calmly. She had realised quite soon that the trick with Vicky was not to let her think she could get a rise out of her, just as the little girl had quickly assessed that the power in this establishment lay with her dynamic grandma not with her docile mother. This rapid rapport between them was surprising, because Vicky had only distantly been aware that there was a grandmother lurking somewhere in the background, until suddenly she had been very much in evidence, taking charge of her mother and herself, bringing them to live in this big old house on a cliff.

217

"I *did* like Plum Close," she whispered, changing her tactic.

"I know you did," her grandmother said softly, also changing her tactic.

Vicky closed her eyes tightly, trying to remember Plum Close. It had been cosier and near the shops and it had an agreeably messed-up smell of greasy lino, dusty curtains and dirty washing. And there were people in and out all the time. Strange people who mostly paid her no mind, but didn't bother her either. Sometimes other children, too: stupid, grizzly children, with snotty noses and scabby knees. Had she really liked it? she wondered.

It was different here. Everything smelt clean and flowery and you weren't allowed to leave dirty finger marks on the white walls and had to wipe your feet before setting foot on the cream carpets. The girl who lived in the little flat above the garage and came in every day to cook and clean had a funny name: Dallas! She was all right. Grandma was all right, too, but not all the time. With Grandma you had to be careful. You were only allowed to watch two hours of TV a day and had to pay attention at school.

She opened her eyes, having paid her dues to Plum Close. She felt suddenly cold and was still dripping water.

"Here!" Rebecca wrapped a towel around her and started rubbing it briskly over her bony little body. "You don't really want to go back to Plum Close, do you? Don't you want to see the lady you played games with in McDonald's? The one you told us about. She's coming to see me. This morning. With Uncle David. We were old friends – once. When we weren't much older than you."

"The looney."

"Who said that?"

"The big fat cow in McDonald's."

"We don't say things like that."

"I do."

"Not any more you don't." Rebecca stopped rubbing her down with the towel. "Here. Finish yourself off."

The child's lips trembled and she felt unsure whether to cry – which would bring her mother running – or laugh – which amused her grandmother. She laughed.

"What's she been saying this time?"

Rebecca scrutinised the sad-eyed woman squatting on the steps leading from the French windows to the garden. Kit was only in her mid-twenties but she looked so care-worn, so weary and, something new, so bored, thought Rebecca. She had been quite right to reject her name, Catherine Howard, she reflected. She must have realised that any reference to a queen of England – even a beheaded one – would have been at best embarrassing and at worst ludicrous to a girl who was more at home in a squat than a castle.

"A big fat cow in McDonald's," Vicky repeated with pleasure, casting a challenging eye at her grandmother.

"Oh yes. I remember her. She called the police." Kit seemed to be having difficulty even remembering the incident. "Go inside and wash up," she told Vicky.

"I'm *clean*! I've just had a swim."

"Well, go and wash up again. I want to talk to Grandma."

"Why can't I stay?"

"Because, *I* say so!" The note of command in her grandmother's voice did the trick.

They watched the small figure trotting off, grumbling to herself, into the house. On the way she deliberately kicked out at the ginger cat who was prowling the grounds, stubbed her toe on the stone step and howled loudly in pain that was largely imagined. She turned to look at the two women over her shoulder, a helpful tear trickling down her cheek. "There!" she shouted and flounced inside.

"I should go to her," debated Kit. "She might have hurt herself."

"I doubt it. She's only making a scene. You know that. Or, if you don't, you should. You're her mother."

"Sometimes I think you're more her mother than I

219

am." She didn't sound as if she begrudged Rebecca that role, rather that she was grateful for the switch.

"I suppose this is leading up to something? That's why Vicky was suddenly sent off to wash up. I wish you wouldn't use those American expressions. It's bad enough with David. But he can't help it."

"Mother!" It was unusual for Kit to sound so positive these days. Ever since she had taken the cure she had seemed so listless, so disinterested. "Ma, I can't go on like this. Living here, like a vegetable, dependent on you."

It was a surprise, but not a shock. Rebecca had almost been expecting it. She just hadn't been certain what direction it would take, this little burst of remembered rebellion.

"You didn't do so wonderfully well when you depended on yourself," she replied carefully. "You and what – whatshisname?"

"Clyde. Don't mention him again."

"I didn't. You did." She took her daughter's hands in hers. The skin was rough and the nails jagged and it seemed as if she could feel a whole, wasted life in those hands. "Kit, why don't you just say what you want to say."

"I want to do things, Ma. I could make my own living now. Get a job. Maybe in a restaurant or a catering firm. I can cook. I used to be a good cook – before – well, before all that." She caught the look of concern in her mother's eyes, the fear. "I know what you're thinking. That I'll go straight back to the old life, the dope and stuff, again. I can't tell you I won't. Ever. Right now I hope not. I'm grateful to you for that. Getting off the stuff was hell enough once. I wouldn't want to face it again and I don't want to die young. But that's how I feel *now*. Maybe – out there – it would be different. Maybe I wouldn't cope. But it doesn't alter anything. I was useless then. But I'm useless now too. I *have* to leave, Ma."

Rebecca swallowed hard. She had been anticipating something of the sort, but something more tentative, enlisting her help, her advice, her guidance. But this was so final and part of her respected her daughter for discovering enough strength of character in herself simply to broach the subject, let alone carry it through.

"And what about Vicky?"

But even this didn't appear to shake her daughter's resolve. She had obviously thought everything through very carefully before facing Rebecca. "I'm no good for Vicky. She's smarter, more self-sufficient, than I am already. You know that. She's better off with you. She pays heed to you and you get on together, even though you battle like cat and dog sometimes."

"You mean you're prepared to abandon your child." The words almost gagged in her throat but she had to spell it out brutally.

"No, of course not. Not exactly. But she'd be better off than trailing around with me. She likes the girl who cooks and cleans and she's settling in at the preparatory school—"

"*She* has a name. The girl who cooks and cleans!" That was petty, thought Rebecca. Was that what she was reduced to? Trading petty grievances with her daughter because she couldn't conjure up any lucid arguments?

"There you go again. Putting me in my place as if I were a kid."

"You are a kid, Catherine, in many ways."

"Well then let me grow up, Ma! You've done your duty, rescued me from God knows what sort of shit. If you don't want Vicky to stay then she can come with me. We'll get along." She began to sound as if the idea was, after all, appealing: Kit and Vicky against the world and Grandma.

Sensing the change, Rebecca realised that the last thing she wanted was for Kit to deprive her of a grandchild who was cheeky, exasperating, sly and half adult, but a companion to match her own mettle.

"No, Kit, don't be hasty. Don't let either of us be hasty. If you're determined to go, I suppose I can understand that. It's been two years. Time enough. And – and as

221

for Vicky. I'd be glad if she stayed with me. But you can't just cut yourself off completely again. It wouldn't be fair – to any of us."

"I know, Ma. It's just . . ."

They heard a car pull into the drive. Kit watched her mother stiffen at the sound. "Later, Kit. We'll talk later," she said. And she stood at attention, waiting, wondering why she was feeling so nervous at seeing an old school friend.

"Becky!"

"Connie!"

"You look good."

"So do you."

They giggled like girls, shrill and full of themselves.

"You were never a good liar."

"But you always were."

As David Levitch observed them, feeling, like his niece, superfluous, it was as if the past had swallowed up the present and everything was as it had been thirty years ago.

Chapter Nineteen

It had been Sam's idea, this get-together to celebrate Holly's first sizeable role in the Chichester Festival season and, although no one actually said it, an acknowledgement too of Connie's apparent return to the land of the living. One happy family and its assorted appendages. A healing process, a reconciliation, a means of exorcising the tragic death of the absent member, Colin, and recalling only benevolent memories of him. That had been the original thought.

But the occasion seemed to have been hijacked by Lewis Diamond. It was he who took charge of the seating in the tiny theatre in the round and then managed to get them re-seated because they were too close to what was a mere step up to the stage. It was he who bought the programmes, cheeked the pretty girl who was selling them and politely enquired if any one was so crass as to want a box of chocolates – Karen, who was snacking for two, did. And then it was he who let slip he had booked a private room in a nearby restaurant a client of his had recommended for supper after the show. He hoped Sam didn't mind, but he knew what hell it was getting something decent to eat late at night in these provincial towns.

"It's a cathedral city," Amy had muttered furiously. She wondered why he was being so embarrassingly proprietorial when it wasn't even *his* family or *his* party. And then she realised that perhaps he was as embarrassed as she was, aware that this supposed reconciliation was, for them, a parting. This was his way of trying to make it as pleasant as possible, but for once his good taste had failed him. He seemed merely pushy and patronising. A city slicker showing the yokels how it should be done. And the infuriating thing about it was that Sam *didn't* mind. If Connie minded she didn't reveal it. And Karen, nibbling Bendicks bitter chocolate mints, couldn't have cared less, and rather looked forward to a lavish supper that she hadn't had to cook herself, even if it did involve being sociable to Sam's baffling family.

"Didn't he used to work in your mother's company?" Sam whispered in Amy's ear. "Nice chap, your young man." (He studiously avoided passing judgement on the unknown quantity – David Levitch – Connie had brought with her who was being extra solicitous to Karen.)

Dear Sam, she thought, better get it over with fast. "Yes – and no. Yes he used to work for Mum. No, he's not my young man. We've – split up." There, that wasn't so bad, she told herself, half believing it.

He looked at her with that old, wise expression she remembered as a child; the kind of expression you could drown your sorrows in. And then quite suddenly, in the middle of this fraught gathering, she found herself wondering whether perhaps that was all it was: just an expression with nothing very profound behind it. "I'm sorry," he murmured hurriedly.

Sorry for what? Her and Lewis? Or . . .? She glanced across at Connie and Lewis who were chatting as people did who hadn't seen each other for some time and had once been quite close. Whatever they were saying they were being studiedly nonchalant about it, smiling a lot and joking and carefully avoiding any physical contact. And as she watched them, she knew that the closeness they'd once known had been more than that of business colleagues. How could she have been so dense not to realise that Lewis's previous reluctance to see Connie again had been tinged with anxiety about how her mother might react at meeting a former lover. But now, of course, it wouldn't matter. He didn't have to conceal anything from her or anyone else. After tonight, he would be out of her life.

"They still make an attractive couple, don't they?" For the first time she detected a hint of malice in Sam's voice and she understood that what had come as a disturbing discovery to her tonight Sam had probably always known. But before she could even think of something, anything, to say, he was fussing over Karen, guiding her carefully up the stairs of the theatre to the seating that Lewis deemed more suitable. The house was only half full which, at the Minerva, meant only a couple of hundred or so people. The buzz of pre-show anticipation was distinctly muted, apart from a large couple in full evening dress who were dead centre front row and talked loudly about theatrical concepts and images and instinctual constructs.

"I've never been here before. It looks very Heath Robinson to me," said Karen complacently, surveying the exposed spotlights and metal girders, bare, uncurtained stage and minimal set dressing. She cradled her bulging stomach as if protecting it from the dangerous influence of such avant-garde pretension. This was not her milieu and, rather than allow herself to feel unsettled in it, she had decided to sink into a comfortably comatose pregnant mode which was quite unlike her usual briskly practical self.

Connie thumbed through the programme. It wasn't right. Not right at all. In the closeness of the small theatre she began to get that old suffocating feeling. It was partly mental, but physical too, as if her oxygen supply was being slowly reduced. Perhaps it had all been too much. Perhaps she was expecting too much of herself too soon, not merely turning over a new leaf in her life but embarking on a new book. Meeting Lewis Diamond after all these years and trying to be casual about it. Seeing David Levitch again and Becky and those long hours they'd spent re-discovering each other and, in doing so perhaps, discovering themselves.

She had talked to Becky about Colin as she had never talked to anyone else: "I always thought there would be time to make good on the things I wasn't doing or feeling for him. And then you realise the only time is now and later is too late." And Becky had understood because it had so nearly been too late for her own neglected child, Kit: "I mustn't let it happen again, Con, and I could so easily." They joked how it was like the halt helping the blind, the two of them, failed mothers sharing their guilts and learning from each other, just a little.

And now here was Amy and Sam and Karen, all behaving not quite naturally, strangers who were vaguely familiar, putting on party manners that concealed more than they revealed. She hadn't been surprised when Amy turned up with Lewis; it had seemed just another item in the chapter of oddities that had categorised the past few days. She wondered how successful she and Lewis had been in covering up the nature of their relationship and thought, probably not very.

And Sam trying not to appear as if he were sizing up what had once been his opposition, David Levitch, while Karen uncharacteristically preened and beamed and enjoyed the indulgences due to an expectant mother.

Only David appeared quite at ease with the company, the surroundings and himself. It was the same as he had been at the seedy disco by the pier and the unprepossessing Indian restaurant. Nothing and no one seemed *faze* to ~~phase~~ him. He had talked knowledgeably to Sam about horticulture; to Amy about financial consultancy; he argued the merits of hard versus soft sell advertising with Lewis and commiserated with Karen about the understandable but groundless fears of rearing a new baby as if he'd been nappy-changer in chief in his own household, which Connie seriously doubted. She supposed when he met Holly he would instinctively put his finger on the underlying meaning of the show they were about to see and the problems of staging it.

She was conscious of his physical presence beside her, the warmth of his body through the slub silk of his tailored jacket which met all the requirements of the occasion: summery, eveningy, but not too formal. He gripped her hand.

His genial smile didn't prepare her for the brutal

directness of his observation: "Sam I can understand, but Lewis!" And he kept on smiling genially, so that anyone not overhearing would suppose he were making some trivially engaging remark about nothing very much. She imagined this was how spies must pass on secret information in public.

"What *can* you mean?" she replied, hoping she sounded suitably cutting.

He kept smiling. "C'mon, Con, you know exactly what I mean. Sam's a great guy. But Lewis! Screwing younger men! You!"

What was the use of denying it? Maybe former lovers give off a special odour when they're together, like cats establishing their territory. "If you dare say 'toy boy', I'll scream."

"No you won't." Still smiling. "And no I won't. He's a smart young man with a big future I'd say. No klutz. No toy boy. Too bad about him and Amy."

"Is there *nothing* you miss?" Acidly.

"Not a lot."

"You really are insufferable, David Levitch. But then, I suppose, you always were. I was just too thick to see it."

She tugged her hand out of his grasp and he gave it up too readily. She searched the programme for the page in which there was a small, practically unrecognisable photograph of Holly and a potted biography which seemed thin even by budding actor standards: bits in *EastEnders* and *Emmerdale*, four episodes in *The Archers*, a week on the Edinburgh fringe in an obscure Latvian folk-play, a Spirit in *The Tempest* and a lady-in-waiting in *Henry VIII* at the National.

If she concentrated really hard on this meagre résumé of Holly's career so far she wouldn't have to acknowledge that she was part of this company and if she breathed deeply the sense of being stifled would evaporate. And then, mercifully, the lights would dim and she could turn her attention to what was going on on the stage.

A tall, thin West Indian hurried through the door at

227

the foot of the stairs, caught sight of Amy, nodded and mouthed something about "Holly" and "after".

"Who's that?" whispered Lewis, intrigued.

"Holly's fella," said Amy and felt lonely and sorry for herself. Why Holly? she thought. Why not me? Lewis seemed not to notice or perhaps he just didn't want to appear to notice.

Then two pianos struck up a medley of 'Where Have All The Flowers Gone?' and a lot of Kurt Weill. When it came to 'September Song' Connie hummed it very softly to herself under her breath; the autumnal mood of the lyrics reflected her own mood or so it seemed to her, until it suddenly struck her as patently absurd to liken herself to some old randy male chauvinist who was reaching the end of his days and on the look out for a young raver with whom to share them. "Stupid!" she muttered and the woman in front shushed her.

On reflection, thought Connie, it hadn't been a wildly wonderful idea – although Sam had proposed it and Lewis had commandeered it from the best of motives. Forced gatherings never were.

The show, in which twentieth century role models interacted musically with each other, was imaginative but under-rehearsed and seriously needed the talents of first rate revue artists to give it lift off. Holly, perhaps too conscious that her family was out front, muffed some of her lyrics and almost fell foul of her sequined train while making her entrance as Mata Hari – or Atam Irah as, for some obscure reason, she was addressed by the rest of the cast, perhaps to denote the deviousness of her calling as a secret agent in the First World War.

In consequence she tried to beg off the planned supper party afterwards, pleading a headache brought on by her elaborate head-dress, but she was persuaded to change her mind by Sam "as a favour to your mother". Which made Connie furious because she could perfectly understand Holly's reluctance to face their united – but hardly honest – congratulations on a brilliant performance.

228

"If Holly really doesn't want to come," she said, "it's not fair to pressure her."

And that in turn angered Amy who turned on her mother with the observation that the least she could do was to show a little interest in her younger daughter's career, a deliberate misunderstanding which probably had something to do with a delayed reaction to the realisation that her mother and Lewis had once had an affair.

Sam looked hurt. Lewis looked uncomfortable. Karen looked hungry. And David Levitch looked amused.

It was John Branco who provided the calming influence, possibly because the only vested interest he had in the occasion was Holly.

"I think," he said quietly, "it would be best if you go ahead to the restaurant and I'll talk Holly round. She's – she's a bit upset."

He ushered them out of the theatre in a comradely kind of way, but very much in command. He winked at Amy and kissed Connie brazenly on the cheek, a liberty she accepted with great pleasure having decided at first sighting that John Branco was 'a good thing' and that Holly should hang on to him.

"Who *is* that guy?" said David. "Makes you feel like a fucking kid."

A Chichester matron raised her eyebrows in passing.

"Yes," said Connie. "Yes he does, doesn't he?" But whereas David sounded aggrieved at being treated like a child by an officious young black man, she sounded as if it were an agreeable indulgence.

"He's a terrible snob," said Amy. "Well, not really, but you have to watch it. He can be touchy." She still felt a little bruised after her first encounter with him.

By the time Holly and John joined them in the rather pokéy private room at the back of the restaurant, Holly had regained some of her usual ebullience. After all, it was only a show and only one performance in the run of the show. She could hold that thought for the rest of the evening, although she knew in the small hours, hopefully curled up in John Branco's arms,

229

she would curse herself for not coming up to scratch on stage.

He pushed her forward gently to the centre of the room where they were all standing around awkwardly holding a glass of wine in one hand and a nibble of ricotta cheese puff or a devil on horseback in the other. (Lewis from experience had elected for a buffet as simpler for late catering and less taxing than a formal sit down dinner with everyone making polite conversation while failing to make up their minds what they wanted to eat.)

"Go on!" John urged Holly. She looked at him gratefully. (Bloody love! thought Amy).

"There's something I have to say," she began, tentatively at first, then more assured. "I was lousy tonight. I know it. You know it. And the director of the show sure as hell knows it – there'll be lots of notes on Monday."

She paused just long enough for a laugh, timing it better than any bit of business she'd enacted on stage earlier. "So, if you don't mind," she went on, "let's forget it. If *you* don't lie, *I* won't lie. Just – I *can* be better." She looked pleased with herself for getting through it as if she knew she'd acquitted herself well at a dreaded audition. "Now if someone doesn't give me a large drink soon I'll take my custom elsewhere."

Perfect! Just perfect! Connie could have hugged her daughter and decided she probably would. Of all her three children Holly had been the one who had somehow escaped her. She had made no demands and, by the same token, she had expected no demands to be made on her. Holly had simply removed herself from Connie, from Sam, from Amy – especially after Colin left home. Not physically, but certainly mentally and emotionally. She had pursued a course far more radical and lonely than that of Amy. She had asked nothing of anyone, somehow insinuating herself into the world of the theatre by her own efforts. And even on the evidence of this evening's clumsy performance it was clear that she had the makings. Not of a star, maybe. But of a good, serviceable trouper. If she had burst out into a chorus of 'I Am What I Am' Connie would have applauded her. Holly was what she was. And I never even noticed it before, she marvelled.

After that everyone felt easier. It came close to being the cheery gathering Sam had envisaged and he stood there smiling in an avuncular way cautiously nursing a lager in anticipation of the drive home with his precious cargo.

He nudged Connie and nodded toward Holly who was being delightful to David, roguish to Lewis, placatory to Amy, charming to Karen and patently worshipful to John Branco.

"Maybe we did something right," murmured Sam.

"Holly! I'd no idea," said Connie. "When I think of all those wasted years."

"If it's any consolation I feel the same." He helped himself to a plateful of seafood pâté and toast triangles with a dollop of caviar on the side.

Connie watched him distribute the food in a neatly symmetrical pattern around the plate. She didn't feel hungry, but consoled herself with the thought that Karen seemed to be eating for all of them. In her bones she knew Sam was about to deliver himself of something that required a certain amount of thought and a good deal of nourishment.

"Damned decent of that chap, Lewis, to lay on all this," he said finally.

"Conscience," said Connie sourly.

"You mean him and Amy?"

Oh, come on, Sam, out with it! She decided to give him a push. "Well, what else? Sam, Lewis and I were a while ago, years. Colin was still alive." The moment she'd said it she shivered. If it hadn't been for Lewis and her maybe he still would be alive. She hoped to God it wasn't that simple. Perhaps only Hubbard Crowther knew the truth. And how much of that truth would he be prepared to tell her?

She bit into a decorative radish to show willing and then remembered she didn't like radishes. "Ugh! Sam?"

"I suppose I guessed," he admitted.

231

"Only it didn't matter, did it, Sam? Be honest! You had Karen by then. I had the business. Our marriage was just a convenient arrangement – until it became an inconvenience and then we did, as they say, the civilised thing. Who's that extraordinary woman – girl – or is it man?"

"Isn't she the one who played Mae West?"

"Nye – you made it!" Holly allowed herself to be clasped to the enormous bosom of Naomi O'Dowd. "This . . ." she spread her arms to embrace everyone – ". . . is my family. And some other people." She was sounding as if the drink someone had poured her had been more monumental than merely large. That and the adrenalin of being centre stage even if it was only in the small private room of an out of the way restaurant; a lethal combination.

She held out her glass for a refill.

"You've had enough, kid." John Branco took the glass from her and put his hand under her elbow to steady her.

The look that passed between him and Naomi O'Dowd was one of deep distaste. "Party pooper!" she said, then sidled across the floor, hips swaying, in the direction of Lewis who looked momentarily panic-stricken until David rescued him by steering Nye toward the buffet while complimenting her on her remarkable impersonation of Mae West whose old movies he watched all the time. He kept on talking and she kept on listening, spell-bound or dumb-struck. Either way it relieved what might have been a tense moment.

"Extraordinary man!" said Sam.

"You think so?" Connie smiled. "He's just playing a game. This – all this – it's just a joke, a diversion, for him. A sort of charade."

He looked at her, puzzled, but she knew, as she passed judgement on David Levitch, that she was right. That's all this was to him: an amusement. She, Becky, Kit, Vicky, all of them, were just players in the show, not serious people with whom he lived his life. That was

232

something quite different. And when he'd finished giving his performance he'd be gone, just as he had when he was barely more than a boy and hadn't quite perfected this illusory role he occasionally played for his own pleasure. And, knowing this, quite suddenly, she felt released from the burden of having to assess her feelings about David Levitch. There was no point. He was an ageing Puck. The comparison made her laugh out loud and she had to assure Sam that she was perfectly sober.

"It's time we left." John Branco was standing beside her, with Holly cosseted in his arms. "And we haven't even talked."

"Is that important?" said Connie. "To you?"

"I think so," he replied solemnly.

"I'd like . . . there's so much I want to say to Holly. Oh, not about the show. She's good. She must know that. Everyone has an off night. But about so many other things. Tonight – it wasn't the night for it, was it?"

She was talking directly to him as if Holly wasn't there and he didn't seem to think that strange. Holly, in any case, was half asleep.

"It's Sunday, tomorrow. Why don't you come over to lunch? I cook up a mean *chilli con carne* – if you can stand it. Amy knows where we live, if you don't."

"I'm glad – about you and Holly. You know . . ." She started to be serious and decided it wasn't the time for that either. "I'm a very unsuitable mother."

"So, I've heard. Mine isn't. I'm not sure whether that makes me lucky or not. Tomorrow then?"

She nodded and kissed Holly who yawned. If she'd heard any of the preceding conversation she didn't show it.

Maybe she had been wrong, thought Connie. Not a brilliant idea. But it had turned out not badly, after all.

Lewis had driven Amy back to London. David managed to persuade Naomi O'Dowd that the party was over, although she insisted it hadn't even begun and she knew a place where the party went on all night if he felt like it. He declined with such grace that she gave every appearance of believing he really was disappointed not to accept and would have done so if he hadn't been responsible for seeing someone else – Connie – home. Which was a lie, but a white one.

Karen overindulged herself on French apple tart with hazelnut cream and retired to the ladies' room, emerging relieved and rosy-cheeked. Sam looked worried.

"When's it due?" asked Connie, equally concerned.

"Soon," trilled Karen, descending on the remains of the buffet before the waiters could whip it away. "I've had a great evening," she beamed. "And so has Tommy or Tilly Tucker." She patted her tummy while Sam restrained her from demolishing the rest of the French apple tart.

Chapter Twenty

"What did she say?"

John Branco was chopping and tossing and decanting from tins the makings of a *salad niçoise* in the chaotic kitchen of the digs he shared with Holly and the others in Chichester. He had cleared and cleaned the area on the work surface for the job, first scrupulously washing and rinsing the implements he needed which tended to be shoved away after use with not too careful a regard for cleanliness. The casual attitude to hygiene of his peers in this country went against the grain of his own upbringing and they, in return, were amazed that he should be so picky; it didn't fit in at all with their assumptions about how Jamaicans should behave.

"And stop stealing the olives!" He slapped her hand lightly. "Well, did you? Phone her?"

She watched him meticulously covering the wooden bowl of *niçoise* with snappie and then measuring out the uncooked pilau rice to garnish the *chilli con carne*. He seemed to be completely absorbed in what he was doing.

"She won't come," Holly sighed. "Dede says if Mum wants to see her and the baby she takes him to the park every Sunday afternoon. But she refuses to make a thing about it. I can't say I blame her."

"You mean *Nye* can't say she blames her?"

"What is this about you and Nye?" she said angrily. "And, come to that, what is it about you and my mother? You've only met her once and everything you've probably heard about her . . ."

". . . From you . . ."

235

". . . From me . . . OK . . . falls pretty short of complimentary."

"Maybe that's why. I always was a sucker for lost causes." He grinned, a wide open grin showing what seemed like more than an average quota of dazzling white teeth. Then his expression was suddenly serious. It was a knack of his to which she had become accustomed, switching from sunny to solemn in a split second.

"Nye's not good for you," he said.

"Why? Because she's Irish?" She latched on to the least likely cause for his dislike of Naomi O'Dowd.

He ignored that. "Because she's a meddler. She winds people up. You've seen it here. She finds the weakness and then puts the screws on, only she kids you she's on your side and when she goes too far its only Nye being Nye, a great joker, doesn't mean half she says."

"You're not being fair," she said, not wishing to prolong the argument. A lot of what he said was true and, if she hadn't been so in love with him, she would probably have felt affronted that he should think her so blind that she was incapable of seeing Nye's faults. But what he couldn't understand was the friendship that could exist between women that wasn't based on perfect harmony, but on something deep and staunch that accepted the other warts and all. If it came to some terrible, unimaginable crunch, she would trust her life to Nye as Nye would to her. No! No-nonsense, masculine John Branco wouldn't appreciate that. She rather hoped it was just the expression of some kind of jealousy.

She nicked a surplus olive and an anchovy before he could stop her. "Nye thinks I have no right to betray Dede's confidence. About her and Colin and baby Colin. Women's solidarity." She smiled. Now who's winding who up? She anticipated his argument: "Women's solidarity doesn't seem to extend to your mother."

But, again, he refused to bite. He shrugged. "Suit yourself. She's your mother. See how you make out together today. Then it's up to you to decide whether to tell her."

236

"I wish you'd known Colin," she reflected.

"I'm glad I didn't. A weak, privileged boy who'd rather commit suicide than face up to what he'd done. Can you imagine how stupid that would seem to people in the third world struggling against poverty and hardship and just trying to keep alive? How stupid and wasteful! It makes me angry."

She sucked, thoughtfully, on the limp little fish. What was the point of trying to make him understand her dead brother? Instead she merely remarked that he was a lost cause, too. Just like Connie.

It was all so vivid, her memory of him on that last day. The day he told her he was leaving home. She had seen him on and off after that, in secret, not often and usually in the company of Hub or Dede whom he had brought to the house now and then. For a time in her early teens she had had quite a crush on Hub, but then she had been given to crushes on teachers, pop stars, soccer players, even rising politicians of the left persuasion, but they never lasted for long.

That's when she had loved her brother most. He always had time to listen, to advise, to tell her she was being silly in the nicest way and to encourage her ambitions in the most positive way. He was a better actor than she but he had never had the drive to pursue that career, so he had urged her to indulge her passion for the theatre on his behalf. "As a sort of surrogate me. You can do it, Holly. You've talent, but more than that you've tenacity, you'll take the hard knocks and they won't get you down. I couldn't. I'd just collapse."

She'd known what he had meant. Without him even confiding as much, she knew that Connie's indifference to him had somehow drained him of that self-confidence she and Amy had in abundance in their different ways. Perhaps he'd demanded more of her mother, she used to reason, and that made her casualness toward him the more demoralising.

And it was worse for him because for so long he made excuses for her, trotting out the reasons to which they all paid lip service – Sam, too. "She's so busy all the time. She's so successful." Even – "She's doing it all for us." The big lie!

Once when he had been reciting that familiar litany she had turned on him: "She's doing it for herself, dummy!" And he had looked so dreadfully pained that she should try to puncture this self-deception of his. But then Colin could never bring himself to be unkind. That was his problem. The story of him as a very little boy wanting to 'do good' had become part of family folklore, deteriorating over the years into a kind of charming joke.

But it had never been a joke to Colin. "If only I could find a way," he would say to Holly who responded to the tone rather than the sentiment which, as yet, she couldn't comprehend. But she enjoyed the secrecy of being a confidante. And when she learned later, as they were sharing their grief over his death, that he had confided in Amy, too, she was quite vexed that he should have divided his trust between them. Over the distance of time she realised that Colin had used his sisters – one older and mature, the other younger and adoring – to dole out the compassion and concern he couldn't win from his mother.

When she could bring herself to be clear-eyed about her brother, which wasn't often, she would admit that he was a problem; the kind of son of whom parents might despair. He drifted from one passionate obsession to another. He worked part-time for one admirable cause only to abandon it when another more attractive admirable cause surfaced. When Sam, patiently, taxed him on what he intended to do with his life he would 'talk' an interesting career but somehow he never got around to following it up. He seemed content to do whatever job was at hand, thus earning enough money to qualify as work, while giving freely of his spare time to 'doing good'. He was, Holly supposed, what was known as a dilettante and she loved him all the more because he was different, not like the rest of them.

And she was always there to listen even if she didn't always understand. "If I had a skill I could really help. Join one of the aid organisations overseas. I've been thinking. Maybe it's not too late. Maybe I could try for medicine. I know it's years of study. And perhaps I haven't got what it takes. But I can apply myself if I have a goal; make up the necessary qualifications for medical school. I'm going to speak to Dad. He'll approve. Mum too – don't you think?"

She could see him now as he spoke, eyes so bright with enthusiasm and yearning. And she felt happy for him, even though she had heard it all before, watched the idea take root, flourish and then wither away and die.

Once it had been civil engineering that would be his entrée to a better, useful life. Once it had been painting, the arts. Another time it had been trekking round the world with Hubbard Crowther and writing a book about it, the funds donated to Oxfam or Save The Children. And always she had believed him because he so desperately wanted to believe himself.

But this time he had sounded more positive. Maybe this time he had found the answer and his new dream would actually bear fruit. If it did she would be happy for him, not simply because he would have found a career he could apply himself to, but because he would no longer be so preoccupied with gaining his mother's attention. Even as his young sister she had wisely seen things of which he didn't appear to be aware.

And then, only a day or two afterwards, he had stood there in her bedroom. She could recall every detail. Her school notebooks open at the page posing an algebraic problem. The screen of the home computer her parents had bought her for Christmas staring non-committally at them both. The busy Lizzie on the windowsill that needed watering. The family photograph hanging lopsidedly on the wall and a new poster of Michael Jackson strutting his stuff pinned to the cork notice board she had rigged up above her bed. And Colin with that crazy look about him. Crazy and cold. She remembered thinking how young he

239

appeared, much, much younger than she, hardly older than the little boy who wanted to 'do good'.

"I'm leaving," he had said numbly. Just that! Nothing about the row with his parents that, she later realised, he had deliberately contrived to disguise the real reason for the row.

She had sat there, stunned, trying to muster the right arguments, to do the right thing that might prevent him from taking the step that, she instinctively knew, would take him away from them forever. But the words wouldn't come. Not the ones that worked. Only the pointless protestations that sounded lame even to her ears.

"But what about your plans? Where will you go? What will you do? Don't go, Colin! It'll come all right, whatever it is."

"It won't," he had said and there was steel in his voice that had never been there before. And she knew that nothing she or anyone else could say would budge a determination that he had probably never experienced in his life before. "I didn't tell them about my plans." He bit down hard on his lower lip and she could see a spot of blood where his teeth had punctured the skin. "It's him – and her." He said it quietly, introspectively, as if talking to himself.

She looked up at him, baffled. "Him? Her? Who?"

"Our *mother* and that man! Lewis Diamond. Her toady! Her lover! I heard them." Then he hesitated suddenly appalled at the burden he was placing on his sister. "I shouldn't have said that. Forget it, Holly. Try to forget it."

Fat chance, she thought, and she continued to stare at him, not baffled now but bewildered.

"You see, it's better I go. I should have ages ago."

He cupped her face in his hands and massaged the high cheek bones she had inherited from Connie with his fingertips, very gently and tenderly. "I'm so sorry, Holly. I shouldn't put it all on to you like this. Don't tell Amy. I think, being older, it might bother her more. It's our secret. Promise." It was hard to follow his reasoning

240

but she promised all the same, while suppressing the uncomfortable feeling that her brother was putting on a performance and casting her as the audience. Perhaps that was the only way he could summon up the courage to follow through on what he had decided to do.

"After a while, when I've sorted myself out, I'll be in touch."

"Maybe you'll come back. It'll all blow over."

"No, it won't." He hugged her tightly and she clung to him until he firmly disengaged himself. There were tears in his eyes. "Don't say anything, Holly. You can't make me change my mind. Hub . . ."

"Oh, *Hub*! Yes, well, whatever Hub says goes, doesn't it?" she said flatly.

"Don't take it out on Hub. We just talk. That's all."

"It seems – it seems such a stupid reason for chucking everything," she said. And it did. It truly did. At school, half the girls she knew had parents who were divorced or committing adultery; nothing much in the family was sacred from keen-witted schoolgirls who watched late night TV and 18-plus videos on the quiet.

"I suppose it is," he admitted.

And she knew that whatever he had seen or imagined between their mother and Lewis Diamond was just the final, demeaning factor, the culmination of the years of slights and oversights that led to this act of defiance.

"It's childish," she said, seeing this defiance for what it was. A small boy's revenge: now they'll be sorry! "Like committing suicide."

"Don't say that." He sounded angry and she suspected she might have articulated what he had actually considered.

"Colin!"

He interpreted the note of alarm in her voice correctly.

"Of course not, silly." He patted her head paternally, like Sam used to, to show how absurd her fear had been.

"What about money? I've a bit. In the Halifax."

He smiled, the rather lordly, lofty smile of an elder brother refusing the pittance offered by a young sister. "I've plenty. Enough anyway. Hub knows a place I can stay for a bit. In London. And some people who can help me get a job. I'll be fine. You see. I won't take the car. It's hers really anyway."

"They'll try to bring you back."

"Now who's being stupid!" He laughed. "They can't. I'm not under-age."

Like me, she thought. Except you're the kid, not me. And then, after another quick hug and a plea that she look after Jagger, he was gone.

She was left contemplating the lopsided family on the wall and Michael Jackson and the non-committal computer screen which became indelibly interwoven in her memory with her sense of loss and her bitterness toward her mother for causing it.

After a fashion he *had* been all right. At least so they had assumed until the day his body had been found at the foot of Beachy Head. For a while he had kept in touch as he had promised. He hadn't let them suffer the anguish of not knowing where or how he was. The habit of kindness, sensitivity to other people's feelings, hadn't deserted him.

There had been no family post mortems after his departure. There seemed to be an unspoken agreement that it should be passed off as a natural move for a young man, as if he had been planning and discussing it with them for ages. After all, if he had gone to university he would be just as absent as he was now. Sam, Holly and Amy kept their private feelings private and Beattie was too far over the edge to understand what had happened. If they expected histrionics from Connie they were disappointed – or relieved. She simply blanked out on the subject of Colin, giving the callous impression that she had more important things to think about than an errant son.

Perhaps they had been too ready to accept the impression for the reality; perhaps the strain of keeping up a front had triggered the disintegration that followed; perhaps if they had reached out to Connie then things would have turned out differently. Sometimes Holly wondered about that and she knew Amy did, too. But not often. They had their own lives to live.

Holly kept her promise not to tell Amy about the reason behind Colin's sudden decision to leave home, although it always seemed a pretty futile promise to her. But it was the least she could do for Colin, to honour his trust and look after Jagger. She had reneged on the latter, but then Jagger was the most cosseted dog she knew, particularly since Karen took over the household and her mother's place.

She looked up at John who was efficiently laying up the table for three. They had the kitchen to themselves. The others were either sleeping in, eating out or tactfully allowing Holly a privacy she hadn't courted in coping with a visit from an awkward parent. They all had them. Awkward parents. Even Nye. But her reason for keeping her distance was John Branco about whom she and Holly agreed to differ.

"I still wish you'd known him. Colin!" she said.

He didn't need to answer her. The doorbell rang and there was Connie, arms full of parcels and bottles of wine, waving off a taxi.

"Here. Let me." John started to relieve her of the goodies. His voice, thought Connie, was soft and mellow, touched with sunshine.

"Beware of mothers bearing gifts," Holly muttered behind him.

"What a wonderful place," Connie enthused, inspecting the disarray in the hall and sitting-room as if she were on a privileged tour of Buckingham Palace.

She's made up her mind to be nice today, thought Holly. "You can't be serious!" she said.

Connie screwed up her nose. "No. It's awful. But at your age awful and wonderful are relative terms." She linked arms with Holly. "I'm here to eat *chilli con carne* not humble pie. Granted. I *should* eat humble pie. God knows!" She took a deep breath exhaling slowly and Holly realised she had been rehearsing this greeting in the taxi all the way from Southdean and maybe through the night. "You know what they say about junkies and alcoholics: one day at a time. I'm trying, Holly!" She hesitated. "Help me!" She didn't appear to mind that she was revealing so much of herself not only to her daughter but to John Branco, a stranger, too.

Holly scrutinised her mother's face with its watchful, anxious expression and she felt the light pressure of John's hand on her shoulder, perhaps trying to tell her something. She tried to recall all that anger she had felt toward Connie. It was still there, wound up in a tight ball of grievance, but she was aware of something else, too, something Colin would have understood.

Compassion for a soul in search of redemption, he would have explained in the preachy language he tended to use in defining the terms of 'doing good'. To Holly it was a simpler urge that was overriding the anger: an urge to make amends. It was time.

"It's time," she echoed her thought out loud and then was surprised to feel a suspicious wetness around her eyes. Ordinarily she would have been embarrassed with herself for being so ridiculously *female*. But now she grimaced and wiped her eyes with a tissue. "It's your damned chilli," she said to John and they celebrated by cracking open Connie's bottle of decent chablis.

It would never be totally right, Holly thought, as they drank the wine and ate the salad and the chilli and picked at the cheeses. There would always be a wariness in her relationship with Connie, a fear that this new-found warmth and openness in her mother were just a sham. You couldn't forget that easily and maybe it would take a nobler person than she to forgive. But one day at a time wasn't too much to ask. She began to feel more relaxed in Connie's company than she had since she was a dependent little girl.

And it was as if Connie wanted nothing concealed. She joked about her breakdown and the folly of being so bound up in business that you ignored the important things of life. She made John laugh with her story about finding herself in Southdean wearing odd shoes and almost being arrested for kidnapping a child and she admitted it did sound pretty funny now but that it wasn't at the time.

She talked about Holly's career and Amy's and Sam's marriage to Karen and the unexpected reunion with someone from her past, David Levitch. And then she talked about Colin and her search for Hubbard Crowther. It all came pouring out, not wildly, but in a measured and controlled way. John and Holly sat opposite her, holding hands, listening, not saying much, just punctuating the recital with the odd comment here and there.

Suddenly she stopped, aware that they were looking at her with a disconcerting concentration. She wondered how foolish she must seem to them with their brave, arrogant youth.

She glanced at her watch. "Goodness, is that the time! I've been running on so much. Such a long time . . ."

She heaved a deep sigh and pressed the palm of her hand to her forehead. "That's not what I meant. Tell me, Mr Branco, John, how do you say sorry to people – without saying sorry?"

He didn't seem surprised at the nature of her question or the fact that she should address it to him instead of Holly. "I suppose," he said thoughtfully. "You don't – say sorry. You do something about it."

She nodded. "Yes. Yes, you do, don't you. I think in a sense reaching out to that child in McDonald's was the beginning of doing something for me. And then finding out she was the grandchild of my best friend at school. A kind of fate, don't you think? I couldn't explain why I feel this but I think that demon child did me a service. The direction of your life is poised on a series of moments of truth. Somehow – God knows how – she forced me to face my truth that morning and the devilish thing is I'd swear she knew it. When I met her again with Becky and her daughter she didn't act like you'd have expected a child to act toward me after that day in the precinct. I'd have been prepared for that. She looked at me, very grave, and said: 'They said you couldn't help it, but you can, can't you?' Isn't that the oddest, grown-up thing? I'd vaguely heard people saying I was off my head and couldn't help it when I fainted. Of course she had picked that up, but then to tell me I *could* help it. Maybe that's what's OK about life: in the end you can usually help it – if you really want to."

She lowered her eyes from their earnest faces. Now she had gone too far, she thought. Better to have kept it light and easy, leave them laughing.

When she looked up again she caught an exchange of glances between them, an unspoken decision. Holly got up. "More coffee, Mum?"

"No, I should be going. I expect you've a million things you want to do on your day off."

"Mum – there's something I think you should know."

Brace yourself, Connie, it can't be that bad. Can it?

The girl looked uncommonly serious. Connie noticed that John Branco was smiling and nodding slightly as if he had won an argument and was offering moral support.

"It's – it's about Colin. Sort of."

Chapter Twenty-One

It took her a few minutes to find her sea legs after speeding to Southdean on the back of John Branco's Harley Davidson. As she leant on the handlebars she felt the *chilli con carne* debating with the *salad niçoise* whether to erupt magnificently into the kerb or to settle down amicably and disperse less explosively in the normal manner.

"Are you OK?" he asked.

She gulped, felt less nauseous, and nodded. "There's a first time for everything."

"Chilli?"

"Riding pillion on a motorbike."

"You haven't lived."

"You're probably right." She regarded him respectfully as he removed his crash helmet. "You're a rare bird, John Branco."

"Not really. I'm just another first for you."

"It was you who persuaded Holly to tell me about the boy, wasn't it?"

"She didn't need too much persuading."

"Why?"

He scratched his close-cropped head. "I'm not sure. I figured from what she'd told me you probably deserved – a lift, I guess. And maybe the kid needed grandparents."

"That was a pretty mighty assumption for you to make. Maybe I'd be appalled at the idea of being a grandmother." ("But you weren't," he interjected. "Were you?") "Maybe the boy would be better off without grandparents," she went on.

He grinned, showing that electric white chorus of teeth. "Just another interfering nigger!"

"You can't get a rise out of me that way," she said complacently. "I'm colour blind. You and Holly? Is it serious?"

He looked guarded and started to speak, but she smiled and waved her hand in front of her as if warding off a confidence she wasn't entitled to. "Just another interfering honky!"

"Wow, lady! Where'd you pick up that kind of talk? From some Second World War GI?"

"Out of date?"

"Centuries!"

"You don't like being serious, do you?"

"Oh, I can be real serious. But just at this precise moment I don't feel it's your business." He sounded quite angry, slicing the air with his hand and with each gesture he seemed to carve more deeply into her self-confidence.

"Sorry I asked," she said. "It's true, I don't have the right. I don't seem to have many rights at all where my family is concerned." She thought about that for a bit and then conceded: "I suppose that's fair."

"Look – Mrs – hell, what do I call you?"

"Connie."

"Connie. Don't take on the world all at once. Your world, that is. One day, one step at a time, that's what you said." He appeared to be regretting that he had spoken sharply to her previously for not much reason. "Out there . . ." He gestured toward the park. "Go see your grandchild. That's a helluva lot for one day, wouldn't you say?"

She took his hand and squeezed it. "Thanks."

"For what?"

"The lunch, the ride, Holly!"

He got back on his bike, a lean, black-clad figure, and pulled the helmet down over his head. He looked, she thought, like the masked avenger. "See you!" She heard his muffled voice through the vizor, returned his

248

wave and watched him roar off down the road out of sight.

It was a warm, sunny afternoon and there were only a few people in the park, mostly snoring away their Sunday lunch in deckchairs or flat out on the grass. On such a rare sultry day with the tide out it was the beach that would be packed with bodies stripped to catch a weak tan or to cool off in the sea. Despite her loose cotton slacks and shirt Connie felt uncommonly warm, possibly because of the unexpected means of transportation to Southdean but more likely because of the meeting that faced her.

She wondered whether she would be up to it, whether she would make a hash of it as she'd made a hash of so much in her life. And, if she did, that would be it. There would be no second chances.

She walked across the grass, skirting the beds of primary-coloured blossom, all neatly regimented in the tradition of council planting as Sam had practised it when he was a Parks' Department gardener.

Her eyes searched the park. There was no sign of a young woman with a toddler. A few tearaways were racing around a wooden seat on which an elderly man was stretched flat out, seemingly dead to the noise with a copy of the *News Of The World* shielding his face from the sun. Suddenly he erupted like a dormant volcano. "Grrr . . . awf, you little bleeders." They stopped in their tracks, stared in disbelief and scattered to a safe distance where they giggled nervously among themselves.

She assumed young Colin wasn't one of them, but feared he might be like them. She didn't dare think how the formidable Dede might bring up a child, although an annoying small voice inside her suggested: "Probably better than you did."

The sound of cool water, gently rushing, drew her to the centre of the park. A mound had been erected as a memorial to the warrior birds of the south coast who 'gave their lives on active service, 1939–1945, and for the use and pleasure of living birds'. You had to negotiate a flight of perilously uneven slate steps flanked by shrubs

249

and tall grasses to reach the summit of the memorial. The inscription was carved in a jagged rock face standing guard over a circular pond with a small fountain in the centre jetting water on the surrounding flags. Although it was scrupulously maintained by public donation, it was on the whole a secret place. The inhabitants of Southdean knew of it and were proud of it, but the difficulty of access daunted the elderly and infirm who would most appreciate it, while protecting it from the attention of vandals.

Perhaps, thought Connie, this is the Sunday she has decided not to take Colin to the park.

But, while she thought it, she knew instinctively this was not true. And as she approached the memorial she heard an achingly familiar chuckle floating through the dense wall of protective shrubbery. It was Colin's laugh; Colin, two years old, before the traumas of growing up had eroded that carefree spontaneity.

She was conscious of a breathlessness that wasn't entirely due to the effort involved in climbing the mound on a sweaty summer's day. There was a patch of well-worn grass by the pond, room enough for a rug on which lay the remains of a picnic. The girl with the scar down her cheek was sitting on the rug, a book – a Margaret Drabble – open on her lap. Her eyes were closed, but there was a sense of alertness about her, the alertness of a mother who never quite allows herself to relax when her child is playing nearby. She was wearing a floppy straw hat with a turned back brim in the front, the kind the chain stores were stocking that season, an ankle length printed cotton sundress, buttoned down the front, and a pair of flat canvas sandals. She looked neater, more normal, than she had appeared before.

Beside her, a chubby little boy was playing with a toy Noah's Ark, made of soft cloth and kapok padding. The brightly coloured outer skin of the Ark was decorated with a riot of bits and bobs, designed to facilitate dexterity in little fingers – zips, poppers, pockets, buttons. The boy was pulling small cloth animals out of the flap that opened up the innards of the Ark and stuffing them into the pockets around the sides. Every time he managed to get one properly anchored in its pocket he laughed out loud and started on another. When he'd placed them all, he stood on unsteady legs and toddled over to his mother, tugging at her arm. "Done! Done!" he cried, triumphantly.

Half hidden by the shrubbery, Connie watched her grandson and felt such overwhelming love as she had never felt before, not for Sam or Beattie or David Levitch or any of her own children.

She drank in the sight of him. The silky sunny, honey-coloured hair; the sturdy little body in its French navy and white striped combination shirt and shorts with vivid red mock braces; the clear golden skin of his legs and the toes peeping out of the navy strap shoes. He was a child, she realised, who was immaculately well looked after and she was ashamed that she should have expected any different.

She felt suddenly like a voyeur who had no business being there because she hadn't earned the right. She hadn't shared this girl's joy or apprehension through her pregnancy. She hadn't been around when her baby was born or bothered about how she might care for him afterwards. She hadn't offered help or even a sympathetic word when it might be needed. She didn't know whether he'd been immunised against whooping cough and measles or whether he had been a contented baby or one who kept his mother up all through the night. She hadn't even been aware how hard it might have been for Dede to manage, whether there'd been enough money or whether she was on social security and where they lived.

Reason told her it wasn't her fault that she hadn't known she had a grandson and Colin a son. No one had told her. Apparently Dede hadn't wanted her to know. Maybe Colin hadn't. But wasn't *that* her fault? That something in her had prevented them from confiding in her?

251

She half turned to leave.

"So soon!"

Dede Crowther's eyes were still closed, but, Connie realised, the younger woman had sensed her presence, perhaps even before she had approached the memorial. She hadn't needed to make herself obvious. She knew Connie would find her and Colin junior.

"I – I wasn't sure I'd be welcome."

Dede opened her eyes and humped the curious little boy onto her lap. The livid scar on her cheek seemed to fade in the light of the expression in those eyes as she regarded his upturned face.

"Why would you think that?" she said. "I wouldn't have let you know where I'd be otherwise." She looked straight at Connie, a touch defiantly. "What did you expect?"

Dede smiled the fractured smile that reached only half of her face. "But I can guess. A slummocky mother dragging up a grimy, whiny little boy with no future and no hope." She hugged the boy to her and kissed him on the forehead. "I can't blame you, I suppose. Hub's place in Rookshaven Lane hardly inspires confidence in the stray caller. Don't worry. Colin and I have a little place in town. It's neat and clean and next door to a kind baby sitter who cares for him when I'm out doing my bit for the oldies in Heaven's Gate. So you don't have to have me or Colin on your conscience. Wasn't that why you wanted to see me? To satisfy yourself?"

Connie sighed. She was conscious of her aching feet, her full stomach, her perilous ride to Southdean and the acuity with which Dede had guessed at her motives.

"Is it all right if I sit?"

"Sure. Free space."

She lowered herself onto the rug and idly picked up the remains of a Granny Smith apple and bit into it. The sharp, juicy flesh of the fruit tasted good.

"May I?" She helped herself to a plastic cupful of mineral water from a polythene bottle and drank greedily.

The little boy observed all this with intense interest. When she had finished drinking and was wiping her mouth with the back of her hand, he pointed to her, glancing up at his mother: "That lady! Who?"

He spoke very clearly for a not quite two-year-old, just as Colin had, enunciating what words he had at his command precisely with none of the gurgling uncertainty that afflicts many toddlers when they start to articulate.

Dede looked over his head at Connie.

"Well?" she said.

Connie was confused. "Is it up to me?"

"If you want. Just remember, though. Whatever you say it's forever. Not just for now."

"You mean on past record you don't think I'm much of a forever person."

"Something like that. But I've been doing a lot of thinking lately. Even before you came down to see Hub. As I've watched Colin grow I began to realise how trivial revenge is. Oh, that's what it was. Revenge. I swore Holly to secrecy about the baby to get at *you*. I hated you because of what you'd done to Colin – or what he *imagined* you'd done to him. It's not the same thing but in his eyes it was."

"You loved him," said Connie softly, hoping that was true.

"No, not really," Dede responded sharply. "That's the bitch of it. I wish I had. Really, truly, madly, deeply – all that stuff. I was sorry for him. And it wasn't enough. But then someone plants a little bundle in your arms and says 'he's yours and he's perfect, a full complement of fingers, toes, limbs and organs'. And then all the other emotions and reasons just – just fade away. That little bundle makes everything worthwhile. For a while anyway. After that you have to start worrying about the bundle and looking out for him. And now and then wishing you were a free agent again. But – hell, didn't you feel any of this? You had three?"

"I wish I had felt all that. As you say: that's the bitch of it. My little bundle was my business and I was blinkered

253

enough to think it mattered most. I'm not apologising. It seemed sensible at the time."

The boy was looking first at Dede and then at Connie as they spoke, his mouth slightly open, his eyes wide, his fingers kept clasping and unclasping a tiny soft toy elephant he had in his hand until it fell into his mother's lap and he didn't notice.

"You haven't answered Colin's question," Dede reminded Connie. "That lady! Who?"

Without asking permission, Connie lifted the boy into her arms. She cupped her hand round the back of his head and he didn't seem to think it strange, but nestled into her shoulder and yawned a slow sleepy yawn.

"I'm your grandma," she whispered haltingly. Good God, she thought, so I am. Saying it made it real.

"Grandma," he repeated, not understanding. Grandmas were a new concept. Obviously Erica Crowther hadn't put herself about in that role either.

"Your daddy's mummy," Dede prompted him. "Of course he never knew his daddy, so that won't mean much."

"A friend," Connie volunteered.

He nuzzled up to her. "Friend," he echoed. Friends he knew about. She stood there for a while, cradling him in her arms, swaying gently, stroking his hair, watching him nod off, his small fists punching the air.

"He's getting to be a weight," said Dede. "He's usually a lot less passive than this. Probably a bit overawed by you."

"Really!"

"He'll put up more of a fight when you're familiar."

It came out so naturally. Not 'if' but 'when' you're familiar. It was as if, almost without thinking, Dede had invited Connie to become part, maybe just a small part, of their lives.

"Dede," she said, "Dede, we don't know each other very well, if at all. Maybe we never will. But, I was wondering, would you let me – just sometimes be another kind baby sitter?"

254

Dede held her gaze for several interminable seconds. "Sure!" she said finally. "Kind baby sitters are in short supply. And he seems to have taken to you." She affected a down-to-earth, practical tone. "Welcome to the family."

She held out her arms for Colin and Connie returned the boy to her. He roused briefly, half opened his eyes, then, reassured that he was in a safe, secure place, he went back to sleep.

"How do you manage those steps?"

Dede pointed to a collapsible buggy. She was, it seemed, as formidably well organised with her child as she had been with her oldies on their jaunt to the picture show.

"We come here a lot," she said. "It's quiet, peaceful. He likes it."

"I imagine it's a struggle for you," said Connie. She wasn't referring to the steps and Dede understood that.

"Yes," she replied simply.

"You could have had an abortion."

"I could. But I didn't." She touched her cheek, for the first time, it appeared to Connie, acknowledging the existence of the scar.

"Was that Colin?" She didn't know why she said it, why she had even thought of it and she feared even bringing up the subject might offend a young woman whom she judged could easily take offence. It was a while before she realised with a shock that she already knew the answer to her question. Colin! Kind, gentle Colin! Why should she be so certain that the inconceivable was true?

"Yes." Dede traced the passage of the scar as if needing to remind herself. "He didn't know what he was doing."

"Why?" Connie gasped. "Was it the baby?"

"He never even knew I was pregnant before he died. No, not the baby. Me! You, partly. Me, because I wasn't you. He'd seen a big piece about you in the paper. Something about the business, maybe going into receivership or being taken over. And there was a bit about

255

Sam and your divorce and a great, splashing, dazzling photograph of you looking so smug and self-satisfied and successful. I suppose it must have been an archive photograph, because you couldn't have been feeling all that smug and self-satisfied and successful at the time. He'd been drinking a lot, really a lot, and I suppose I said the wrong thing. There was a kitchen devil on the table and . . ." She shrugged. "He just stared at me and the blood. There was a lot of blood. I think I screamed. Then he screamed, only it was more like a howl of pain, much greater than the pain of the cut. And he took off. The next I heard he was dead." (So that explained the 'God forgive me' suicide note, thought Connie.)

"Did you go to the police?"

"No. Hub came round. He had a chum who was a third year medical student and they got me patched up. It wasn't legal but that way we didn't report it."

Connie took a step toward her but Dede stopped her. "Don't, please, don't! It's done. I don't even think about it any more, don't even see it – or register it – when I look in the mirror."

"Did Holly know this?"

"We never told her, but she may have suspected. I don't know. And if you care for little Colin at all, even me, don't bring it up again. I'd rather remember the best of Colin. So should you."

"That's why you were fending me off." She knelt beside Dede and took her hand. "Don't worry. I shan't throw a fit. I might have once. But I'm learning. You must understand that."

She got to her feet and busied herself dusting shreds of grass off her slacks. "I shan't tell Sam. My ex-husband. If you don't want me to."

Dede nodded and almost managed a smile. "You're not so bad."

"That I take for a compliment," said Connie.

"By the way, about the baby sitting. I didn't think you lived here now."

"No." She took a deep breath. "But I think it's time

256

for a change. Is there anything I can bring when I come to see you?"

Dede frowned thoughtfully, then shook her head. "It'd be too expensive."

"Try me."

"A rocking horse. If there is such a thing. A hand-crafted rocking horse. He saw a picture of one in a book and fell in love with it. Anything to stop him growing into a TV vegetable. Hub used to have one when he was a boy, but I'm afraid we aren't on speaking terms with my parents. Sad, when you come to think of it."

"A rocking horse! Hand-crafted!" Connie grinned broadly. "I know just the man."

She bent down and kissed the sleeping boy, then, hesitantly, his mother – on the cheek with the scar.

It was a three mile walk back to the house but Connie didn't notice the journey or the heat. She felt strong and sure and invigorated. "It won't last," one voice kept telling her. "Oh yes it will," said another. Meanwhile there was a spring in her stride and she smiled at strangers so infectiously that most of them smiled back, if a little nervously at such an extravagant display of good humour.

"Thank God you're back!" Sam had just brought the car round to the front door. "Karen. She's asking for you."

"Karen! For *me*! She doesn't even *like* me." She was still enjoying her sense of well-being and didn't immediately take in what Sam wasn't quite saying.

"Whatever!" he replied. "She's asking for you. Same gender I suppose. I've phoned the doctor. He's meeting us at the hospital."

"Sam! What is it? The baby?"

"Of course," he said irritably. "What else would it be? She's upstairs. Go to her, Con. It's not like her at all."

Karen was sitting on the end of the bed, nursing her stomach and gulping as the spasms of labour pains increased.

"Come on, Karen, we've got to get you to the hospital!" said Connie with an authority she didn't feel.

She put her arm round her waist and heaved Karen to her feet.

"Con!" she gasped. "I'm scared!" She turned appealing eyes to Connie, searching for reassurance. Sam had been right. This was quite unlike the calm, sensible Karen who seemed so in control of everything.

"That's just silly. You of all people! You know there's nothing to be scared of. Breathe! Deep!" She steered her to the door and the staircase. "You've had all the tests, attended all the clinics, done all the exercises, read all the books. Why, with you it'll be like shelling peas from a pod as my mother used to say. You were born for babies, Karen. Honestly! Come on. Breathe! Easy."

They took the stairs slowly one at a time.

"I know I'm being foolish," Karen panted. "But right now I'm scared! It's a – a judgement for being too cocksure that nothing would go wrong."

"Nothing *will* go wrong. Now stop talking and lean down hard on me."

"Were you scared?"

"As hell," Connie assured her.

As they reached the bottom of the stairs, Sam took her arm, guided her to the car and between them Connie and he lifted Karen into the back seat. "I should have called an ambulance," he worried.

"No time," said Connie.

"Will you come with me, Connie?"

"Doesn't she have any woman friends?" Connie asked Sam.

"Connie!" shrieked Karen.

"Wouldn't miss it," lied Connie and climbed into the back beside her.

Who would have thought, two days ago, that I'd be the one Karen wanted to comfort her in what she imagined to be her hour of need? She pondered the irony of it as she gripped Karen's hand tightly and the car sped toward Southdean hospital.

The baby boy bounced into the world two weeks premature ("It was probably the French apple tart that did it," said Sam) weighing in at a healthy seven pounds one and a half ounces. It was, one of the maternity nurses assured Connie, a record. Karen was barely in before the baby was out. As Connie had predicted it had been like shelling peas. Mother and child were doing spectacularly fine.

At midnight, Holly and Amy had been informed, Karen was sleeping ecstatically and another tiny addition to the earth's population was being cooed over in the maternity wing along with a dozen other future inhabitants of the planet – a good weekend's trawl.

Sam and Connie drove back to the house. Jagger barked a noisy welcome and Sam looked mightily pleased with himself, if still slightly shocked.

"Thanks, Con," he said. "I just don't know what came over her. I don't think she's been scared of anything in her life before."

"Well, she's never had a baby in her life before, either. You never can tell till it happens."

"Anyway. Thanks – for being here."

"Glad to be of service," she joked and realised she actually meant it. She really was glad to be of service. It was a good feeling.

She wondered when would be the right time to tell Sam that he had a grandson who was nearly two years older than his newly born son. But she decided not quite now. Later.

Chapter Twenty-Two

"You look whacked."

Hub Crowther didn't sound sympathetic, but he had been right. Monday morning was quieter, even in Heaven's Gate, as if the whole of Rookshaven Lane was recovering from a riotous weekend.

"Sort of," said Connie. "I spent most of last night nursing my ex-husband through the shock of becoming a father in his fifties. Lots of men think second families are a lovely idea until they're faced with them. Although I think Sam will hold up pretty well."

He wrinkled his patrician nose. "I can't think of an answer to that."

"It wasn't a question." She looked around the dreary hall with its single electric light bulb. "Is there somewhere we can talk? I think you owe me that."

She was determined not to be intimidated by him this time. He pursed his lips, nodding, as if pleased at her show of spunk.

"This way," he beckoned her through to the back of the house and a small room off the kitchen which at some much more affluent time must have served as a maid's pantry. He opened the door with a flourish. "My den!" he proclaimed. "That's how Erica, my sainted mother, would refer to it – sight unseen, of course."

She surveyed the chaos in the tiny room, dominated by a huge desk, with papers strewn all over its top, a home computer propped up precariously on the window ledge and a battered TV set dumped on the floor, alongside a pile of old clothes and shoes and a telephone trailing its cord to trip the unwary.

"Den!" she echoed.

"Well, pigsty, if you prefer. Except pigs are tidier. Coffee?"

A kettle was bubbling away in another corner of the floor. He scooped spoonfuls of instant into mugs, sloshed the boiling water into them and at the same time swept a pile of pamphlets off the only serious chair in the room so that she could sit down.

He handed her a mug. "No milk."

"No need," she said and sipped the vicious brew gratefully. She hadn't been kidding. It *had* been a long night.

All the time she was conscious that he was scrutinising her carefully, perched on the edge of the desk, his long legs stretched out in front of him, ankles and arms crossed in a deceptively languid posture.

"Well!" she demanded defiantly.

"I hear you saw Dede and the boy yesterday."

"You could have told me the other day."

"That was up to Dede. And anyway I don't think you could have taken it the other day."

"Probably," she agreed. "He's a beautiful child. Very like Colin."

"You don't really hope that, do you?" he pressed her.

"In looks," she elaborated, then, "no I don't suppose I'd want any boy to go through whatever Colin went through. How could he have *done* that to your sister? It was horrible." She was genuinely perplexed that Colin should have been capable of such a brutal act.

Hub shook his head. He sounded unperturbed and she sensed he and his sister had been over and over that question time and again without reaching any acceptable conclusion. "Frustration. With himself mostly. Perhaps it gave him a reason for suicide."

"'God forgive me!'" she quoted the note he had left behind. "Why would he need a reason that harmed someone else?"

"Because he wasn't frightfully good at pulling it off

261

when it only harmed himself." He caught her look of surprise. "Oh yes, a couple of times, Dede and I caught him before it was too late. Pills, slit wrists – the classic cry for help of failed pop stars and wronged lovers. Poor old Colin, he couldn't even do that right – until eventually he did." He didn't sound callous, just regretful at the pointless waste of a life.

"Why on earth couldn't you have contacted us? Any of us? Sam – at least – even if not me?"

"Then we really would have had a basket case on our hands. Not that we didn't anyway," he ruminated.

He gulped down his coffee in one almighty swallow. "You see the trouble with Colin was that he couldn't hack it. He never could."

"What do you mean – hack it? Sex?"

"No. Achieve something worthwhile. Devoting himself to others. Redressing the balance. You're his mother. Didn't you know?"

"I suppose I must have. You're saying I – my success in business – was the balance he wanted to redress!" She gave a hollow laugh. "Good grief! There *has* to be a God after all. If Colin couldn't redress the balance, He bloody well did, bankrupting the company, turning me into a vindictive neurotic."

He gave her a sceptical smile which made her feel as trivial as the remark she had just uttered. "You really *do* believe in divine intervention. Well, maybe you're right. God pays debts and all that. I learned that in the nick. I was an arrogant bastard even when they sentenced me for dangerous driving while under the influence. It should have been manslaughter, but the boy didn't die instantly, but some weeks later in hospital and the magistrate knew my father and spouted some rubbish about how I'd carry the guilt of what I'd done for the rest of my life and he had to take into consideration my age. But I didn't give a toss about what I'd done. And the poor buggers of parents didn't know enough – or their solicitor didn't – to kick up a fuss about the leniency of the sentence. My mother and father rallied round, a united front, with

262

all their stupid friends who used to joke about driving offences and sweet-talking the police into not charging them when they were caught speeding. Only Dede had the guts to call me a bastard to my face. But Dede was a lost cause. . . ."

". . . Another lost cause. . . ." murmured Connie.

". . . Because she'd taken herself off to join the Greenham women when she should have been learning how to be beautiful and useless and a suitable consort in the fullness of time for some wealthy bigwig. She was always wiser than her years, Dede. I think that's what attracted Colin. In a funny way she reminded him of you without the aggravation."

"You make it sound as if he had some kind of Oedipus complex," she said, hoping he would contradict her.

"Nothing as positive as that. Positive wasn't part of Colin's nature. I suppose the only three positive things he did in his life were to leave home, father a child and commit suicide. No, with him, it was just a fixation he had on you. He was like a punter in a restaurant trying to attract the attention of a waiter who refuses to notice."

"The waiter being me?"

He didn't answer, didn't need to.

"So how did this arrogant bastard, Hubbard Crowther, become the caring, compassionate human being we now know and love?" She laid on the irony in exchange for his cutting assessment of her non-relationship with her son.

He didn't mind her tone, indeed he seemed to relish it. "I thought it would be a doddle. Prison. Out in a year with good behaviour. Then back to the old routine. Having a good time, playing at a career, lording it over the peasants."

She smiled, remembering him at the school speech day. He and his mother and their cool condescension toward her.

"Well, it wasn't a doddle. It was bloody awful. And maybe I'd have slit my throat if it hadn't been for a skinny little runt named Maurice Priddy. I'll never forget

263

that name. He was always being picked on, but he always came up smiling, not minding. He was inside for killing his wife who was having it off with every guy in town over seven and under seventy. But it was premeditated, you see, so it was worse. Yet in a funny kind of way he was a true Christian. He helped me anyway, not just to fully appreciate what I had done, but to see myself truly as well. What family he had had never visited and, so far as I could see, he had no friends who cared outside. When I got out I vowed I'd do something for him and others like him. But I was so afraid that I'd forget as soon as I got back to my old life and everyone, at any rate my parents, were urging me to forget."

"But you didn't." She looked around her at the grubby, cluttered room.

"No, I forced myself not to. I spent some time with the Salvation Army and then I got the idea of buying this place, as a sort of shelter, somewhere for no-hopers to come and it all grew from that. And that's the rub, the worm, the pitcher of gall I have to keep swallowing. These people I try to help couldn't do what I did because *I* was privileged and *they* weren't. Dede and I, we're both privileged. We had money left to us in trust by grandparents. We may have had to fight against the odds, but they're nothing like the odds most people have to fight against. There are two totally demoralising things: being penniless in a capitalist society and being unloved. I suppose all you can say for me and Dede is that at least we've tried."

"And succeeded," she prompted. "What happened to – what his name?"

"Maurice Priddy? He had a heart attack and died a few days before they were due to release him. I went to the funeral service. There were just a few old lags there and the prison governor and a warder who had become a sort of chum. No one from outside except me. The padre went through the motions and then Maurice went up in smoke. They gave me the ashes and I scattered them in the nicest place I could think of. There's a wood just outside Southdean, not many people know of it, it's too tucked away. In the spring it's a riot of wild daffodils and primroses and that's where Dede and I laid his ashes to rest – among the daffodils and primroses. I think he'd have liked ending up that way. Better than out and alive.

"He'd been a bank clerk and the likelihood of him getting a job was pretty remote. His home had been repossessed. But he believed, he really honestly believed that the Lord was watching over him and that life was worth living. His faith was awesome. I thought if this pitiful little guy could have that much hope, what right had I to throw away my life? I tried to explain all that to my parents, would you believe? They just thought I was cracked. I tried to explain it to Colin, too. I really tried," he said earnestly. "But look what happened! So don't talk to me about succeeding."

"You shouldn't be so hard on yourself." She thought for a moment and she felt his eyes searching her face for a clue to what she was thinking.

"Now let me see if I can guess the next question," he said, screwing up his mouth in mock concentration.

"You make it sound as if I'm interrogating you. I don't mean to."

"You – want – to – ask – but – don't – know – how," he spaced his words and then gabbled, "whether-Colin-and-I-were-gay. Lovers. Right?"

"No." It wasn't true, just that it didn't matter.

"It must have glanced through your mind," he prompted her.

"Glanced. When I read his diary. It was full of you."

"Odd! He turned me down in no uncertain terms. *I'm* gay, you see. He was straight – whatever that means. Satisfied?"

"You brought up the subject, not me," she reminded him.

"So I did," he conceded. "We'd settled that hash a long time ago at school. After that, we were just – chums. You know, like in *Beano* and Rudyard Kipling. Only we didn't conform to the traditional stereotypes. I should have been the picked-upon little blighter who needed protection."

"But it was Colin who needed protection." She spoke softly, from memory. "He said in his diary that something happened that was awful and you were splendid. Those were his words. And he didn't mind the thrashing so much, but what they said that made him feel dirty. Who were 'they'?"

"There were gangs of them from the council estate. They used to lie in wait for boys in uniforms from good schools and if you didn't run fast enough they'd beat you up. Sometimes they picked the wrong boys and got a beating themselves. It was really no big deal. But it was to Colin. He was alone one day and they cornered him, kicked him all over, threw a rock at him and called him everything from a fucking snob to a grizzly crawler. Stuff like that. A few of us weren't far behind and we waded in. Didn't he tell you any of this?" He sounded amazed.

"He said you told him it was better not to say anything or it would get worse."

But she knew that was no excuse. For she remembered the day. He had come home bruised and fairly bloodied and his jacket was torn. It had been one of her rare evenings at home early. "What on earth has happened to you?" she'd asked. He'd given her some cock-and-bull yarn about an impromptu wrestling match he and another boy had had after school. He'd made it sound quite amicable ("you should have seen the other boy") and she'd accepted his explanation because it was easier than delving deeper for the truth. She had patched him up and Sam had remembered a funny story about how he had fared in a local amateur boxing tournament when he'd won the medal for best loser. And then she had forgotten about it because the telephone rang with a more urgent concern about misdirected orders.

"Did I say that?" queried Hub. "I suppose I must have. Like I said: I was an arrogant bastard. He should have let you know. That's the sad thing about Colin. He wanted so much to believe everything he was told, to believe that other people understood more than he did. Low self-esteem, I suppose you'd call it these days."

"You always kept in touch."

"Well, not after I went to prison. I gather he was off bumming around in Europe or working for charitable organisations. He made out somehow. Then when he came back to Southdean I'd been released and we met up again and he and Dede took a shine to each other. He helped out here for a while, too. But there was a terrible unease in him." He shook his head. "That's when he made the feeble attempts at suicide."

"Why did he take his car?" she said suddenly. "The one I bought him? He left it at home in the garage for ages, then suddenly it was gone. We assumed he took it or had sold it."

He smiled. "He said it was collateral. It would be useful. Frankly I didn't see how an open top sports car could be useful around here, except as a gift for vandals. But that was Colin for you. His mind had a weird logic that made sense only to him."

"But how come the police found it wrecked in a lay-by after he died? I mean – what happened to it and why? Have you any idea?"

He pondered that for a moment, then shook his head, as bemused as she was. "I honestly have no idea. And I suppose we'll never know now, will we? I assume he vandalised it himself before dumping it and . . ." There was no need to elaborate. They both knew what the 'and' meant.

Connie fidgeted with her mug, peering into it as if searching for a sign and avoiding Hub's eyes. There was a catch in her voice when she spoke. "You think he ruined it because I gave it to him. It was like inflicting pain on *me*. But it was only a *thing*. Things don't matter." Is this me talking? she thought. There had been a time when things were *all* that mattered to her.

She looked up abruptly, challenging him to agree

267

with her. And he measured his answer accordingly. "Who knows? What's the point of tormenting yourself about it?"

"I think," she said slowly. "I was the one he wanted to carve up with a kitchen devil, not Dede. She just happened to be the unlucky one who was handy. It just goes on and on, doesn't it? I've been blaming myself for Colin. But it doesn't end there. Because of what I did or didn't do Dede suffered too. And if she weren't so level-headed little Colin might suffer. It just grows and grows – like a cancer."

"Dede doesn't think that," he said quietly.

"That doesn't help, Hub. It doesn't help."

"Just – give it time."

Enough, she thought, I can't go through any more. Why was it that she could reveal herself so completely to this young man whom she felt still vaguely disapproved of her, more as a symbol than a person? Reveal herself in a way she never could to the analyst who refused to be judgemental. Judge! Judge! she silently cried. That's what we wanderers in our mental nightmares need: judgement!

But to Hub she merely said: "I can see why you're so good at counselling your no-hopers."

"Counselling's the least of it," he said.

A boy presumably in his teens shambled into the room without knocking. Hub didn't reprimand him. It was, Connie assumed, an ever open door.

"I've got this form," he said without any preamble, thrusting it at Hub. "From the social."

"I'll look it over," said Hub. "How's the job-hunting going?"

"I'm trying," he said.

"So try harder."

The boy frowned. "It's the words," he said as if that explained it all and mooched out.

"What did he mean? The words?" said Connie.

"He's illiterate. Well, semi-illiterate. He can just about read road signs. And innumerate. Nothing fancy, like

268

dyslexia. He's just thick. He wasn't a tearaway or a truant, just backward, and there weren't enough time or teachers at school to encourage him to learn. He used to be on drugs but he managed to kick it all on his own. He had that much courage and gumption, as much gumption as it takes to learn your ABCs. He does odd jobs around here, helps out in general. He's a good worker. But he probably won't get a proper job because he can't read and write and add up properly. That puts 'sad' into perspective, don't you think?"

"I wish I could help," she said and wondered if she really meant that or was just saying it because it seemed appropriate.

"You could. But you'd have to really want to. Teaching scruffy lads like Tony to string a few words together on paper and understand them takes training, patience and a high threshold of tolerance to swallowing insults and abuse and general nastiness. I don't think you've got the guts, Mrs Remick," he said in the lofty, patronising tone he had adopted toward her when they had first met. He was, she realised, testing her and, rather than respond, she changed the subject.

"You know Andrew Deeley, don't you?"

"Now, *there's* a guy who's got the guts!"

"He's offered me a sort of job. Advisory, really. In that workshop project of his." She didn't know why she was telling him except perhaps to restore some self-esteem.

"Well, aren't you the lucky one? Two job offers in as many days."

"You don't have to be facetious," she rounded on him.

"No I don't. I can just tell you to take your affluent bourgeois neuroses home and kid yourself you're suffering."

She stood up, picked up the mug and, taking careful aim, chucked it at him. He ducked and it shattered satisfyingly against the wall above his head. She had to admit she felt a lot better. He clapped slowly and admiringly. Anger he appreciated. It was whining indifference that bugged him.

269

"You don't get rid of me that easily," she said dismissively. "I've got a grandson whose mother I respect and they're both related to you. So don't you forget it."

As she left the house, she came upon Tony studying a scrawl of chalked graffiti on the retaining wall. He was frowning intently. "The word is 'dead-end'," she said in passing. "But don't you believe it."

"Stupid cow!" he yelled after her. It was a normal response with no trace of rancour in it or even any understanding that it might sound insulting.

I've been called worse, thought Connie, feeling not nearly so desolate as she had expected.

It was uncommonly quiet when she got back to the house. No friendly bark from Jagger. He had been farmed out with Bill Daley until Karen was settled back in again with the baby.

Sam was at the hospital, having passed out cigars and champagne to the staff at the garden nursery in the time-honoured manner of a new father. He preened, decided Connie. That was the word. She'd never seen such preening, even when their own three were born, and she was pleased for him. She was relieved, too, to learn that Karen fancied the name of Arthur for her son. She had feared they might feel obliged to call him Colin and two baby Colins would be awkward, not to say inconvenient.

She would visit Karen later in her private room when the first rush of enraptured visitors had subsided.

She made herself a tuna sandwich, poured a glass of Sam's best dry sherry, settled herself comfortably in his study and foraged in her bag for the dazzling calling card Andrew Deeley had given her. As she punched out the number on the telephone she realised she was taking some kind of crucial step in her life and she wasn't surprised to notice that her hand was shaking. Not just: am I doing the right thing? But: am I capable of doing the right thing? Well, she'd never know if she never tried.

A wary female voice answered. A speak-easy kind of

voice which she half expected to demand that she knock three times and ask for Joe, just like in the movies.

"Who wants him?" it queried.

"A friend. Tell him it's Connie Remick."

"Oh – only sometimes his family get on to him and that upsets him."

"Is that what he said?"

"No." Truculently. "But *I* know."

I'll bet you do, Boadicea!

"Who is that dragon that stands guard over you?" she said when Andy Deeley came to the phone.

"Mrs Battleaxe? I told you about her. Lillian Biggs. My housekeeper. Her one big virtue is that she has less regard for my sons than I have. So – don't waste my time, Connie. What have you decided?"

"I've decided to make a deal with you, Andy. I'll consider your option to see how I could help you with your workshop project if you can find someone who can make me a rocking horse – a good-sized quality rocking horse for a little boy. Something he'll keep and treasure and hand down to his grandchildren and great-grandchildren who will bring it along to the *Antiques Roadshow* when they visit Southdean in the next millennium."

She could sense him beaming with pleasure at the end of the telephone, either at managing to get a decision out of her or at the prospect of producing a rocking horse or both.

"I'll make it my personal priority. Deal!"

"Deal!" she said and put down the receiver.

There, she told herself, that wasn't so hard, was it? And she answered her own question by pouring another glass of Sam's good sherry.

Chapter Twenty-Three

Karen was sitting plumped up in a comfy chair by the window, looking extremely pink and extremely self-satisfied. Connie had never seen her oozing such a pleasurable awareness of her own femininity.

"Isn't he the most beautiful baby you've ever seen?" she enthused. To which Connie replied that he was indeed the most beautiful baby she had ever seen, not wanting to puncture Karen's delight in the little miracle she had produced by observing that he seemed just like every other baby she had ever seen, including her own. Red, wizened and grumpy.

Amy sat on the bed, not uttering, and looking wistful. They were the only two visitors, but that wouldn't last long. There had been a constant stream of them all bearing gifts. Connie's freesias, which she had thought rather tasteful and suitable to the occasion, were lost in a blaze of ornate sprays and arrangements and pot plants. "We'll never find enough vases," said the nurse with just a touch of acerbity because she really meant it and envisaged having to commission chamber pots into service.

They'd sent Sam off to find himself some food and put up his feet. He hadn't wanted to go, but, as Connie pointed out, he'd have Karen and little Arthur for the rest of their lives so half an hour's absence wouldn't make much difference.

Arthur! She rolled the name round her tongue. It was a nice, solid name with no uncomfortable emotional baggage attached to it, she thought. Its only significance apparently was that a favourite uncle of Karen's had been named Arthur.

"We thought Arthur, Samuel – and Colin," said Karen tentatively. Colin very much the afterthought.

"I always think three Christian names are a bit much, don't you?" Connie suggested.

"You're probably right," breathed Karen, relieved. "You know, Con, I don't think I'd have made it without you."

Connie shook her head, laughing. "What kind of anaesthetic did they give you?"

Karen frowned. "None." Then she got the point. "No, honestly, Connie, I know I was behaving like an idiot, but having you there, telling me *not* to be an idiot . . . It was nice, really nice."

"Well, maybe it's time I started being nice for a change."

"What's this?"

Amy had picked up a slim volume from the side table, placed apart from all the other volumes of current best sellers that Sam had scooped up in the mistaken belief that his wife might actually have the time or the inclination to read them. ("You'd never think he'd been a father before," reflected Karen.)

"It's a Kate Greenaway Alphabet book."

"I can see that." Amy handled the volume with its delicate Victorian illustration of a mother and child on the cover, with the reverence of a connoisseur. "It's a first edition. Lucky you!"

"I know. It was so thoughtful of him. It came this afternoon by special delivery. From your friend – Lewis Diamond. I thought you'd have known."

"No – no I didn't. I spoke to him on the phone last night and told him about the baby." She was about to add "in passing" but restrained herself, realising that to Karen her baby would have been headline news in any bulletin. She couldn't even recall what they had talked about, except in a roundabout way 'goodbye'.

"It's a tremendously thoughtful gift. I hardly talked to him the other evening. I'll cherish it, of course. Won't let any grubby little paws get near it until they appreciate

273

what they're handling." She positively swelled with the sense of her own importance being the giver of life to those grubby little paws.

Amy smiled ruefully, touched by Lewis's gesture and Karen's pleasure in it. "Yes, he can be very kind." But not to me. She shrugged. "I ought to be going. Just a quick nip down to see you. You're a clever mum, Karen. He's an angel. Holly will probably be around either later or tomorrow morning."

"You're all so good to me," Karen ruminated.

"Does that surprise you?"

"It could have been otherwise. That young man of Holly's? Are they – you know?" Now that she was comfortably fortified in a comfortable marriage with a comfortable family Karen felt she owed it to the others to take an interest in their domestic arrangements.

"John? I expect she'll end up marrying him," said Amy. "I'm sure he's terribly proper."

And Connie thought she detected a note of envy in her voice.

She walked Amy out to her car.

"Amy—" she began.

"I'd just as soon you didn't, Mum. I can't think how I didn't guess about you and Lewis. I suppose it was a case of mother and father and Queen Victoria. No, that's not quite right, is it? Anyway. It's tough to see that your mother might be desirable, sexually I mean, especially to someone you yourself find desirable."

"I don't think I was particularly." Connie linked her arm in Amy's. "It was just we worked together. We got on well together. And it was sort of like an extension of business. A brief affair, a nice cup of tea and what's next on the agenda! That's what drove both of us. Business. I imagine it still drives Lewis. I'm so sorry, Amy, you seem to be the one who's drawn the short straw. Lewis. Me. These past two years."

Amy took a deep breath, pulled herself out of her ribs and faced her mother squarely. "No I haven't. I'm considering joining the company's office in Brussels.

274

Get in on all that EC plunder." She seemed to be daring Connie to give her an argument or, worse, a show of sympathy.

Connie merely nodded appreciatively as if her daughter's proposal was eminently sensible, which in fact it was, she supposed. "You'll be near Lewis, too," she added, chancing her luck.

"Why not? After all – tomorrow *is* another day!" Amy chuckled, giving a pretty fair imitation of Scarlett planning her strategy for recapturing Rhett. It was the first time Connie could recall her serious daughter making a joke.

She had been summoned to Becky's eyrie on the cliff. There was no other word for it: summoned! A phone call, an agreed time convenient to both, a hire car to pick her up.

"You've become very grand," Connie chided Becky. "You give audiences, like royalty."

"Do I?" Becky sounded surprised as if she hadn't seriously considered how she was behaving for quite some time. "I suppose it's a habit I picked up from the Howards." She shivered in mock horror. "I really must kick it or you won't come to see me again. Drink?"

Connie shook her head.

"I would. It's David who wanted to see you. That is – now, now, now."

"He's not capable of picking up the phone himself?"

"To tell you the truth, Con, I think he feels a bit embarrassed and that I might provide some moral support. I won't, by the way. I'm very fond of my brother, but I feel he's old enough to fight his own battles."

"Good grief! What battles has he got to fight with me?"

"You'd be surprised. Or maybe if you're as astute as I think you've become you won't." Her hand hovered

275

over an assortment of bottles on a side table. "Do you think that's what drove Kit away?" she mused.

"What? Who? David?"

"No, of *course* not. My being grand?"

Connie considered. Over the past few days she felt she was beginning to get the hang of what tips the balance one way or the other in the relationship between parents and their children. "Possibly," she decided. After all, why should she spare Becky the anguish of guilt she had experienced herself?

"She's leaving, you know. Wants to strike out on her own. But I suppose she can't find me *too* much of a tyrant. She's leaving Vicky. It's awful to say it, Con, but you know I really think I get on better with my granddaughter than I ever did with Kit."

Connie smiled. "I'd believe it," she said, but she didn't explain why. It was still too private.

In the rear of the house she heard Vicky sassing her chosen sparring partner, the housemaid Dallas, and getting back as good as she gave. "At least you don't have to worry about Vicky," she laughed. "She'll grow up much grander than you. A regular bossy boots."

"She likes you," said Becky. "She thinks you're funny."

"Not peculiar?"

"No, funny. Anyone who wears odd shoes and creates a diversion in the shopping precinct has to be an improvement on the rest of the great, grey mass of humanity." She jerked her head toward the terrace overlooking the sea. "He's out there. Waiting for you. He's going back to the States tomorrow."

Connie shrugged her shoulders in a gesture of baffled irritation. "Why all the mystery?"

"You know David. He likes his little dramas. Always great on striking attitudes. Remember?"

Connie nodded, still faintly irritated. "I remember Maltesers and winkle picker shoes, too, but they don't play an important role in my life any more."

She stood for several moments observing him, as he

276

leant on the railing staring out at the sea. She liked his easy posture, the set of his profile, the aura of confidence he exuded. And then she stopped admiring and thought what a poseur he was, too, and even before they'd spoken she knew what he was going to say and what she would reply. Considerately, with just a hint of regret, but definitely.

"It was a good evening." He didn't turn round to face her.

"Holly's play? A bit of a homespun evening by your standards, I'd imagine."

"Homespun is nice sometimes."

"That's the point. Sometimes! Like vacations from whatever happens to be real life – your real life."

"Is that supposed to be a significant remark?" he said and this time he turned round, but he didn't make a move toward her, as if he needed to keep some distance between them.

"I didn't think so. But perhaps it is. A lot's happened since Saturday. Karen's become a mother and I've become a grandmother." The puzzled expression on his face amused her. "It seems Colin left a son behind him. I only learned about it on Sunday."

"I see." He was staring at her, but she felt not really seeing her. He was lost in some ruminative debate within himself. "That makes a difference?" he asked finally.

"It makes a very big difference." She watched him digest, not so much what she said, but the cool determination with which she said it.

"You know I'm going back?"

"Becky told me."

"I was thinking you might like to visit. I could show you Chicago. You'd love it." He sounded, thought Connie, like a travel agent making a sales pitch that had grown weary with over-use and she felt unaccountably sorry for him, for the emptiness at the heart of that swaggering self-assurance.

"You mean stay with you," she asked directly.

277

"I've a big place," he said. "But now I'm feeling a fool. Like I've missed my cue and can't pick up the gist of the play."

"That's so typical of you, David. It's a play! It's theatre! And you've missed your cue!"

He looked hurt. "That means no."

"It means – I don't know, maybe. Maybe sometime. But not now. Not yet. There are too many missed cues of my own that I have to pick up – and, I'm sorry, they don't include you. Not right now."

He shrugged and she had the feeling she was being dismissed, like a pleasantly recalled holiday relationship that was no longer relevant. "I guess we were thirty years too early, Connie. We hadn't yet grown into the people we were meant to be."

"I don't think so." She couldn't quite suppress a sense of sadness that crept into her voice.

"I've changed," she corrected him. "But you, you're exactly the same David Levitch, plus a few pounds and wrinkles. I think maybe temperamentally you were born whole and complete."

She proffered her hand. "I'm really glad we met again, David. Have a good trip."

She didn't wait for him to say anything but walked slowly back into the house. She heard him call "Connie!" and paused deciding whether or not to respond. But she knew if she did she might not be able to keep her resolve not to be trapped again by his charm and her own susceptibility to it.

Sam was there when she returned to pack her suitcase. He had been ordered by Karen to take a break and in any case she would be out in a day or two.

As she waited for the cab to take her to the station they sat together on the settee in the sitting-room, holding hands like two very old friends. And indeed, Connie decided, that's what they had become. Perhaps that's the most they ever had been and the illusion of love had been just that: an illusion.

278

"I thought you might take off — that chap, David Levitch."

She sighed. "It was a long time ago, Sam. I hadn't realised just how long."

"What'll you do now?"

"Sell up in Richmond, first." The thought crystallised as she articulated it and she knew then it had been at the back of her mind ever since she had come back so unexpectedly to Southdean, although she hadn't understood that.

"Why? I thought you liked it there."

"I do — did. But not any more. There are things that I can do down here. I'll stay with Becky for a bit."

(She had a fleeting memory of Becky's reaction on learning she had turned down David Levitch's proposition: "I'm glad, Con. He's not right for you. He never was. I told you that once when we were girls. But I couldn't tell you again now that we're grown women. You had to know that for yourself." "Maybe I don't really know it, Becky?" she'd wondered. "Well, at least, you've given yourself time to find out.")

"You'll probably end up fighting like cats and dogs," said Sam.

"Probably," she conceded.

But she could tell Sam wasn't really concentrating on her immediate future but on his own. "I suppose I'll have to get used to the patter of little feet again," he said, enjoying the relevance of the hoary cliché.

Now, thought Connie, now! There'll never be a better opportunity. "As a matter of fact, talking about the pattering of little feet." And she proceeded to tell him about their grandchild, editing out the more gruesome details.

He took it rather well, considering he didn't approve of Hubbard Crowther, didn't recall meeting his sister Dede and regretted that Colin hadn't lived to see his own son or even been aware that he was to become a father. "It might have made all the difference," he murmured with the certainty conferred by his new status that babies were born to make a difference to their fathers.

"You mean he might have been alive today?" she said. "Don't delude yourself, Sam. Colin had departed long, long before he took that plunge over Beachy Head." She didn't tell him about the physical legacy Colin had inflicted on his child's mother. She reckoned one shock at a time was sufficient for Sam in his present state and she registered with surprise that she was actually beginning to consider the feelings of someone other than herself.

On the train to London she looked out at the pleasant southern landscape now pock-marked with ill-considered housing developments, industrial sites and dual carriageways. She started to think back over the past days, but her brain rejected the overload of thoughts and she found herself nodding off instead.

What amazed her was how unchanged it all was when she finally got back to her apartment block in Richmond.

The same surly contractors attacking the lawns venomously as if they were settling grievances with a mortal enemy. The same courtly smile from the same courtly porter who stood guard against dubious visitors and expected a tip for the time of day. The same lush view over the river. The same smell of Johnson's wax polish as she mounted the stairs to her first floor flat.

All just the same, as it was when she left it in a kind of dream only a week before. How could this be? It should have been transformed, just as she felt herself to be transformed.

Her neighbour, a sprightly little lady with a yappy little dog, was just locking her front door. She beamed a greeting and expressed surprise.

"Why, Mrs Remick. I haven't seen you for days. Where have you been?"

Normally Connie would have resented this blatant display of curiosity. Nosey, she'd always thought her. But, today, she didn't mind.

280

"On a voyage of discovery," she said, enjoying confounding her. "No – rediscovery."

"A package tour?" enquired her neighbour brightly.

"You could call it that." A reflective smile spread slowly across Connie's face. "A package tour." Then she let herself into her flat, kicked off her shoes and poured herself a stiff, satisfying gin and tonic. The shoes, she noted with a comforting sense of order restored, were a matching pair.